The Corpsman's Wife

A Novel

Sabine Chennault

HELLGATE PRESS   ASHLAND, OREGON

THE CORPSMAN'S WIFE

Published by Hellgate Press

(An imprint of L&R Publishing, LLC)

Hellgate Press

PO Box 3531

Ashland, OR 97520

email: info@hellgatepress.com

Interior & Cover Design: L. Redding

ISBN: 978-1-55571-987-6

First edition 10 9 8 7 6 5 4 3 2 1

For Lance

Sarah,
I'm so happy we
met and I see our
friendship growing!
Lots of Love

Contents

The US Navy Hospital Corpsman's Pledge

I solemnly pledge myself before God and these witnesses to practice faithfully all of my duties as a member of the Hospital Corps. I hold the care of the sick and injured to be a privilege and a sacred trust and will assist the Medical Officer with loyalty and honesty. I will not knowingly permit harm to come to any patient. I will not partake of nor administer any unauthorized medication. I will hold all personal matters pertaining to the private lives of patients in strict confidence. I dedicate my heart, mind and strength to the work before me. I shall do all within my power to show in myself an example of all that is honorable and good throughout my naval career.

SABINE CHENNAULT

A Corpsman's Prayer

Grant me, oh Lord, for the coming events;
Enough knowledge to cope and some plain common sense.
Be at our side on those nightly patrols;
And be merciful judging our vulnerable souls.
Make my hands steady and as sure as a rock;
When the others go down with a wound or in shock.
Let me be close, when they bleed in the mud;
With a tourniquet handy to save precious blood.
Here in the jungle, the enemy near;
Even the corpsman can't offer much lightness and cheer.
Just help me, oh Lord, to save lives when I can;
Because even out there is merit in man.
If it's Your will, make casualties light;
And don't let any die in the murderous night.
These are my friends I'm trying to save;
They are frightened at times, but You know they are brave.
Let me not fail when they need so much;
But to help me serve with a compassionate touch.
Lord, I'm no hero—my job is to heal;
And I want You to know just how helpless I feel.
Bring us back safely to camp with dawn;
For too many of us are already gone.
Lord, bless my friends if that's part of your plan;
And go with us tonight, when we go out again.

—*Author Unknown*

As of today, a staggering number of veterans commit suicide every single day. Twenty-three percent of all homeless Americans are veterans, often homeless because their benefits did not come through before they lost their homes. Of all those feeling that there was no other way than to end their life, sixty-eight percent annually were in the Navy. Sixty percent of all veteran suicides are committed with a personally owned firearm, not a military issued one.

These are our husbands, wives, fathers, mothers, brothers, sisters, and children.

They go to fight a war, which at some point no longer makes sense to them.

They grew up protected in a country with the prime purpose of instant gratification and are thrown into countries where people not only live by different rules but also will not stop killing those who disagree with their beliefs.

When the Navy, Marines, Army, Air Force and Coast Guard are done with them, vets all too often feel cast aside with nowhere to turn and without the ability to make sense of anything.

Any one of them may be living in a loving family but feel lost and alone without anywhere but the wrong end of a gun to turn to.

THEY SERVED FOR US, WHY ARE WE TURNING OUR BACKS ON THEM?

Acknowledgments

A SPECIAL THANK YOU TO my husband, Lance, for serving twenty years as a Navy Corpsman and often feeling, especially after his retirement, lost and alone. You are my rock and inspiration for everything I do in life.

A million thanks to Joshua Hood (*The Treadstone Resurrection*) for saving my sanity and walking me through the process of taking this book from mediocre to great.

To my friend, Tiffany Hale, for sharing her picture (cover). To her husband, Jon Hale, for his continued service in the Navy. It was Tiffany's picture and my husband's stories that inspired this book.

Thanks to those who shared their stories of the terrible things they witnessed, experiences they never could have imagined, and the loss of brothers and sisters they endured.

A note of immense gratitude to organizations like Wounded Warrior Project (WWP), Red-White-and-Blue (RWB), the United Service Association (USO), and other veterans associations for all you do for America's veterans to make them feel appreciated, loved, and whole after giving so much of themselves for us.

Most of all I'd like to thank all of those amazing men and women who continue to serve with little regard to their own physical and mental well-being. You are true heroes and deeply loved.

We believe in you,
We are here for you,
You will never be alone.

No matter what, help and a listening ear are never more than a phone call away.

The Corpsman's Wife

and sat on the blue-and-white checkered couch. *I'm gonna have a bonfire with this thing if he doesn't take it.* Susi pulled the phone off the end table on her right and sat it on her lap, took a deep drink of her wine and dialed.

"Hello?" the male voice at the other end stated.

"Gene, listen, 'cause I'm only going to say this once." The wine gave her courage, and she took another drink. "I'm gonna be gone from Tuesday to Thursday. There will be no more of these little trips here and there to get your shit. Make arrangements to get what you want and then stay the fuck away from here. You do not live here anymore."

"Why are you so hostile?" he wanted to know.

"I'm not interested in a conversation with you, just please get your stuff," she sighed. "Whatever is left when I get back will get donated or burned. Got it?"

"Fine," he scowled and hung up. She really needed to call Tracy back. She pressed down on the cradle to get a dial tone and dialed her number. At that very moment, she remembered that with Tracy in Texas, she was two hours ahead. It was past eleven at night there.

"Jesus Christ, woman, what the fuck took so long?" Tracy announced at the other end. "Do you know what time it is?"

"I'm sorry, sweetheart." Susi kissed the phone. "I called Dr. Carl from the office, came home, poured a glass of wine and called Gene."

"How did that go?" Tracy asked.

"I told him that I'm gonna be gone from Tuesday till Friday and he needs to get the rest of his shit out of the house. What's left when I get back is going to get donated or burned."

"So, you're going?" Tracy inquired.

"Looks like it," Susi announced with the enthusiasm of a sloth. "Dr. Carl wanted me to take the whole week, but I told him Tuesday to Friday is fine."

"That works great," Tracy replied. "I'm relocating for my new job and I have to start there Monday after next."

"Nice, where are you moving to?" Susi asked and emptied the rest of the wine in her glass.

"I thought I'd fly back down with you since my new job is at McDonnell Douglas in Mesa." She waited.

"What?" Susi jumped off the couch, and her mood improved instantly. "Are you serious?"

"Yup, they've been bugging me for a year, and they finally made the right offer, and I accepted." Susi could feel her smiling at the other end. "I don't have a place yet, and since you have the house to yourself, I thought maybe I could bunk with you for the time being."

"Absolutely, it'll be like old times." Susi was elated. "Oh my god, I can't believe this, this is seriously the best news I've had all year."

They ironed out the details of the flight while Susi munched on some cheese and crackers.

Tracy was flying with Alaska Airlines from Dallas to Chicago. She was scheduled to arrive at Terminal 3. Susi booked a flight with Alaska as well, which would also arrive at Terminal 3 half an hour after Tracy's. They planned to meet at Bubbles for some sparkling wine and some snacks. Susi would rent her own car since Tracy and Tony would have other family in town. Susi wanted to go to the Sears Tower and stroll along Lake Shore Drive. She was looking forward to the trip. She hadn't seen Tracy in over a year, and it had been at least fifteen since she saw Tony.

****

"Don't we have to be back by midnight?" someone behind Susi yelled. She had just gotten a glass of red wine at the bar. The bartender had suggested a Washington red blend, and she loved it. She took a small sip, smiled at the bartender and nodded. She turned and ran right into one of the many sailors in the restaurant, spilling her wine all over him and herself. His beautiful white uniform was drenched in the red liquid. She just stood there staring at him, her red hair framing her face like a burning halo. The look on his face was priceless. Everyone around them fell silent as they both started laughing. She hadn't laughed this hard in she couldn't remember how long. Tears were rolling down her face, and she had to grab hold of his arm to steady herself.

"I really don't see what's so funny." She could tell he was trying to be serious. "I didn't plan on having to go change."

"Get over yourself, sailor," she snickered. "You're not the only one who's wet here."

They looked at each other and started laughing again. Several of his friends along with hers had gathered around them to see what was going on.

"Hey, Susi, I have a sweater in the car you can change into," her friend Tracy yelled from somewhere in the crowd.

"Susi, huh?" He smiled at her.

She held out her hand. "Susi…Susi Jury. Pleasure to meet you, sailor." He took her hand, and she almost pulled away. He had never felt anything like that before. It was unexpected, almost like an electrical surge. She held on, her tiny hand felt good in his, and there was something familiar in her touch. Susi turned bright red, leaving little difference between her hair and her face.

"Lance…" That was all he managed to get out before one of the other guys pulled him back. "Please, don't leave," he managed to yell as someone pulled her towards the door.

"Didn't know we were chasing tail tonight," Cory, one of Lance's fellow boot-camp graduates, stated.

"Do you have to be such an ass?" Lance countered. He hadn't cared much for Cory; he always had some derogatory comment handy when it came to women. Lance went to the restroom to assess the damage; it wasn't that bad. She must have gotten the most of it on her.

He went back out to the bar, which was somewhat separate from the main dining room, Whether it was Chili's, Applebee's, or Bennigan's, they all looked pretty much the same.

He couldn't find her anywhere and went out to the parking lot. He saw her and another woman standing by a car under one of the lights. She was pulling off her wet blouse to put on something else, and he could see her silhouette under the light. Despite the fact that it had been a warm July day, since the sun had gone down, it was rather chilly.

"A true gentleman." Susi smiled. He could tell how blue her eyes were even in the dark.

"Damn, it's cold." He rubbed his hands together in front of his mouth and blew warm air into them. After a few moments of silence, he gently touched Susi's hand. "Can I tell you something?"

Susi nodded.

"Honestly, it's not just the air that's giving me chills. I have no idea where this is gonna go, but right now, in this moment, nothing feels more right," he confessed. "You know I can see you blush, you don't have to hide it." He laid his hand on her shoulder.

"What's next for you?" Susi changed the subject.

"You mean with the Navy?" Lance inquired, and she nodded. He could tell she was nervous and hoped that some small talk would help her relax. "I'll be staying here for a few more months to go through A school. Are you from around here?" He smiled at her in the dark and gently squeezed her hand.

"I'm sorry, but no." He saw the smile fade from her lips. "Right now, I live in Arizona, but I don't want to stay there for long. I was just here to get away for a few days and to attend Tracy's little brother's graduation."

"I see," Lance stated matter-of-factly. "Anyone waiting for you back there?"

"Not really," she said with a slight sigh.

"What do you mean by not really?" he wanted to know. "If there are things you're not ready to talk about, I understand."

She took a deep breath. "It's not that, I'm just not sure how to lay out the last few miserable years. It's not something I'm proud of. The guy I was married to, whom I came over here with from Germany, wasn't what one might consider nice. You know what I mean?"

"Abusive?" Lance saw her nod. "I'm sorry," he said quietly and squeezed her hand again. "I can't stand guys like that; in my book they are sorry excuses of human beings. Sorry, just my opinion. One can only hope karma will take care of him."

"Thank you, I really appreciate you saying that. I've filed for divorce, so that will all be over soon." She forced a smile.

They pulled up to the hotel and she parked.

"I'm in 203." She handed him the keycard. "I'm just going to stop in and tell Tracy good night really quick."

They walked in together and made their way up the stairs without saying a word. Susi knocked on Tracy's door while Lance inserted the key card just opposite of where she was standing. As he opened the door to Susi's room, Tracy opened the doors to hers.

He closed the door behind him and looked around the room. A small kitchenette with basic appliances and necessities made way to an area with the bed and armchair on one side with a desk, chair, lamp and television on the other. The brown carpet made the room seem darker. He investigated the bathroom with its cool grey tile, white walls and shower curtain. Moments later he could hear the girls talking in the hall and looked through the little peep hole in the door.

Tracy gave Susi a gentle nudge out the door, but Susi quickly turned and pushed her hands against the door so Tracy couldn't close it.

"I am really nervous!" he heard Susi quickly state. "Anyway, I really just wanted to know what time we have to leave in the morning?"

"We need to leave here no later than ten to make it to the airport on time." Then she smiled. "I was gonna go and have breakfast with Tony, but you don't need to go."

"Okay, thanks. Give him my love and tell him to stay safe wherever they send him." Susi leaned in to hug her friend and then turned and knocked on her own door. It startled Lance since he was so focused on their conversations.

He opened the door and smiled at her almost sheepishly. It was more than obvious that he was no less nervous than her. She stood by the door smiling at him. "Now what?"

He reached for her hands with both of his and, turning both of her hands palm side up, he kissed each palm gently, then looked at her and smiled.

"You have the most amazing blue eyes I have ever seen," he declared and saw the warm blush rising in her cheeks, and she looked at the floor.

He gently lifted her chin and moved closer to kiss her. He could feel her melt against his lips.

"Shall we have a little nightcap?" He pointed at the limited variety of small bottles he had pulled out of the minibar.

"Sure," Susi beamed and laughed. "Something should help make my hands stop shaking so bad." She held both arms straight out in front of her, and he saw how nervous she really was.

He took two small bottles of rum from the counter along with a Coke and a couple bottles of water. Quickly depositing all the items on the small table at the end of the desk, he stood and wrapped his arms around her.

"My insides are shaking as bad as your hands." He leaned down to kiss the top of her head, and she ran her hands down his back. He loved how small she was. She laid her head against his chest, and he leaned his against hers. They fit together like two odd puzzle pieces.

"I cannot recall ever having been so comfortable and content in someone's arms," she spoke softly. He breathed in the scent of her hair.

"It might sound silly for me to say this, but I have never felt so at home in anyone's arms either," he said tenderly. "Not to sound weird, but I felt it the moment you touched my hand."

She pulled her head away from his chest and looked up at him, her big blue eyes filled with tears. "How am I supposed to let you go?"

"Don't say that right now," he urged. "Don't even think that. Right now, we are together and right now is all that matters." He lifted her chin with his right hand and gently wiped away a tear with the other, noticing how soft her skin was.

"We will figure this out," Lance whispered as he took her face in both of his hands. "Right now, I don't know how, but I promise you I will not lose you or let you go. It may be hard in the beginning. We both have a lot to deal with, but we will make this work." With that he closed his eyes as his lips gently kissed hers. He could feel her body relax as she sank into his arms. Right now, in this moment, she was completely in tune with him. As they gradually began undressing each other, they moved slowly, their lips never separating. He picked her up and gently laid her on the bed. There could not possibly be a more perfect moment than right now.

****

The next morning came all too quickly. Susi lay in bed next to Lance. His eyes were closed, but he wasn't asleep. He liked how gently she moved when she had to get up and how soft her skin felt against his when she snuggled against him. He had dated plenty in his time, but she was a first in every way. There was nothing fake about her.

"You look a lot more rugged with that three a.m. shadow on your face," she had said. Her long red hair draped across his broad chest. At one point during the night he had held his hand against hers and his fingers were significantly longer than hers. She could make a fist, and he could close his fingers around hers and cover her whole hand. Was it possible to feel this much love for anyone this fast? She snuggled in close to him without opening her eyes, and he pulled her closer. Her skin against his gave him a level of comfort he had never experienced. He had been adopted when he was three years old, in and out of foster homes from the time he was six months old. Abused from early infancy, everyone had written him off as a loner never able to really feel emotions or a deep connection with anyone. Being honest with himself, he had never allowed himself to feel anything. He'd been afraid to; nothing was worse than the pain that could result from deep emotions, and he'd had friends who were crushed after a breakup.

A couple of hours later, the rising sun woke them both. "Good morning, beautiful," he greeted her. "That brain of yours already hard at work?"

"Oh, hush." She rolled on her back. "You're not supposed to be awake yet."

He yawned and raised his arms behind his head in a long stretch. The comforter slipped to his waist, and his firm chest and stomach were exposed. She gently touched his stomach and he quivered.

"Don't take this the wrong way, but I really don't like those soft touches, but I noticed that you really do." He smiled and winked. She gently smacked his bare chest as she blushed.

"I think we need to get ready, so you can drop me at the base before heading to the airport." No sooner had he said that when he saw the tears rise in her eyes, and she swallowed hard.

He got out of bed and grabbed a notepad on the desk. He scribbled something on it and handed her the piece of paper.

"This is my address, this is good until December. Now, can I have yours?" He handed her the pen, and she wrote down hers along with her phone number.

"Are you sure it's okay to call?" he asked. She had told him that she filed for a divorce, but he didn't know if her soon-to-be ex-husband was still in the house.

"He is supposed to be out of the house by the time I get back, but I will write you and let you know when he's gone for sure."

"We can go have a little breakfast somewhere or we can grab something downstairs on our way out the door if you'd rather play a little longer." With that he picked her up and carried her back to bed. Gently laying her down, his lips never left hers.

They made love one more time before sharing a shower, and he helped gather her things while she packed, and they left the room. They had been on the second floor, and there was no need to take the elevator. They walked down the hall, down the stairs, to the lobby, holding hands as if they had been together forever, but neither of them spoke a word. Lance wondered what either of them could possibly have said to make the next hour any easier?

They had a cup of coffee and a Danish before making their way to the car. It was getting warmer outside, and there wasn't a cloud in the sky.

"When do you start A school again?" Susi asked.

"Next week," he stated firmly. "Not looking forward to the dead of winter here though." He looked at her and smiled. "Don't get me wrong, I love snow. We get plenty of it in Washington, but from what I hear, it's just insane here, not to mention below zero temperatures and the wind coming off the lake, brrrrr." He shuddered just talking about it.

"I bet fall is very pretty though. Anything is better than that terrible heat in the desert," she proclaimed.

They were at the base in a matter of minutes. Susi pulled up close to the gate where Lance had directed her to stop. She put the car in park. He followed her every movement and could tell from her quivering lip that she was trying not to cry.

"What are we going to do?" she whispered. He knew it was a rhetorical question. He got out of the car, walked around to the driver's side, opened the door and knelt down. He could have cared less at this point how much dirtier his dress whites got.

"Look at me," he spoke softly, but she didn't turn. "Please look at me." Her head slowly moved. The tears made her blue eyes seem even brighter. He wanted to wrap her in his arms and tell her to stay, but he knew that wasn't possible.

"I told you last night, right now there are things we both have to do," he continued. "There is just no way around that." He grabbed her hands the best he could with her sitting in the car. "I don't know what will happen down the road, but I promise you right here, right now, there will never be anyone else in my heart...ever."

She stepped out of the car while he held her hands and looked at him with all the hope of the world reflected in her eyes. He felt as if his heart were ripping in two as tears slowly rolled down her face.

"I need you to be strong, not just for you but for both of us," he confided, smiling. "I will write as often as I can and as soon as it is alright for me to call, I will." He pulled a handkerchief out of his pocket, softly wiped the tears from her eyes, and gently kissed her.

"I have to go," he said, pulling her in close and hugging her tightly.

"I love you," she whispered softly. He looked at her eyes while kissing her hands.

"I love you too, more than I ever thought possible." He kissed her forehead, let go of her hands, and whispered, "I'll see you soon." With that he walked away.

The Corpsman's Wife

TWO

The "+" on the Stick

"Distance is temporary, love is forever."

S USI TURNED, HOLDING ON to the top of the car, and watched Lance until he disappeared. Tears fell down her face as she climbed back into the car and shut the door. How could life be this cruel? Hadn't she been through enough? A knock on the window startled her, and her head spun around.

"Are you okay?" the face on the other side of the window wanted to know. She wiped away the tears and nodded yes. She forced a smile and rolled down the window. "I'm fine. I just hate saying good-bye." The woman on the other side of the window nodded and continued on her way. Susi checked herself in the mirror, turned the key, slowly put the car in drive, and made her way to O'Hare International Airport. By the time she got there, and the rental car was returned, she had little recollection of the drive. She methodically went through everything she had to do at the airport and was more than relieved to find Tracy already sitting by the gate.

"You look like...you just lost your puppy!" Tracy exclaimed.

"Thank you, dear." Susi jokingly glared at her friend. "Good morning to you too."

Susi sat her small bag under her seat and plopped down in a chair next to her friend. Tracy moved in closer, urging her to share some details.

"What's to tell?" Susie asked. "The whole night was amazing. I love you like my own sister, but you are not getting a play by play." Her eyes wandered around the faces of other passengers.

"I will tell you this, as cheesy as it may sound, with him I feel whole, complete, like the part of me that has been missing all these years has been found," she said, smiling. "I really had no idea which way my life was going to go, but now I feel as if I have a purpose."

"Wow." Tracy's smile had vanished. "That sounds really deep."

"If you had asked me just last week if I'd ever want anything to do with someone in the military again, I would have told you to go to hell." Susi looked serious. "Something happened when he took my hand last night. I can't explain it, but I've just never felt anything like this before."

"So now what?" Tracy asked, and Susi figured that was the only logical question.

"I can honestly say I hope more than anything that Gene is gone by the time we get back," Susi stated in a practical kind of way.

"Any idea where he's going to be staying during the divorce?" Tracy inquired.

"I think he's going to be at his mother's." Susi couldn't help but snicker. The last thing she had expected was for her husband to move back in with his mom. "I would love to be a fly on the wall when she lectures him about drinking." She laughed. "The lawyer said since we don't have kids and don't really have any common debt or assets, this should be done pretty quickly."

The boarding call came across the loudspeaker, and both women checked their boarding passes for their seats and sections.

"Don't get me wrong, but I have to ask, I don't understand how you can trust again so quickly," Tracy noted. "Sorry, didn't mean to come across so cold. That is not what I meant." She blushed.

"No worries, I know what you mean, and trust me, I've asked myself the same question multiple times since last night." Susi grinned. "We better line up."

The two women gathered their things and joined the crowd already waiting to be herded onto the plane.

"It wasn't always as bad as everyone thinks," she continued, "but, yes, I should have left him a long time ago."

"You've got to be kidding me." Tracy seemed angry. "You are seriously going to make excuses for that jerk? Do I have to remind you of your broken nose?" she announced rather loudly, and several passengers looked at her.

"Tracy, please," Susi urged, "not here."

"Sorry, you know I get irritated when it comes to that piece of shit," Tracy apologized but shook her head.

"How are you today?" The gate attendant asked with a smile that seemed all too mechanical. She checked Susi's ID and the boarding pass. Tracy followed right behind her friend, and for now they had dropped the conversation. Susi knew that she was right; not everyone on the flight had to know what that man had done to her.

****

Susi and Tracy had gone to college together in Wiesbaden, Germany. Susi had met Gene and some of his friends at a pizzeria near the Army base. They had only been dating for two weeks before they had their first big fight. Tracy and everyone else had told her to reconsider dating him but, given the positive outlook Susi always seemed to have, there was no changing her mind. Six months later he shoved her so hard during an argument that she hit the wall. She didn't tell anyone about it, but several days later when Susi and Tracy had played tennis, Tracy saw her friend's back in the shower and asked what had happened. Susi looked as if someone had hit her with a bat. Tracy begged her back then to break up with him, but Susi was stubborn and assured her friend that Gene would change and that he was under a lot of stress because of his promotion and the exam he had to take.

Tracy had been openly reluctant when Susi approached her the following year and asked her to be the maid of honor at her wedding. For months Susi had ignored her friend's questions about her increasing bruises and had explained them away with the all-too-common explanations of running into things or just being clumsy. Susi knew that Tracy had no doubt that it was Gene causing the bruises and took it upon herself to call Susi's parents. When they confronted Susi about the matter, Susi did not speak to Tracy for three months.

Susi's parents refused to attend the wedding, and they had not spoken to each other since then. There was some communication through Susi's Aunt Anni, but that was it. A month after the wedding, Tracy called Susi and tried to work things out. Susi told her in no uncertain terms to mind her own business. Gene and Susi had not been married two months when he announced he was going back to the States. He had orders to Fort Hood. He hadn't told Susi earlier because he felt she was going where he told her to. He made sure she wouldn't have a chance to go home and see her family again before they had to leave, and once again, she'd made excuses.

She asked Tracy if there was any way she could follow her. The night before they left, Gene went out and Susi called her friend to talk to her. She told Tracy that she wasn't ready to give up yet but some part of her was beginning to get scared. Susi knew that it would be difficult for Tracy to get an immigration visa but since she was a top-notch translator, she could easily get hired by a company and that would give her the needed visa. Tracy was not attached to anyone and getting a visa for no reason was nearly impossible. It took some time and while Tracy had to wait, the two of them were in constant contact through letters. Susi would call Tracy when Gene was passed out drunk or just not home, and more and more she began to confide in her dear friend.

One day the doorbell rang, and Susi went to answer. She opened the door, and there was Tracy. Susi could see the shock on her friend's face. She knew what she looked like with her black eye and hair as short as when they were teenagers on the swim team at school.

Susi threw her arms around Tracy and burst into tears. She told her that his violence had gotten worse since they had arrived in Texas, and he would not allow her to call her aunt or anyone else. He had literally put a lock on their phone so she couldn't use it. She was only allowed to call her family when he was home, so he'd be sure she wouldn't tell them what was going on. Not that she would; she was so embarrassed by all of this. Susi told Tracy that his outbursts mostly happened when he was drinking, which was daily, but he was always sorry when he sobered up. Tracy told her she didn't want to hear anymore, and she was not leaving until she talked to him.

When he got home that night, Tracy confronted him. Susi wasn't sure if she was glad it happened or if she was scared he'd completely flip out and hurt Tracy too. The three of them sat, talked, and yelled until the early morning hours. Susi knew that Tracy didn't trust Gene, but Tracy told him that she would give him one chance to get cleaned up and start treating Susi better.

She told him that she was staying just a few minutes away and she would be by the next day with a list of AA locations. She also told him she would take him until he had a sponsor, that an hour drive was no big deal, and if he missed as much as one meeting, she would go to his commanding officer. When she left in the early morning hours, Susi was scared to death of what he might do. She'd become so numb that she thought she couldn't feel any more pain or fear, but here she was. Much to her surprise, he managed to go to Alcoholics Anonymous for three months and during that time didn't lay a hand on Susi. He worked the steps and even brought her flowers on Fridays after work. Life seemed as if it was going to get better. They stayed in Fort Hood until 1983, and then he left the Army. He was in no rush to move, and they remained in Texas until 1985. He stayed clean and sober the whole time. In the meantime, Tracy had gotten a job at the airport in Houston. In August 1985, from one day to the next, Gene decided that Arizona was where he wanted to be, and they packed and left. He had no job lined up and they had nothing saved. Everything she had gotten from her family–furniture, heirlooms, and things holding precious memories–he gave away to neighbors or threw in the trash. He wanted nothing more than a U-Haul trailer on the back of the car.

Once they arrived, he was in no rush to find work. He had been sober for over two years and hadn't laid a hand on Susi the whole time. Slowly she began to trust him again but remained cautiously optimistic. She'd found a job with an optometrist, and he began to drink again. By Christmas that year, the violence began again, but now Susi was much stronger. Tracy was still in Texas but came out to visit as often as her job allowed. The first time Susi went to work with a black eye and her boss asked her what happened, she told him the truth and said that her husband was bored and needed a job. The elderly doctor provided the needed job. Gene went to work at a garage the doctor's son owned and returned to AA meetings.

Both Susi and Gene knew the marriage was going nowhere, and several months later the day came that she went home during the early afternoon, not feeling well. Their house wasn't that far from the office where she worked, and she could easily walk to and from work if she wanted to exercise a little. When the temperatures hit triple digits, she drove. She was surprised to see his car in the driveway but in no way shocked or surprised when she walked in and found him at the kitchen table with the receptionist he worked with. They didn't look like they had been sitting there sipping coffee the whole time. Him having an affair was the best thing that could have happened.

He spent less and less time at home in the evenings, and it gave Susi time to read, knit, and study for her optician's exam.

A month before Tracy invited Susi to go to Great Lakes for her brother's boot-camp graduation, she told him that he could be expecting the divorce papers. She'd smiled at him but somewhat expected him to hit her. Susi was shocked that he stayed so calm, and when she asked him if he'd expected her to throw a fit about the affair, he just said he didn't guess so but did expect her to at least ask him to stay with her. She laughed.

That night Susi called Tracy and told her everything. They were on the phone for hours, and Susi didn't leave out a single detail. Tracy told her she would see about transferring to the Phoenix area and if that wouldn't work, she would just find a different job. Within a month she had gotten hired at McDonnell Douglas where she would be starting her job the Monday after their weekend at Great Lakes.

Tracy had told Susi that she had to fly from Dallas to Chicago on a one-way ticket and would be flying back to Phoenix with her. Susi had offered her a room at her house; it would be fun to spend time together.

****

Susi kept thinking about Lance during the four-hour flight, which was smooth. They landed in Phoenix around four in the afternoon. Since neither of them had checked baggage, they were outside quickly. Tracy told Susi that she did not want to wait for a shuttle and decided on a cab. Susi objected, but Tracy insisted and told her that she would be making enough money to treat them a little. They decided to go home, freshen up, and go somewhere for dinner.

The cab pulled up to the house, and Susi got out while Tracy paid the driver. Gene's car wasn't there, and the two women went inside. He had left the blue-and-white checkered couch Susi had purchased a couple months ago, a small white oak shelf, and the TV. He took his stereo and most of the things in the bedroom except the bed.

"I think we should have a bonfire with that." Tracy smiled, pointing at the bed.

"That's not a bad idea at all," Susi quipped. "Why the hell would I want that damn thing?"

"What's your money situation?" Tracy asked.

"Not bad at all. I have some in savings, and I've sent a bunch back home over the last couple of years that he doesn't know about. Anni put that in a savings account for me."

The doctor she worked for had arranged a financial advisor to meet with Susi as soon as he found out about the abuse she dealt with at home, and a small percentage of her earnings went directly into another account. Gene had no clue how much she made. Susi was trying to calculate just what she had available.

"We could go look at some furniture before dinner," she told Tracy. "I have enough to get what I need with what I have in savings here without touching what I have in Germany." She looked pleasantly at her friend. "You'll need a bed and dresser for your room as well."

They put their things away, freshened up, and headed out. It didn't take long at all to pick out some new furniture, and by seven that evening, they were sitting at Aribba's Mexican Grill, enjoying some refreshing, and much needed, margaritas while waiting on their food.

"I have to be honest," Susi announced. "I am really glad you are here. I would not want to spend tonight alone." She stared at her drink. "Not after meeting Lance."

"Is there any way you can get a hold of him?" Tracy questioned.

"Not really," Susi sighed. "Since I didn't know if Gene was going to be at the house, I figured it would be better for Lance to not call. I told him I would write and let him know if the coast is clear. He doesn't go back to school till next week."

The two enjoyed a pleasant dinner and by the time they got home, they were both tired. The furniture would be delivered the next morning, and Tracy shared Susi's bed. She felt a lot better with her friend there than she ever did with the man who was about to be her ex-husband. Tracy fell asleep in minutes, but Susi couldn't come to rest.

She got back up and wrote what was meant to be a short letter. She spent three hours telling Lance as much about her life as she could and ended the letter saying that she would understand if he'd changed his mind. After all, she did have a lot of baggage. She got her purse to get the note with his address out of her wallet and found another note tucked into the side pocket of her purse. She had no idea when he'd written the note. It must have been sometime during the night at the hotel while she had been sleeping. It read, *Dearest Susi, never in my wildest dreams could I have imagined meeting someone like you. No matter what our future brings you will forever own my heart. With all my love, Lance.*

She kissed the note. How long would she have to carry this with her until she could see him again, until she could hear his voice? She went back to bed with the note in her hand. His scent was still on the paper. It made her relax, and her body remembered how safe she felt in his arms. This time she quickly drifted off to sleep.

****

A month later Susi and Tracy had worked out their daily routine and enjoyed each other's company. Susi had written Lance that the coast was clear and did not have to wait too long for his first call. It came on a Sunday night, three weeks after they had met. It became their weekly ritual that he would call her on Sunday evening. Two weeks after the first phone call, she woke up early on Saturday morning. Her mouth was watering, and she knew at any moment last night's dinner was making a repeat visit, sadly not in the same form. She ran to the bathroom, pushed open the lid and seat, and threw up.

When she was done she leaned against the wall and thought about the conversation she'd had with Lance the Sunday before. He had settled in his new quarters and A school to learn the fundamentals of his Navy job. Everything was going well. He was getting anxious to be done and get to San Diego where he would be closer to Arizona, and it would be a lot easier for them to visit.

She hadn't told him that she had missed her period last month, and since Tracy had told her that it was more than likely because of the stress of the divorce and the occasional arguments with Gene, she didn't pay much attention to the lack of the monthly visitor. Susi threw up again and began to wonder if Tracy felt okay. The two of them had gone out to dinner the night before, and if Tracy also felt sick, they might have gotten a touch of food poisoning.

Susi found Tracy in the kitchen making breakfast, and the smell of the cooking eggs made her feel sick again. She headed to the pantry and grabbed a box of saltine crackers. The kitchen was small but had enough room for a table with four chairs, some counterspace, the stove, a dishwasher, and refrigerator. The old china cabinet she had inherited from her grandmother was against the wall of the dining area. It had been the only piece of furniture she had been able to rescue when Gene was giving away all of her things. Susi had painted the kitchen a soft beige when they first moved into the house and had done similar earthy tones in every room of the house.

"Glad it's Sunday and we don't have to work. I'm not feeling good at all today," Susi stated, holding her stomach with one hand and shoving a cracker into her mouth with the other. "Are you okay?" she added and looked at her friend.

"Yeah, fine, why?" Tracy turned and looked at her. "You do look a little green around the edges." She patted Susi on the back and proceeded to finish breakfast. Tracy generally worked longer hours than Susi, so Tracy cooked on the weekends and Susi during the week. Tracy placed a plate of pancakes, bacon, eggs, and fruit in front of her friend, grabbed her own, and sat down.

"Did you ever get your period?" Tracy wanted to know. Susi shook her head and nibbled on a pancake she was holding in her hand.

Tracy set down her fork. "You don't think you're pregnant, do you?" she asked while shoving a piece of bacon in her mouth. Susi's arm stopped in mid-air with her pancake just hanging there.

"No!" She shook her head. "You don't think...that's really what I need right now. Lance being almost two thousand miles away and me working full time and saving as much as I can. I couldn't tell him this!"

"If you are, you're gonna have to, sweetie." Tracy dipped a piece of bacon into the soft egg yolk and it exploded. A drop of yolk dripped on her chin when she maneuvered the bacon to her mouth. "I think we should go get one of those tests." The bacon crunched. "Just to be on the safe side. I can go get one." She looked at Susi with a huge smile on her face.

"I really don't see how you think this is even remotely funny." Susi felt a little irritated. She could, however, understand why Tracy would be tickled pink about this. There really wasn't anything the two of them hadn't done together, and so why not add a pregnancy to that? Susi knew no matter what, her friend would be there for her; she always had been. Tracy kept talking, but Susi heard little of what she said. What would she tell Lance?

He would be done with A school in December and then head straight to San Diego for pharmacy school. How would a pregnancy affect him? She would poke around when they talked that Sunday and decide then. Being able to discuss her week with him made each day go by faster, and life seemed less stressful. Even all the anger and stress the divorce was causing she could vent about. He just always listened and was there for her with his full attention. All too often he didn't say a word about how life was treating him, and she felt bad about that. When she said something to him about it, he would joke that someday she'd get a chance to make up for it.

"I'm just trying to cheer you up, honey," Tracy joked, then got up and gathered the dishes to put in the dishwasher. Susi had barely eaten anything. "I have to run to the store anyway, so I'll just pick one up."

Tracy turned to look at Susi, but she was no longer at the table. She had sprinted back to the bathroom and threw up what little she had just eaten. She sat on the cool bathroom floor and cried. Why couldn't she be with Lance now?

"Susi, are you okay?" Tracy knocked on the door, her voice conveying her strong concern. "Hey, maybe it is just a touch of food poisoning."

"We both ate the same thing," Susi stated from behind the closed door.

Susi knew what Tracy suspected was most likely right, but it really wasn't what Susi needed.

"I'm gonna run to the store, okay? I'll get the test. Do you want anything?" Tracy asked.

"Some apple juice if you don't mind," Susi responded, "and some potato chips," she added as she lifted herself off the floor. She pulled the door open. "Thank you, Tracy."

The two friends hugged. "Go back in there and brush your teeth." Tracy grinned and held her nose.

"I'll just get in the shower while you're gone," Susi told her.

Tracy left, and Susi got in the shower. The hot water felt good. She pressed her hands against the wall and let her head fall forward. The water ran over her head, draping the red hair against her face, shoulders, and back. Her mind began to wander. At twenty-nine she was more than ready for a baby. She had just never planned on making it happen under these circumstances.

Relieved was the only word she could think of for not having gotten pregnant with Gene, but she had taken every possible precaution. She knew with every fiber of her being that Lance would be different, but she couldn't tell him, not yet, and not on the phone. She would do nothing to jeopardize his Navy career. Her mind raced in every possible direction, and she noticed that the water was getting cooler.

"Hey, are you still in there?" Tracy yelled.

"Yeah." A chill hit Susi. "Guess I got lost in my thoughts. Be right out."

She quickly cleaned herself, dried off, applied her lotion, and dressed. By the time she got back out to the kitchen, Tracy had put everything away. Nothing was out except for two pregnancy tests.

"You got two?" Susi picked up one of the packages and read the back.

"Yeah, it says you should do it first thing in the morning." Tracy picked up the other box. "But I figured you could do one now and the other in the morning. If they have different results, we'll get another one and go with two out of three."

"Even though your logic often escapes me, this time you're making a lot of sense." Susi smiled. She took a deep breath, looked at Tracy, and said, "Well, here goes nothing." Heading down the hall to her bedroom, she felt the all-too-familiar butterflies. Once in her bathroom, she opened the box and read through the directions. It did say that, for best results, the test should be done in the morning, but there was no hesitation on her part that it would be accurate now.

She sat on the toilet, began to pee and stopped, placed the stick in position, and finished. The instructions had said not to shake or vibrate the stick, so she put several layers of toilet paper on the counter before she began. She gently laid the stick on the tissue and avoided looking at it until after she had washed her hands. Though the bathroom was small and there was only one sink, she had enough room to keep the test away from the sink. She dried her hands and looked at the test without picking it up.

A bright pink plus sign stared back at her.

"Tracy!" she screamed from the top of her lungs. Only seconds later her friend came running.

"What?" Tracy looked at Susi standing in the middle of her bathroom with an expression on her face as if she had just seen a ghost. There was absolutely no color left in her usually pink cheeks. She held the test stick out in front of Tracy and wanted to say something, but her mouth was too dry.

"I understand you think this is funny, but please tell me how?" Susi demanded.

"Honey, this is not a bad thing." Tracy smiled at her. "You've talked about wanting a child, and you were always happy that it never happened with Gene. Well, how did you think it was going to happen?"

Susi knew she was right. "I'll do the other test in the morning," she said in almost a whisper, "but I have a strong feeling it will have the same result."

"Yeah." Tracy nodded her head. "Me too."

Susi, who had moved to sit on the edge of her bed, slowly slid off, almost knocking Tracy on her butt. The two of them sat on the floor with their legs pulled in. Susi rested her face on her knees.

"What am I gonna do?" she asked her friend with a slight hopelessness in her voice.

"You're not going to do anything," Tracy responded assuredly. "We are going to do this together. I am here for you, my friend, and I will hold back your hair when you puke. I will go to classes with you and, best of all, I will go maternity clothes shopping with you." She patted the top of Susi's head. "This will be fun for both of us come hell or high water, and you don't really know yet what Lance will say."

"Exactly," Susi stated firmly and rearranged herself to sit with her legs crossed. "I don't think he planned on being a daddy at the beginning of his Navy career. Besides, we have been together less than twenty-four hours and…"

"Theoretically speaking, but given that the two of you are very lovey-dovey every Sunday for a little over six weeks now, I'd say this is a little more than a causal relationship."

"I guess until I talk to him, there is really nothing solid that I can decide." Susi smiled. "I mean I can make plans for myself but nothing that really includes him…for now, anyway."

The two of them sat on the floor and talked about fixing the spare room up as a nursery, when the best time would be for Susi to go on maternity leave, and much more. They talked straight through lunch time. It had to have been a good six hours. There was very little they didn't cover and before long, Susi realized it was almost time for the weekly call and she was hungry. Tracy offered to go get a pizza. No sooner had she decided that and Tracy had left, the phone rang.

Susi took a deep breath and exhaled slowly.

"Hi there, sailor." She faked a smile, but she knew that he would see right through that.

"Hi, baby, is everything okay?" he asked.

"Yeah," she lied. "It's just been an odd day, how are you?"

"Not that good." There was sadness in his voice.

Susi sank down on the bed. "What's wrong?" she asked with concern.

"Just feeling blah," he said before sneezing. "I think I'm getting a cold, and that sure isn't what I need right now." Another sneeze. "Hold on, honey, I need to find some tissues." She heard him set down the receiver.

A voice at the other end asked if he was done with the phone yet, and she heard him say not yet, that he'd be right back. Only moments later he was back on the line.

"I miss you like crazy, and I wish you were here." He sounded awful. There was no way she was going to spring this on him right now, not while he was feeling this bad.

"I miss you, too." She felt, in a way, relieved.

"Honey, can you send me a couple pictures?" he wanted to know. She had settled back against her headboard, and they spent the usual one to two hours on the phone. Tracy popped in to bring her a plate with pizza, and she ate while he excused himself to blow his nose. It seemed most of the guys on his floor were pretty understanding and didn't complain about him dominating the phone every Sunday. Just before six he brought the conversation to an end.

"Honey, are you sure everything is fine?" he urged. "I feel like you needed to tell me something and I totally dominated this conversation. How are things with the divorce?"

"We've got the final hearing in a couple weeks." She had successfully avoided the first question. "I got a letter this past Thursday. I'm a bit nervous about it. Maybe that's why I seem off." She figured there was some truth in that.

"I wish I could be there with you." He sneezed again. "Damn."

Susi laughed. "You poor thing. I wish I could make you chicken soup and tuck you in."

"Me too. I love you, baby." She could feel how sincere he was with every word. "Can't wait till next Sunday."

"Be good, my love." She wanted to kiss and hold him more than anything. He had no idea how much she needed him right now. "Please take care of yourself," she urged him.

"I will," she heard him say, and she closed her eyes to see his smiling face in her mind. Seconds later, as usual, they hung up the phone at the same time.

Susi went to the living room where Tracy was sitting with a glass of wine and watching TV.

"And?" she spouted out as soon as Susi entered the room. "You didn't tell him, did you?

"No," Susi quickly interjected. "He's not feeling good. Getting a cold or the flu. He seriously sneezed a hundred times."

"Nice way out for you, little mommy, isn't it?" Tracy stated with a smile.

"Oh…my…God, don't say that." Susi seemed shocked. Tracy grabbed the remote, turned off the television, and hopped up.

"Let's go to dinner!" Tracy announced; Sunday evening had become the one night a week they'd go out. "We need to get your mind off all this. Lance will be alright, and tomorrow is another day." Susi knew that there was no need to argue with Tracy. She went to her room and got dressed for the first time that day. Somehow she knew there was really no reason to take the test again.

They weren't gone too long, went home, chatted over a glass of wine, and turned in for the night. Despite knowing what the result would be, Susi took the second test–positive. Susi let Tracy know and waited for the Told you so. Instead Tracy hugged her and assured her that they would get through that and to not give into any negative thoughts.

"That's something you could small talk about on the phone this Sunday." Tracy laughed and startled Susi. Then both girls laughed.

****

Susi had gotten enough clothes to get her through the first few months. She had been paying attention to what expecting moms were wearing, and it seemed that showing off that growing belly had become somewhat fashionable. On her own time, she wouldn't mind wearing some of the fun things she'd gotten, but at work she would have to keep it more contemporary.

The fact that she still had to tell Dr. Carl about her pending motherhood gave her anxiety. Both he and his wife were very active in their church and knowing that Susi was in the process of getting divorced, the fact that her estranged husband had moved out a while ago and now she was pregnant by another man wouldn't sit well. A lot of lectures were in store for her from both the doctor and his wife. The phone rang. It startled her.

"Hello, baby." She could feel Lance smiling and the butterflies went wild in her stomach.

"How was your week? Anything fun happen?" he inquired.

She laughed and thought if he only knew. "Hasn't been too bad. Tracy and I got some more work done around the house and work is going okay."

"What's wrong? You sound sad?" Lance's voice turned serious.

"I just miss you." She had to hold back the tears. These days her mood switched faster than she could blink her eyes.

"I know, little one, I wish you were here with me," he whispered, and they both fell silent for a moment. "It'll only be a couple more months till you come up. You are still planning on coming up, right?"

"Of course," she replied. "Can I ask you a silly question?"

"Shoot." He giggled.

"I had a sort of funny dream last night." She blushed and was almost afraid to continue. "It really was silly…I was pregnant, and we were sitting on the couch."

She waited for a response but none came.

"You had your hand on my stomach and were talking to our baby." There was still silence at the other end. "Are you there?" Her heart began to pound. Maybe she shouldn't have gone there.

"It'll be nice when that won't have to be just a dream." His voice seemed to echo through the line.

"Really?" She sank down several inches with a sigh of relief. "When it does happen, would you prefer a boy or a girl?" Somehow that just seemed to slip out.

"A girl," he answered as if he had rehearsed what to say. "Preferably one as pretty as her mom."

"Hmm," she mused. "I would have figured you more for wanting a little boy, someone who can learn football and all that."

"Who says a girl can't play football?" he noted, and they both laughed.

They continued talking about their future kids and the family they would eventually have for a while longer before Susi drifted to sleep. She was out for almost an hour before something startled her and she woke up, the receiver still in her hand.

"Hello?" There was silence. She was sad that she didn't get to tell him good night as she laid the receiver in the cradle. A mere second later the phone rang again.

"There you are, princess." Lance laughed. "Did you have a good nap?"

"Oh, wow." She rubbed an eye. "You waited all this time?"

"Well, the line disconnected. I tried a few times, waiting for you to wake up and replace the receiver. I just got a busy signal till then, but now we both need to sleep, so I'll talk to you next Sunday, okay?"

"Okay." She could not have sounded sadder. "I wish this were all over and we were together."

"I know, baby, I know." He sounded compassionate. "Soon, I promise, very soon. Good night, honey, I miss and love you."

They exchanged a few more loving words before hanging up. She knew Lance had no problem falling asleep quickly. She, on the other hand, lay in the dark with her hands on her stomach and smiling to herself. Maybe she could tell Lance about the baby when she went up to see him in December. As she drifted off to sleep, she was sure she felt an ever-so-slight flutter under her hand.

****

Susi woke up from a beautiful dream. She was watching Lance sit on the couch holding their baby and talking to her. No sooner were her eyes open that she felt the vomit working its way up.

"I really can't wait for this part to be done," she muttered to no one in particular while leaning her head over the toilet. Maybe she should talk to her doctor about the morning sickness; it didn't seem to be getting any better. She was four months along and there had been no change in how severely intense her morning sickness had remained. Last month he had told her that she was a bit underweight and if she continued being sick, they would need to do something about it. Since her last checkup, she had not gained an ounce, and she was getting scared. Her doctor had ordered an ultrasound to make sure the baby was growing as it should, and a week ago, she had found out that everything was fine. The doctor wanted to see if possibly her diet was causing her continued morning sickness. She was to write down everything she ate and drank for a week. She sat across from Dr. Miles' desk while he studied her list.

"You should certainly not be losing weight," he stated as he looked at her above his glasses. "Let's try switching you to bottled water." Before she had a chance to answer, he continued. "I have seen this with some of my other patients. You do drink a lot of water and that might be the cause. Our tap water around here, especially in summer, tends to be rather hard, and you might be a bit sensitive to it."

"Wow, really?" She seemed relieved. "I don't see any problem with switching. You really think that is all it is?"

The doctor nodded. Susi felt as if a weight had been lifted, and after a few more minutes of discussing her diet, his gaze went back to her file.

"When you had your ultrasound, did they let you know the sex of the baby?" He smiled at her.

She felt a knot in her stomach. "No, the technician said she had a hard time seeing it."

"Well, she must have been able to because it is noted on their report." He looked at her. "Would you like to know?"

Susi felt herself blush. She hesitated for a moment only to wish with all her heart that Lance was sitting next to her, holding her hand, and hearing this with her. Then she nodded.

"It is a girl," he said. "She appears very healthy."

Susi wanted to cry with happiness.

"Are you all right?" the doctor asked her.

She nodded. "I wish her dad was here."

"I see." Dr. Miles looked back at the file. "Does he know?"

"Sadly, no." She quickly thought. "He's in the Navy and I haven't had a chance to tell him. With him on a ship, we don't get to talk," she lied.

The doctor looked at her. "When do you expect him back?"

"Not until after she's born," she replied with sadness in her voice.

"Is anyone here to help you with all of this?" He handed her a box of tissues. "Someone who will be with you for the delivery and to help you a bit afterwards?" He seemed genuinely concerned.

"Yes, my best friend is staying with me and she'll be here for the whole thing."

He got up off the chair. "Well, that's good to hear."

Susi got up, thanked him, and shook his hand.

"Let me know if the bottled water helps clear up the morning sickness," he stated.

"Will do." She left his office, checked with the front desk to see when her next appointment was scheduled, and walked out to her car. Glancing at the time, she noticed that there really was no need to go back to the office, and she was rather anxious to tell Tracy what she had learned. On her way home, she stopped by the grocery store and got several gallons of bottled water and some juice. She couldn't help but feel happy. Lance had said he'd like a girl. No sooner had that thought passed, she felt the knot in her stomach come back. How would she tell him? Not just how but when? Pulling up to the house, she noticed that Tracy's car was already there. She must have gotten off early again.

"Tracy?" Susi called out as she walked in with a couple of the water bottles.

"In the kitchen." Susi walked through to the kitchen, sat the water on the table, and smiled. Tracy did a double take.

"Did you go to your appointment?"

Susi nodded.

"Well, what did he say?"

"Oh, he thinks I'm sensitive to the hard water and he wants me to try bottled water and see if that helps." She continued grinning.

"You look like the cat that ate the canary and you expect me to believe that all he told you is to try bottled water?" Tracy smiled sheepishly, but before she could say anything else, Susi was jumping up and down with excitement.

"It's a girl, it's a girl!" She grabbed Tracy by her shoulders and then hugged her. Tracy pulled away. "Are you serious?" Her face lit up with a level of excitement that came close to Susi's.

"Didn't he say he'd like to have a little girl?" Tracy mentioned. The phone rang, and she went to answer it. Moments later she held out the receiver in front of her. "For you, it's your boss," she sneered.

For a few moments the only thing that left Susi's mouth was "Uh-huh" and then, "I'll be there in a minute." She hung up the phone.

"Everything okay? What the hell does he want after hours?" Tracy blurted out.

"The computers arrived." She rolled her eyes and slipped her shoes back on. "He just wants me to come up and make sure everything is there that is on the shipping order. The damn thing got here three weeks early; we can start adding the information and get done quicker."

She went to the door. "I won't be long. This shouldn't take more than an hour or so." Susi tried to squeeze out a smile. "We can go out to dinner when I get back." Without waiting for a reply, she walked out the door only to arrive at her office a few minutes later to find Dr. Carl frustrated.

"I can't make sense of any of this." He looked completely helpless with his chair parked in the middle of the front office surrounded by computer components, more than one would think would fit into those few boxes. Thinking quickly, Susi saw an opportunity. "I will help you with this under one condition." She put her hands on her hips. "I want to go to Chicago at the end of December and I need three days off no matter what."

"I don't know." He shook his head.

Susi dropped her hands and leaned forward. "I either get your promise right now that I can have those three days, or I'll go home right now and let you figure this out on your own."

"Fine." He shook his head again. "You know just what to do to get your way, don't you, young lady?"

She smiled and nodded. "I also would like for this to not take more than an hour. I haven't had dinner and I'd like to eat at a reasonable time."

He agreed. She sat on the floor, and he handed her four sheets of paper, which turned out to be the shipping slips. Each component had a sticker on it that matched a number on the sheet. She had him read the numbers to her while she marked them off the papers, and they were done in forty-five minutes. Dr. Carl thanked her with obvious relief and handed her a hundred-dollar bill.

"What's that for?" she asked.

"Your help and your never-ending patience with me," he answered, smiling. "Enjoy dinner on me."

They laughed, he turned out the lights, and they walked out together. She bid him a good night and got in her car. Before he shut the door on his, she rolled down her window. "Dr. Carl?" she called.

"What is it?" He had his hand on the door to close it.

"There is something I need to talk to you about sometime soon."

"You're not quitting, are you?" He got in his car.

"Oh no, nothing like that." There was that damn knot again.

He told her that they could talk during lunch the next day. He got back in his car and moments later they both drove off.

Within the hour Tracy and Susi were sitting at Applebee's, and once again Susi was beaming.

"Now what?" Tracy shook her head.

"I'm getting my three days off and he gave me a hundred to pay for dinner." She grinned while sticking French fries in her mouth.

"He gave you a hundred bucks and we came to Applebee's?" Tracy whispered.

Susi shrugged her shoulders. "I wanted a burger." Tracy had a couple of smart comments about the good old doctor. The two women hadn't laughed this much in weeks, and towards the end of the evening, Susi noticed that it was the first time in weeks she didn't feel sick after eating.

When she went to bed that night, she thought about what a great day it had been, and within the blink of an eye, her smile turned to tears. If she only knew how Lance would react to the baby. Another five weeks until she was supposed to go up north. Telling Dr. Carl about this was nowhere as scary as telling Lance. What would she do if he didn't want this?

There was a knock on her bedroom door. "Susi?" Tracy called from the other side of the door.

"What's up?" she answered.

The door opened, and Tracy stuck her smiling face in. "Honey, everything will be fine."

"What?" Susi sat up, and Tracy went in and sat at the edge of the bed.

"I know that behind all of your laughter and everything else, you show throughout the day there is one thing constantly occupying your mind, and that is how Lance will react." She took Susi's hand. "I know how he feels about you. Anyone who has seen him look at you can tell, and he will feel the same about his little girl. There is no doubt in my mind."

They hugged. "I hope so, I really do."

FOUR

That Little Bump

"You can't give up, even if all you can do is cry. Swallow your tears, stand up on your own two feet and show them you're not giving up, no matter what."

"WHEN ARE YOU DUE?" Dr. Carl asked Susi with a very stern expression, and she felt as if she were facing her own father, about to be punished.

"March twentieth of next year," she replied timidly.

"You said the father is in the Navy and has no idea?"

"Yes," she swallowed hard. "He is in A school right now and he's done with that at the end of December. That's what I want the three days off for, to go see him." The way he looked at her, she felt a tinge of embarrassment, and she couldn't help but think that she needed to call her aunt the following weekend and tell her about the baby as well, so she could tell her parents; maybe this would help bring them back into her life.

"You know how my wife and I feel about anyone having a child out of wedlock?"

Dr. Carl snapped her out of her thoughts.

"Yes, yes, I do." Susi's face lit up. "But if you could meet him and if you could understand how much we love each other...something like that can't be wrong."

"Then why haven't you told him?" he countered.

"I don't want him to make career decisions based on a child." She felt anger rising within her. "This is not just his fault, it is just as much mine, and face it, Doc, you're not the easiest to talk to when it comes to these things. You make me feel as if I'm talking to my own father."

He looked at her without expression for a moment, turned away, and took a deep sigh. Susi knew she'd gotten to him. When he finally broke the silence, he had just one question.

"How will your pregnancy affect your work?" He didn't wait for a response. "I need you fully focused on your job, especially while we are switching to the computers. I need…"

Susi interrupted him. She did not want to get angry and wanted this interrogation to be done with. He really had no right to meddle in her life this much, and she certainly wasn't his child.

"Dr. Carl, nothing will change in my work performance, and I spend enough time in this office to take an occasional day or half day off for a prenatal check." She stood up as if that would give her more authority. She had been working for him for the last few years and had never taken any time off. "I will go to Great Lakes at the end of December as planned. I will go to my prenatal check-ups as needed, and two weeks before my due date, I will start a two-to-three months' maternity leave." The more she spoke the stronger she felt. "I will make sure that Casey is familiar with everything I do, and you have nothing to worry about." She turned to head back to her desk. Once the door was open, she turned back to look at him. She opened her mouth to speak but paused for a moment to think. When she looked back at him, she had a soft glow in her eyes.

"Do you really believe this could be bad?" She looked him straight in the eyes. "I mean, God created this child, he allowed this to happen, this can't be wrong."

He smiled at her with a fatherly gentleness. "I know."

Within an hour, everyone in the office had heard about the expected baby, and Susi was bombarded with well wishes, hugs, and more questions than she'd wanted. For the most part, no one had issues with the news, but a couple of the girls wondered why she hadn't told the father. At the end of the day, she was exhausted just from explaining her decisions.

****

"I can't believe you let them question you like that," Tracy scoffed. "What the hell business is it of theirs what you do? You don't meddle in their lives, and they have no right to stick their fat noses in yours." Tracy slammed a pot on the stove a little harder than she had meant to. "Sorry," she mumbled.

Susi walked to her friend and hugged her. "Thank you for always being so worried about me. You really need to get some hold of that temper of yours, it is really not attractive."

Tracy gave her a little push and chuckled. "Whatever, dork."

The two women laughed. It only took a short time for dinner to be done, and the two sat at the kitchen table and shared childhood memories. What they had wanted their weddings to be like, their children and husbands, not that Tracy ever planned on getting married. She had been telling Susi that since they were sixteen and Tracy's parents divorced.

"I sure missed the mark the first time around, didn't I?" Susi grimaced her face.

Tracy laughed, "Uh, yeah, just a little. By the way, have you heard from him anymore?"

"Remember we have our final hearing next week, it'll be done and over with. I can't believe he had it postponed all this time, but I guess my attorney, and his, have had enough of his games."

"Not that I care," Tracy shrugged her shoulders, "but I am a bit curious. You know how I believe in karma, and I can't wait for that to bite him in the ass."

"Tracy," Susi scolded, "that's not very nice."

"Neither is he!" Tracy declared and raised her head in a defiant manner.

"Well," Susi sighed, "guess things with his girlfriend aren't the best. Seems that now that he is officially available, she's not that interested anymore."

"And that, my friend, is karma," Tracy exclaimed as she stacked the dishes on the table to take them to the sink.

Susi went to the bedroom to change and get comfortable for the evening. As she pulled down her shirt, she got a glimpse of herself in the mirror. She held the shirt up under her breast and turned sideways, giving her sweatpants a little nudge downward to fully expose her abdomen.

"Tracy?" she called out.

"Is everything okay?" the voice came back from the kitchen.

"Yeah, I just want to show you something," Susi responded. Tracy walked in the bedroom, drying her hands on a blue checkered dishtowel and immediately noticed what she had been summoned for.

"Wow! That is really noticeable." She laid her hand on Susi's stomach. "Can you feel it yet?"

"I think so," Susi said, "especially at night when I'm really still. I hadn't even noticed this…well, not this strongly, maybe because I wear scrubs all the time."

"I can understand how that could happen." Tracy gave the little bump a rub and took a step back. "Pull your shirt down," she instructed her friend, and Susi did as told.

"You can still hide it well, and I think you won't get that much bigger by the end of December," she stated matter-of-factly. "Besides, it will be freezing cold up there and you will be bundled up."

"Dr. Carl thinks I should tell Lance when I go up there. What do you think?" Susi looked at her friend.

"I think you should wait and see how things go," Tracy replied. "Maybe you can poke around some more when you talk."

"My concern is that he will notice it when the clothes come off, so I may not want to wait until that point to tell him," Susi shared. That thought had crossed her mind many times lately.

****

"How are we feeling today?" Dr. Miles asked.

"Not bad at all, actually." She smiled. "I haven't thrown up in the last three weeks or so, and the bottled water seems to have helped."

"I'm glad to hear that." He paused to look at her file and check over the notes the nurse had jotted down. "It looks like you have gained eight pounds since we last saw you," he said with a smile.

"Good grief." Susi was shocked. "Eight pounds in less than three weeks?"

"There is nothing wrong with that," he assured her. "Keep in mind you haven't really gained anything, and you are approaching the fifth month."

"That's true," she agreed.

"In another month or so, I'd like you to have another ultrasound." He looked her right in the eyes.

"How come?" Susi felt herself blush and that knot in her stomach tighten again.

"Didn't you say a while ago you planned on flying up north at the end of December?" he inquired.

"Yes, sir, I did."

"That's why," he stated. "I just want to make sure everything is good for you to fly. You'll be almost six months by then. Have you felt the baby kick yet?"

"I think so." She laid her hand on her stomach. "At night, when I'm really still, I can feel little flutters."

"That will increase significantly very soon, and it will be unmistakable," he concluded.

They chatted a moment longer, and then he told Susi to schedule her next appointment on the way out. He also told her they would schedule the ultrasound for her, so she should expect a call with the details. She felt good for the first time in weeks, and when she left the doctor's office, she decided to invite Tracy to dinner; maybe Mexican would be good. She just felt like celebrating; it didn't matter that there was nothing to celebrate. Two more days till Sunday and she would get to talk to Lance and then just five more weeks till she would fly up to see him. Every time she thought about being in his arms again, she got butterflies. A quick trip to the store for some essentials they needed and then home.

As she turned the key to open the door, she heard the phone ring.

She slammed the door shut behind her, which caused a picture to fall off the wall, dropped the bags on the couch, and ran the few steps to the phone.

"Hello?" She was out of breath.

"Hi, baby." Lance's voice seemed to beam at the other end of the line.

"Oh, my goodness." She was so thrilled, "I miss you so much. Thank you so much for calling. Is everything all right? Are you okay? Nothing happened, did it?" She caught herself, how could he answer if she kept rambling on?

"Everything is fine." He laughed. "I just wanted to tell you that I booked your flight and you can go to the airport when you have time to pick up your ticket, or I can get it and send it to you."

Susi squeaked with delight. "You are incredible. Really, you are so amazing."

"It's almost time. I can't wait to see you," he said. Susi could feel his warmth through the receiver.

"I love you so much. Do you think I can go tonight to get the ticket?" she asked.

"I love you too, honey." He chuckled. "I'm sure it's fine if you go get it tonight."

"Are you still gonna call me Sunday?"

"Of course, silly." He seemed to be in a great mood. "I wouldn't miss hearing your sweet voice tell me that you love me for anything."

They talked for a bit longer, and Tracy came home just before they hung up. She was as surprised as Susi that he had called two days ahead of schedule. Susi told her that he had called to let her know about the ticket, and that she wanted to go to dinner, and that she felt like Mexican. Tracy laughed. "Okay."

Not two hours later they were on their way to Sky Harbor Airport to pick up the ticket and then on to dinner. Susi decided she wanted to start getting some baby clothes, so they looked at some stores after dinner and got a couple of little outfits. Doing that seemed to add to Susi's overall level of excitement.

****

The next few weeks seemed to fly by. The ultrasound results were fine, and Dr. Miles gave her the all-clear to go. The morning of her departure arrived, and she could not have been more nervous. Her flight was at seven thirty in the morning, which meant that she should be at the airport no later than six thirty. She had told Tracy the night before that she would like to leave at least ninety minutes before in case of traffic, given that they were leaving right before morning rush hour. Highway 60 to Phoenix could turn into a parking lot in a matter of minutes. The sun had not yet peeked over the Superstition Mountains when the two young women got in the car to leave.

"You really should have eaten something more than half a bowl of oatmeal," Tracy scolded.

"I'm too nervous to eat and I don't want to get sick on the plane." Susi reached for the power knob on the radio and turned it. Music began to play, and both women began to sing along. Moments later a news update, weather, and then traffic. Nothing that would affect them, and Susi let out a sigh of relief. They made their way west on Highway 60 towards Phoenix when they heard the unexpected traffic update. A huge accident on the 60 and I-10 interchange. This would affect them in the worst way, as they had to go that way to get to the airport. They both looked at the clock at the exact same moment.

Five fifty, they had forty minutes to get to the airport. Not a half mile later, traffic had come to a complete stop. No one was moving, and the next exit was over two miles away. By the time they made it to the next exit, it was six fifty. They were not the only ones who had thought about getting off the freeway, and there were back-ups at every single light and every single intersection. Susi couldn't help but look from the road to the clock and back again. With every minute passing, her fear of not making the flight increased. At seven forty-five they pulled up at Sky Harbor. Susi could only hope that there had been some kind of delay.

They parked the car and went to the ticket counter.

"I'm sorry, miss, that flight left fifteen minutes ago," the agent at the

"Are you sure?" Susi felt relieved. She had been reluctant to take this trip by herself, not so much for the drive but breaking the news alone and having him ask questions.

"Yes, I'm sure. I don't suppose you and I being so close has anything to do with that." They both laughed.

Within what seemed only minutes, Tracy had called one of her co-workers to let him know that she was taking a few days off. Being in a higher position, that seemed to be no problem.

Tracy glanced at the kitchen clock with a sheepish grin on her face. Susi knew those smiles. "Oh my god, what are you conjuring up now?"

Tracy grinned. "Just a crazy idea. It's only two thirty on Friday afternoon, we both have the day off. Instead of just being lazy, why don't we try to get out of here by three? We will be in San Diego around nine. Well, let's say ten if we stop and have dinner."

"That's a great idea, but what about Lance calling this evening?" Susi was excited.

"We can just record something on the answering machine for him. I'm sure he'd be thrilled to know that you'll be there sooner and that you'll actually make it this time."

"True!" Susi shouted. "Let's do it."

Together they cleaned up the kitchen, finished packing, and were on the road just minutes after three. Traffic was a breeze that Friday afternoon, which Susi noted as a positive sign. Despite the energetic conversation and light heartedness between the two of them, Susi felt increasingly tense and excited, happy but somewhat worried. There were mild pains that she knew she should not be feeling, but she wanted to keep going. She had always been such an optimist, and it really had not crossed her mind that he might not be as happy about this as her.

She knew he had been adopted as a small child, and his birth mother had been instructed to avoid all contact until he was eighteen. He was about to turn twenty-seven and still had never heard from her. Susi had no idea how this news would affect him; when they had talked about children, he always seemed excited to, someday, be a father. That was the word that bothered her: someday.

He had joined the Navy to get away from home. His adoptive parents had divorced when he was sixteen and he hadn't liked life much since then; for some reason he had always blamed himself a little for their split. Susi felt she had a fifty-fifty chance he'd appreciate the situation, and she knew how very much in love she was with him. For now, nothing else should matter.

At the second rest stop in Quartzsite, close to the state border to California, Susi knew something was wrong. After she had used the toilet, she could barely stand up. She went out to the car holding her stomach.

"What's wrong?" Tracy asked with concern.

"I'm really sorry, I should have told you sooner." Susi sat on the seat with the car door still open. "I've been having some pains and they seem to be getting worse."

"Holy shit, Susi!!" Tracy jumped out of the car and walked around to her friend. "Yes, you should have told me sooner, but right now we need to call your doctor. We are over two hours away from home." She grabbed Susi's purse from the back seat. "His number is in your little book, right?"

Susi nodded.

"Are you okay to sit here for a moment?" Tracy stood up.

Susi said, "It's not that bad. I'm just a little concerned, especially since it's getting worse."

"Are they like labor pains?" Tracy's heart was racing.

"No, I don't think so." Susi recollected the last few pains. "They aren't regular."

"Well, I don't think that means anything," Tracy stated. "Stay put, I'm gonna go call. Hopefully, I can get a hold of him this late on Friday afternoon." She walked to the pay phone. Susi could see her drop the change in, dial the number, then hold the receiver to her ear. She could see her talking but couldn't hear what was being said.

"I got his answering service," Tracy shouted. "I told them what's going on and they are checking to see if they can get a hold of him."

Moments later Tracy gave Susi a thumbs up. She assumed that meant Tracy had Dr. Miles on the phone. When she hung up, Susi could see by her expression that something was coming that she would not like.

"I know you won't like this," Tracy said reluctantly. "We have to go back. Doctor Miles wants to see you at the hospital as soon as we can get back there."

"This is just fucking great," Susi snarled. "How am I going to explain this to Lance? This is the second time I'm not showing up. I swear I thought everything in the world wanted us to be together, but the way it's going, it seems like that is no longer the case." She fought the tears.

"Don't say that, Susi." Tracy smiled at her. Susi knew it was a fake but sympathetic smile. They made their way back onto I-10 heading east.

"You know he loves you and you know he will understand. He's not expecting you until tomorrow, and maybe it was your nerves that caused this." Tracy looked over at Susi in the passenger seat and saw tears rolling down her face. "You can call him when we get home and explain that you'll just be a little later tomorrow."

Susi tried to stop crying. What Tracy had said made sense. She wasn't really supposed to go till tomorrow anyway. Maybe all she needed to do was get a hold of her nerves.

****

Tracy tried to engage her in light conversation for the next couple of hours and, luckily, the traffic wasn't too bad. Susi hadn't noticed that Tracy had been speeding most of the way and they made it back by just before nine. By the time they got to the hospital, Susi's pain had gotten so bad that she could not stay focused on their conversation. Tracy parked right in front of the emergency doors and yelled for help. An orderly came running with a wheelchair.

"She is Dr. Miles's patient and he is expecting her," Tracy told the orderly as they helped Susi into the wheelchair.

He told Tracy to park the car and then come in.

"Ma'am, are you going to be able to get into a gown by yourself?" the orderly asked Susi in the emergency room unit. He held his hand out for her to take before standing up.

"I think so," she responded.

He looked at Tracy, who had joined them. "If you can help your friend change, I can go let Dr. Miles know that she's here."

"Absolutely!" Tracy took Susi's hand, and the orderly closed the curtain as he walked out. Neither of the girls managed to say a word. No sooner had Susi settled on the bed, Dr. Miles walked in with the orderly in tow.

"What are you doing, my dear?" He took Susi's hand and smiled.

Susi shrugged her shoulders. "This could not have come at a worse time."

"She is going to tell the dad tomorrow," Tracy chimed in.

"Aha," Dr. Miles said, "I guess that is why you were on your way to San Diego?"

Susi nodded as she fought the tears again, and Tracy took her hand and nodded at the doctor as well.

"Well, let's see if we can still make that happen, shall we?" He checked her pulse and blood pressure. Susi noticed the frown on his face. He took her pressure a second time.

"I'd like to see why your blood pressure is so high." He turned his attention to the orderly. "Let's get her on an IV, bloodwork, and an ultrasound." Looking back at Susi, he said, "Don't worry, dear, we will take good care of you. The last thing you need to do right now is worry too much. I'll be back with you right after the ultrasound." He gave Susi's hand another squeeze and disappeared on the other side of the curtain. Only seconds later a nurse came in to connect the IV and get some blood. The ultrasound technician was polite and reassuring as she completed her test.

It seemed like hours before Dr. Miles popped back in. When he pushed the curtain aside, Susi could tell from the expression on his face he was coming with bad news.

"I'm really sorry, Susi, but we are going to have to keep you here overnight."

"Is everything okay with the baby?" Tracy wanted to know.

"Yes, the baby is fine, but for some reason Susi's blood pressure is rather high, causing the baby a lack in oxygen. We need to get this under control to make sure your little one continues being fine." Susi could feel the tears well up in her eyes.

"Susi, one thing I need you to do is stay as calm as you can. Any spike in your blood pressure can cause more problems." He squeezed her hand. "I know this is not what you wanted to hear, but I know that your main concern right now needs to be your health and that of your child." She nodded.

"I will have a nurse come in to get you admitted and take you upstairs. I will check on you in the morning. We will give you a mild sedative tonight and see how things are tomorrow."

Susi couldn't speak. The doctor gestured Tracy to follow him out so he could speak to her without Susi.

"I'll be right back, sweetie, okay?" Tracy hugged her friend and then followed the doctor.

Susi heard them walk away, but not far enough for her not to hear what the Doctor was telling Tracy.

"This is not an uncommon condition, but we need to get it under control. If the placenta is deprived of oxygen for too long, it will create big problems for the baby and could result in a miscarriage."

Susi heard Tracy gasp. "Is this an actual condition, or just a fluke thing?"

"Yes," Dr. Miles said. "It is known as preeclampsia. We can control this with medication and, most of all, she needs to avoid all forms of stress and, for now, travel. She only has three months to go. The baby is showing no signs of distress, so everything should be fine."

"Oh, great." Susi heard Tracy and figured she'd be rolling her eyes. "It'll be fun explaining that to her."

"I am counting on you!" he told Tracy, and then Susi heard him walk away as Tracy slowly shuffled back to Susi's ER cubicle. She stopped at the other side of the curtain and sighed.

"You can come in, I heard you guys anyway," Susi announced. Tracy pulled the curtain aside and smiled.

"You suck at faking it, you know that, right?" Susi asked. "So I can't go to San Diego at all, did I hear that right?" Tracy nodded.

"You're not going to be able to travel until after the little terror is born." Tracy played with the edge of the blanket and avoided Susi's eyes.

"Hey now, it's not her fault," Susi stated firmly. "Well, this is just fucking great. Lance is not going to believe that I am standing him up again." The tears were welling up in Susi's eyes. "Maybe we aren't meant to be together. Maybe I'm just meant to be a single mom." The tears rolled down her cheeks, and she looked so sad that it made Tracy cry as well.

Tracy moved to her friend's side and hugged her.

"Do you want me to call him?" Tracy whispered.

"And tell him what? Susi's in the hospital and oh, by the way, she's six months pregnant with your child?" Susi mocked. "I'm sure he'll hop in his car and come right out here."

Tracy backed away a step. "At least let me try. Neither of us really knows what he'll do."

"All right." Susi wiped her sleeve across the bottom of her nose. "His number is in my purse. What have I got to lose at this point?"

Tracy grabbed the purse as the nurse came in to move Susi to an upstairs room.

"Why don't I go home while they get you moved?" Tracy offered. "I can make that call and grab whatever you want or need. Toiletries are in the bag in the car already."

"Well, there's not much choice is there? I guess you can bring me some PJs." Susi looked as hopeless as she could. Tracy hugged her and gave her a kiss on top of her head. "I love you."

"Love you too." Susi faked a smile. "You know what, why don't you just run home and when you come back, we'll call from the room?"

"That makes sense," Tracy agreed. "That way you can tell him the good news." Tracy winked. "I promise I will be back within an hour."

****

As promised she got back quickly. Susi had been moved to a small single room and was settling in. Tracy helped her change out of the gown into the pajamas. As soon as Susi had settled back against the pillows, she asked Tracy to call Lance.

She dialed the number that was on the piece of paper. The phone rang a couple of times before a male voice answered.

"Master Chief Miller, how may I help you?" he asked.

"Hello, I am trying to reach Lance Wells," Tracy hesitantly replied.

"One moment, please, I'll get him." She heard the receiver being set down and then the voice shouted Lance's last name. Moments later there was a voice at the other end of the receiver.

"Hello, this is HM3 Wells."

"Hi, this is Tracy," she stated with a slightly shaky voice.

"Oh, hey, I figured you guys would be out here already. Is everything okay? Where is Susi?" They both heard the worry building in his voice.

"Well, since you mention it, we are actually in the hospital. She's in a bed, I'm not. The doctor says she'll be fine, but they want to keep her overnight," Tracy explained. Susi heard Lance trying to say something, but Tracy interrupted him. "Let me explain."

"Sorry, I'm listening," he said.

"We were on our way out there. We were getting close to the state line when she started not feeling good. We'd stopped for a bathroom break and called her doctor, and he said we needed to turn back and meet him at the hospital. For some reason her blood pressure is too high and she's having some abdominal pains. That is why they are keeping her overnight for observation."

"Is he still there?" Susi whispered.

"Are you still there?" Tracy asked softly.

"Yes," Lance stated firmly. "Are you sure she even wants to see me and didn't just put you up to this? I mean, we haven't seen each other in six months."

"I promise you I am telling you the truth." Tracy was holding the receiver with both hands. She covered the mouthpiece with her hand and asked Susi, "Do you want to talk to him?"

Susi nodded and Tracy handed her the receiver.

"Hey, it's me." Her voice was shaky. "I need to tell you something. I didn't want to do this on the phone, but I have no other choice."

"What is it?" Lance sounded stern.

"I'm sorry this shit keeps happening. I mean, the accident last time really wasn't my fault." Susi took a deep breath. "I didn't know I had this preeclampsia condition."

"Wait, isn't that a blood pressure condition some pregnant women get?" He paused and waited.

"Yes!" was all Susi could say. The tears were running down her face and she had a lump in her throat. This wasn't going well.

"You are pregnant. Who's the father? I mean, I haven't seen you in six months." His voice was cold, and Susi didn't know what to do with that.

"I'm six months pregnant. I missed my period after I was at Great Lakes and took a test. I haven't been with anyone else." She was on a roll now. "I wanted to tell you when I came up at the end of December, but we both know how that turned out. This was not something I wanted to tell you on the phone when we had physically only been together once."

There was silence at the other end.

"Lance, I by no means expect anything from you. Like I said, I would have rather done this face to face," she added.

"When are you due?" he asked. There was no change in the tone of his voice.

"March twentieth," Susi responded just as coldly.

"Which hospital are you at?" he asked.

"Banner Baywood in Mesa," Susi replied. "Like I said, I do not expect anything from you. I am sure that this is not something that fits into your plans right now. Just know that I love you more than anything, and I will always love you. All I can say now is that I am sorry...sorry for not telling you, sorry for being careless, sorry for allowing this to happen, sorry for everything. Take care of yourself." Without hesitation she hung up.

Tracy who had been staring at the silent TV flung around.

"What the fuck just happened?" she asked.

"I don't think this is what he wants," Susi answered and laid her hand on her rounded belly. She felt the tears welling up. "You should have heard the tone in his voice, like ice." The tears began to roll down her face.

"Susi, please don't think that way." Tracy stood up, walked to the bed, and laid Susi's head against her chest, trying to comfort her. A nurse interrupted them to give Susi a sedative and to tell Tracy that she needed to leave since it was well past visiting hours.

"I'll be okay." Susi faked a smile and took a deep breath. "We knew it was a fifty-fifty chance. Will you be back first thing in the morning?"

"Of course, sweetheart." Tracy looked as if she wanted to cry. "I'll set the alarm for six, take a quick shower, and come right down. I'll get us a coffee in the cafeteria after I get here."

As the door closed behind Tracy, Susi began to cry again. She found a million reasons why this was all her fault. She buried her face in her pillow and cried until the sedative took over and she fell asleep.

****

"Susi?" Lance had heard the click. "Hello?" He starred at the receiver. He thought to himself that he really could have handled that different, better. His mind was racing. She's pregnant. He was going to be a dad. Did he just completely push her away. There was no way to call her back. Surely, this late the hospital wouldn't put a call through to a room. He had to try to get a hold of Tracy.

He went to find Tony, Tracy's brother, woke him up, and told him what was going on.

"I can give you the house number," Tony muttered. "Don't you have that anyway?"

"Oh shit, you're right. Sorry for waking you up, man," Lance apologized.

"What are you gonna do?" Tony asked.

"I'm gonna call Tracy, tell her that I didn't mean to come across the way I did, something in my mind just clicked," he began to explain. "I love that woman more than life. I don't want to lose her. Then I'm gonna wake up Chief and tell him I'm going to Arizona because of a family emergency. Then I'm gonna talk you into going with me so I don't have to make that long ass drive by myself."

"I wouldn't wake up the chief. As long as we're back Monday night, we're fine," Tony assured him.

"So, you'll go?" Lance asked.

"Fuck yeah, man." Tony smiled. "Wouldn't mind seeing how this turns out and give my sisters some crap."

Lance went to his room and packed a few things; his roommate was gone for the weekend. He had told Tony to come get him when he was ready. Lance sat at the brown desk and stared out of his window for a moment. The hills in the distance were just a shade of black and grey at that time of night. He picked up the receiver and dialed the number to Susi's house.

"Hello," Tracy answered sounding sleepy.

"Tracy, it's Lance," he began, and she cut him off.

"You've got some nerve, mister." She was angry.

"I know, I fucked up, hear me out, please," Lance begged. There was a knock on the door and Tony came in. Lance motioned that he was on the phone.

"Tracy?" Tony whispered and Lance nodded.

"Listen, I do not want to lose her. I handled this whole thing completely wrong," Lance admitted. "Tony and I are leaving right now, and we should be there by six."

"Really?" Tracy was surprised. "What do you plan to do?"

"I haven't quite figured that out yet, but I will be on the way," Lance said. "I'm gonna hand you to your brother so you can tell him where we need to go. In my state of mind, I'll forget."

Tony wrote down some instructions and then they headed out. It would take them just about six hours to get there, and it was close to midnight when they left. Lance had told Tracy that they would call as soon as they got there. She had told him that she planned to get up at six, shower, and head to the hospital. They agreed to meet in the lobby of the hospital at seven.

They took turns driving so they would have a little time to sleep along the way. Lance had asked Tracy if she went to Susi's room before meeting them to please not tell her they were coming.

****

At six thirty the next morning, they were in the hospital lobby. Tracy was waiting in one of the chairs. She looked tired.

"Hey, sis," Tony announced, and she got up.

"I told her last night that I would get coffee and then go up to her room," Tracy told them. They got the coffee and headed for the elevator. Lance got the butterflies as soon as the elevator doors opened. They stopped at the nurses' station. There were two nurses on duty, and Susi's room was three doors down. Tracy explained what they were all doing there and wanted to make sure that they were okay to go in. A short blonde nurse told them it was fine and said that Susi had been restless during the night.

"That would be my fault," Lance stated.

"Stop saying shit like that." Tracy had her stern tone of voice that Lance had heard a few times. "Tell you what, why don't you take her coffee and go in and surprise her?"

He took the cup from Tracy and walked the short way to room 301. He gently knocked and slowly pushed the door open.

Susi must have fallen asleep again. It was still dark outside, and there was just a dim light on the nightstand with lights on her monitors. Everything he had felt for her the first time he had seen her was right there again. He placed the coffee cups on the small table in the corner, smiled gently and softly walked towards the bed. He stood, watching her sleep for several minutes and then leaned to kiss her forehead. She slightly moved, reaching up to rub her nose, and barely opened her eyes. He kissed her lips and whispered, "I'm so sorry." Not fully awake, she wrapped her arms around him and pulled him close. Needing his hand to balance himself, he brushed against her stomach and paused. He felt the little movement through the blanket.

"Is that...?" His eyes widened. Susi nodded. "Can I?" He began to pull the blanket back while Susi nodded again. He gently laid both his hands on her stomach and stared intensely. He didn't have to wait long before he felt the strong kicks of the little being hidden beneath its mother's belly. He leaned down to gently kiss her stomach.

A light knock on the door broke his concentration. The door slowly opened, and Tracy stuck her head through the crack.

"Can we come in?" Tracy asked.

"Check this out!" Lance almost shouted, smiling from ear to ear.

"I know, I've lived with her, remember?" Tracy smiled and pushed the door open with Tony right behind her. All the troubles of the last few hours and months seemed to vanish, and the four friends enjoyed a conversation and fantasizing about the baby for the next hour while they had their coffee. While Susi had breakfast, Tracy and Tony went to the cafeteria. They told Lance they would bring something up.

By the time Dr. Miles made his rounds, they were all back in the room. There was a soft knock at the door, and the doctor came in. He seemed surprised to see that many people in Susi's room that early in the morning.

"You've got quite the support team, don't you?" He smiled and looked at Lance. "Are you the father of that little princess?"

Lance smiled, nodded, and stood up to shake the doctor's hand. "Yes, sir, I sure am. I just hadn't known that it was a girl. Susi hadn't had the chance to tell me yet." He squeezed Susi's hand and pulled it up while he leaned down and kissed it.

"I guess I let the cat out of the bag, I'm sorry," the doctor apologized. "This little mom is going to need some rest and as little excitement as possible," he said. "I highly advise against her traveling until after she's had the baby."

"I can stay for the weekend but need to be back in San Diego by Monday night." Lance looked concerned.

"When will she be able to go home?" Lance asked Dr. Miles.

"We are getting her paperwork ready now." The doctor turned to leave.

"Hey, Doc." Lance stood up. "Can I have a word?" The doctor nodded, and the two men walked out into the hall.

"I was hoping to take her back to San Diego with me. Would that be at all possible?" Lance waited for the response.

"Well, I can't say I'm thrilled about that, but if you drive and she is well rested, it should be okay. I would want her to come by my office Monday morning just to check her again. When would you be leaving?"

"We'd have to leave no later than three on Monday afternoon to get back in time," Lance stated. "My friend Tony suggested I call and see about getting a couple extra days, but I don't know."

"Okay. Well, bring her in Monday morning, and we'll see. If she rests over the weekend and excitement is avoided, she should be fine. We will check her pressure and heart rate one more time and then the nurse will bring the discharge papers if everything checks out." Dr. Miles shook Lance's hand and walked to the nurses' station. Lance stood outside of the room, laid his hand on the doorknob to open it, and hesitated for a moment. He knew what he had to do right now. He pushed the door open and walked into the room.

"Is everything okay?" Susi was puzzled by his facial expression; she had no idea what to make of it. Lance walked to the bed, took her hand, and asked her to sit up. Susi rearranged herself while looking at Tracy and Tony, both shrugging their shoulders. Lance took her hand again and got down on one knee. "Susi Jury, I have been in love with you from the moment I met you. There were times I wasn't sure if you felt the same, but I now know that you do. I know this might seem crazy right now, and if you need time to think about it, I'll understand, but I would be the happiest man on earth if you agreed to become my wife."

Tears rolled down her face and she smiled the biggest smile while nodding yes. She had no words. Lance stood up, still holding her hand. So much for no excitement. "I haven't gotten a ring...yet...but we can do that together. Am I understanding your nod to mean yes?"

"Of course," Susi answered. "Yes, yes, yes."

Lance leaned in to kiss his brand-new fiancée and then looked at their friends; they both seemed struck. Tracy was the first to recover and literally jumped and yelled, "Woo-hoo!" Tony shook his head, walked to the bed, and gave Susi a hug. "Congratulations." He shook Lance's hand, smiled, and shook his head again.

"Oh my god, how exciting, congratulations." No one had noticed that the nurse, Emma, had come into the room. "I don't think in all of my years of nursing I have ever seen a proposal before. This is awesome." She walked to the bed, leaned over, and hugged Susi. Moments later she explained the instructions Susi was to follow at home and let her know that an appointment with Dr. Miles had been scheduled for eight thirty Monday morning.

The guys stepped into the hall to give Susi privacy to get dressed.

"I can't believe you did that. You have literally only spent one night with her, not even a whole twenty-four hours," Tony said as the door shut behind them.

"I love her, she's having my baby, and I want to marry her. Where is the confusion?" Lance looked stern.

"Isn't this a little spontaneous?" Tony inquired.

"It may appear that way." Lance was confident. "But there is nothing I have been surer about. I was going to tell you on the way back to San Diego. I talked to Chief about switching to FMF. You still in?" He had decided to go with the Fleet Marine Forces, a special unit within the Navy.

"You seriously want to go FMF now?" Tony didn't wait for a response. "How do you think your bride-to-be is going to take that?"

"She knows that it was either pharmacy school or FMF." Lance shrugged his shoulders. "I really don't want to be a pill pusher."

"I got ya, brother!" Tony chuckled.

"Since I have you here alone, you want to be my best man?"

"Absolutely," Tony answered.

The door opened, and Tracy emerged with Susi right behind her. The four of them stood there in silence for a moment. Susi finally spoke. "Well, now what? When do you guys have to be back?"

"We need to head back Monday afternoon. I want you to come with me." Lance stared firmly into her eyes. "Your doctor wants you to come in Monday morning, and he'll make the decision then."

"Oh, wow!" Susi didn't get a chance to say much of anything else.

"Did you not hear the doctor say strict bed rest?" Tracy pointed out.

"Tell you guys what." Tony took charge. "I saw some restaurants not far from here. Why don't we go grab lunch and make plans?"

The four of them agreed, as they were all getting a little hungry. Susi knew she would have to call her boss and let him know that she would not be coming back to work for a bit. She knew he'd not be happy; she had promised that this pregnancy would not affect her work, but she had not planned on this, and she was not risking her baby for his office.

The group walked into Applebee's and waited to be seated. Susi seemed to have gotten her appetite back, and her friends had to laugh at her order combination.

"Funny how these restaurants all more less look the same. Applebee's literally reminds me of Bennigan's." Lance smiled.

"Just a different color scheme, different décor, and different food. Other than that they're the same," Tracy stated.

"I have no idea what to tell Doctor Carl. He is going to be so pissed." Susi started to get emotional. She slid into a booth, and Lance sat next to her. Tony and Tracy sat across from them, and Tracy grabbed the flip-menu with all the cocktails and happy hour items listed.

"I'm gonna call Doctor Carl when we get to the house." She had worked for the man for years, and though he was a grouch, they always figured things out. The group was quiet for a moment, but they all knew she was right.

"Let's get back to this getting married business for a minute." Tracy broke the silence. "What's the plan?"

Lance took Susi's hand and laid it on his lap under the table. "Here is my suggestion. Tony and I will head back to California tomorrow after lunch. I do need to talk to the chief."

"You're switching to FMF, aren't you?" Susi got teary eyed again.

"Yes, my love, but you know how much this means to me." He put his arm around her and gave her a gentle squeeze. "I'll get a little time off to switch from San Diego to Camp Pendleton. We can get married and get you moved out there during that time." He gently rubbed her tummy. "Of course, it is all up to this little lady." Susi leaned her head against his shoulder.

The small group finished lunch and headed to Susi's house. She told the guys to make themselves comfortable and knew that Tracy would take care of them. She hugged Lance, and he gave her a glance that made her feel stronger. She made her way to the bedroom, arranged the pillows, sat on the bed, and leaned into the small pile of fluff. It felt good to get her feet up again. She reached for the receiver of the phone and dialed the number to reach Dr. Carl. He answered in his usual grouchy tone of voice.

"Hi, Dr. Carl, it's Susi."

"I thought you were in California for the weekend," he growled. "Is everything okay?"

"Well, as a matter of fact, no." Susi swallowed hard. "I just got home from the hospital after spending the night there. I have this condition that causes my heart rate to spike really high. They've moved me to a high-risk list, and I am on strict bed rest for a few days." She waited for his response, expecting him to be really upset.

"You and the baby are fine now though, right?" he calmly inquired. Susi was sincerely surprised by his concern. "Yes, we are both fine, and the baby's dad surprised me. He came from California when he found out about my trip to the hospital. He proposed this morning."

"Does that mean you are moving?" he asked.

She started to feel discouraged again. "If I want to marry him and be with him, then yes, I will have to move."

"That does present a problem." He sounded withdrawn. "I do understand though. Honestly, Susi, the missus and I had sort of been expecting something like this. You have been such a loyal employee and have grown to be just like a daughter for us. You know we will hate losing you, right?" Susi was very surprised and had to fight the tears.

"I know," she whispered.

"Susi, we will figure this out. I am sure you have a recommendation for who is competent enough to take your place. You had mentioned Casey before. You have written such a good office manual that training someone new should not be that hard." He was on a roll. "If at all possible, stop by the office Monday. I'd like to see you before he sweeps you away."

Susi chuckled through the tears and told him she'd be in the office Monday afternoon during lunch.

SIX

A Decision Has to Be Made

*"The military is my husband's mistress and sometimes
that bitch gets all of his attention!"*

M ONDAY CAME, SUSI WAS at the office to see Dr. Miles as
instructed. He gave her a prescription and checked her pressure.
He also told her that he wanted her to get with a new doctor as quickly
as possible when she got to California. Susi told him that she wasn't
going for a couple of weeks and that they were going to Camp Pendleton, near Oceanside. She went to visit Dr. Carl right after her appointment, not just to say her goodbyes but also to recommend her
replacement. She was beyond shocked when Dr. Carl handed her a
check for twenty-five thousand dollars. He had told her now and then
that she was his most valued asset and that she had become like a daughter to him and his wife, but she'd always figured that was just something
he said. This would surely come in handy with getting a place, getting
married, and having the baby. She couldn't wait to tell Lance. Dr. Carl
had told her to consider that a wedding present.

Susi spent a few minutes with Casey and explained that she would still be
in town for a couple of weeks, so if she needed any help she could call. She
had lunch with Tony and Lance before they headed out, and Lance asked her
to take it easy as much as possible; the next two weeks would fly by.

"You are not going to believe what Dr. Carl did today," she said,
hugging Lance. "He gave me a check for twenty-five thousand dollars
as a wedding gift."

Lance and Tony were both speechless. "Are you serious?" Lance finally responded. "That will really help with the move and everything." Susi smiled and bounced in her seat a little.

Tony looked at his watch. "I think we need to head out." Lance nodded. Tony took care of the check, gave Susi a hug, and told Lance he'd be waiting in the car.

"Here we go again, one of us leaving," Susi stated as a tear rolled down her face.

Lance took her face in his hands. "Don't cry, honey, it's just a couple weeks. I'll call you tonight, all right? Please promise that you will take it easy." Susi nodded. She watched them drive away and then went to her own car. She had a few more errands to run and then went home. She hadn't realized the day had flown by and before she knew it, the phone rang.

"Wow, you guys got back quick for a weekday," Susi said.

"Yeah, Interstate Eight wasn't bad at all, which was surprising," Lance told her. He sounded sad.

"Everything okay, my love?" Susi asked.

"I got approved for FMF school, so I'll be training in Camp Pendleton for twelve weeks. It'll be tough, and I'm not sure where they want to send me after that. We could get base housing, but once we get married, it's still gonna take a minute to put in all the paperwork and get you on DEERS benefits. What do you think?" She could tell he was nervous waiting for her response.

"I'm near the end of my sixth month." She was counting on her fingers while talking and it wasn't easy. "That means two more weeks for January, four in February, and then three-ish in March. The little one should be here before you are done with training. Maybe we can get a short-term rental?"

"We'll figure it out, baby." Hearing the relief in his voice made her feel better. "Just a suggestion, but how about using some of that money to hire movers? I'd rather you not do all that work, especially since you aren't supposed to."

"That's a great idea. I will make some phone calls tomorrow. I miss you so much." Now she began to cry.

"Don't cry, my love, it's only a few more days." She wished he could hold her. "I hope we can have you out here within the next ten days or so and get married. I'll get all the paperwork in the next couple of days."

"I know, my love, it's just hard without being able to touch you. You'll call tomorrow?" Susi wanted to know.

"Of course, babe, have a good night, I love you so much."

"I love you too, good night."

They both hung up at the same time as usual, and only moments later Tracy came in.

"Hey, where are you? Wanna go to dinner?" She headed down the hall to find her friend in the bedroom. "Just get off the phone?" She could tell when Susi had talked to Lance. "Everything okay?" Tracy noticed that Susi seemed a little upset.

"Yeah," Susi sighed. "Just this FMF school thing kinda screws with the wedding and even more so, with getting a place."

"Let's go eat." Tracy grabbed her friend's arm and pulled her gently towards the kitchen.

They headed to Scottsdale and spent the evening eating, talking, and making plans. By the time they headed home, they had decided that a small wedding would be best, given the circumstances that really made the most sense. The next morning Susi called the moving company to make the arrangement but was quickly faced with the next challenge. Not letting the morning get the best of her, she drove to Home Depot to get as many boxes as she would be able to fit in her car, along with other supplies, drove home, and began packing. By the time Tracy got home, she had most of the bedroom non-essentials in boxes and labeled.

"What on earth are you doing?" Tracy looked shocked.

"Well," Susi said, sitting at the edge of the bed, "I called the moving company this morning. You would think with our combined common sense one of us would have figured out that they would need an address to deliver everything to." Tracy looked stunned and smacked herself on the forehead.

"Are you kidding me? None of us thought of that. Now what?" She joined Susi at the edge of the bed.

"I guess I'll wait for Lance to call and see what we can figure out. Wanna have pizza?" Her mind seemed to always have a little pre-occupation with food these days. "And I'm thinking popcorn and a movie a little later?"

As neither of them felt much like going out, Tracy called in the order and the two of them were interrupted by the phone ringing moments later. Tracy answered and then handed Susi the receiver. "It's your honey," Tracy told her.

"Hey, sweetie, what's new?" Lance asked.

"Not much, other than the movers can't come, pack, and load stuff." She felt like being a little sarcastic.

"Why not?" Obviously, he couldn't understand what the issue might be.

"Well, my love, they don't know where to deliver the stuff to once they have it." She chuckled. "We do not have an address of where they can deliver the stuff to!" Susi waited for a response.

"Shit, I can't believe we didn't think about that." Susi heard him smack his head.

She could feel his frustration through the line. "What should we do? I can't really come out there in a hurry to find us a place."

"Yes, you can," Tracy interjected. Susi looked at her puzzled. "The cat's out of the bag, so to speak, so there is nothing for you to get your blood pressure up about or your heart rate in the danger zone. Call Dr. Miles and we can drive out there."

"Great idea," Susi heard Lance shout at the other end. He'd apparently heard the announcement.

"You two can't be serious?" The question was directed at both Lance and Tracy.

"Why not?" Tracy pronounced. Lance echoed the same at the other end of the line. Susi felt outnumbered but had no clue how this was all going to work. She handed Tracy the phone and muttered, "You two work this out, I have to pee."

By the time she came back, the phone was on the receiver. "He didn't wait for me to say good night?"

"He got called away," Tracy explained. "He said to tell you he loves you and sleep well."

"So, what did the two of you hash out?" Susi tried hard to ignore the sinking feeling in the pit of her stomach. Tracy stood up, hugged her friend, and motioned her to go sit on the couch.

If Susi could get the go-ahead from Dr. Miles for a short trip, then the two of them would drive out first thing in the morning. The doctor had told her Monday that everything looked good. He had given her a prescription, which she had gotten filled and overall, she felt really good. Lance had said he was fine with the two of them finding a place. If Dr. Miles was against the trip, Tracy would fly out for a couple days to take care of the housing issue on her own. Susi knew she would make the right decision.

"You trust me, right?" Tracy wanted to know.

"Of course," Susi assured her. "I just don't think the doctor is going to let me go, but right now we have to make the best of the situation."

They finished their pizza, packed a few things, just in case, talked a bit longer, watched Grease, and headed to bed.

****

"I think you should be fine," Dr. Miles informed Susi over the phone. "You've been on the medication for a few days. I do want you to stop frequently to walk around a bit and rest for a while when you get there."

"Of course, Doc." Susi was beyond thrilled. "Thank you so much!"

"I also want you take one day to rest once you get there and one before you head back. Any issues, spikes in your heart rate or blood pressure, pain, I want to know about it immediately," he added.

She got further instructions before hanging up, and as soon as the receiver hit the cradle, she let out a loud howl. Tracy came running from her room to see what was going on and immediately figured it out when she saw the huge smile on Susi's face.

"Well, all right then." She turned on her heel and collected their bags. Only moments later she was back in the living room. "We can grab breakfast on the way out if you want."

By noon the two women were well on their way to San Diego. When they stopped by early afternoon to have a late lunch, Tracy called and made a hotel reservation at the Hilton San Diego Bayfront near the base in San Diego and then called the Wyndham Oceanside Pier Resort to make a reservation for two nights. That should give them enough time for Susi to rest as needed and to find a place, maybe even set up something for the wedding.

They reached San Diego before dinner and found the Hilton. The trip had taken longer than it should have, but Susi had Tracy stop every ninety minutes, when possible, so she could walk around a bit. The Hilton happened to be just a short drive to the naval hospital. They parked and checked in. The hotel was stunning, and even Tracy with her high standards was pleasantly surprised. Floor-to-ceiling light brown wooden section dividers, the chandeliers were huge iridescent circles, and there were tables of different sizes and chairs in various shades of brown. It was luxurious, and Tracy noted that she had great taste.

After four o'clock Tracy called her brother and let him know that they were in town and the guys should come down. By five thirty that evening, the two sailors had made their way to the hotel and the four of them had dinner in the Vela restaurant inside the hotel. Tony told his sister she was nuts and asked if she'd forgotten what their income was.

"Don't worry about it, little brother," Tracy proudly announced. "I've got this covered. I never would have thought Susi would meet someone that would treat her like a most precious gem. Not that I didn't know that was what she deserved, but I just honestly think that breed of man has died out. Tonight is a celebration for Susi and Lance. I chose this hotel because I've heard of its grandeur, and I am not disappointed. Susi ordered the Reuben, her favorite sandwich, Tracy and Lance had the filet mignon, and Tony had the Bayfront burger. Not much was said during their meal other than the occasional comment on how delicious everything was.

"I figured we can take tomorrow for Susi to rest and maybe roam around San Diego a bit, and Saturday morning, or tomorrow evening, we can head up to Oceanside." Tracy suggested. "I have to say I am proud of how organized I am." Susi shook her head but agreed.

SABINE CHENNAULT

"Sounds like a plan." Lance seemed impressed. "You really thought of everything, didn't you?"

Tracy shrugged her shoulders. "Yeah, like making sure the movers had an address!" They all laughed.

"You got two rooms in Oceanside?" Susi inquired.

"Yes, one for me and little nerd, and one for you lovebirds."

"If I'm a little nerd then you must be the bigger one," Tony kidded his sister.

She gave him the finger. "I figured you and I could share a room. I got one with two queen beds just in case," she informed him.

"We are all going to get spoiled hanging out with you," Tony joked.

By Tuesday morning everything had been arranged. The big news came Monday night when Tracy announced that her transfer request to San Diego was approved. She'd be off for the next two weeks, and that would give them time to get everything done. She had secretly sent her assistant to San Diego to find her an apartment for the time being. They found a nice little two-bedroom house that would serve Susi and Lance for the time he had to be at Camp Pendleton, and they were able to rent it on a month-to-month basis. They would find something more permanent when Lance was done with training and they knew where they would be sent. Susi was glad Pendleton was only a forty-five-minute drive from San Diego, so Tracy could come up whenever she wanted.

They even had time to make arrangements for a small wedding two weekends later. Tracy made Susi promise that she would allow her to handle everything. Susi had full trust in her friend and knew she'd pull off something amazing. Tracy had kept her promise and made all the arrangements. Susi could not have been happier that everything had worked out so well and that she had such a remarkable friend in Tracy.

"You know, you don't always have to rearrange your life for me. I mean, I am thrilled and I'm beyond happy to have you so close, but don't you want to live your own life?" Susi asked at some point while they were driving along I-10 on the way back to Arizona.

"Listen, we have been best friends for as long as I can remember. Not only that but living in San Diego, I don't just get to be close to you guys, but I actually get to hang out with my brother more often." Tracy looked at Susi. "I feel good. All of my decisions seem to have been the right ones, and right now life could not be any better than it is." Susi agreed.

SEVEN

A Wedding Dress and a Baby

*"Life will never be the same because there has
never been anyone like you... ever in the world"*

ONCE BACK IN ARIZONA, Susie needed a night to rest before she could immerse herself in packing, the movers, and the finalization of the wedding. The day after they got back, Tracy arranged for a moving company. They would come Wednesday, which gave them time to pack what they didn't want the movers to mess with and to go find a wedding dress.

"I made an appointment at David's Bridal in Scottsdale. They told me they have lots of nice things to accommodate your baby bump." Tracy smirked.

"Funny girl," Susi responded, shaking her head, "but I suppose you have a point." They did some work in the morning and headed to the bridal store in the afternoon. Susi was nervous. "Are you okay?" Tracy asked, concerned.

"Yeah, I just can't believe all this is real." She paused. "Lance is such an amazingly sweet guy and I get to spend the last few months of the pregnancy with him. It's awesome."

"You deserve someone who really loves and appreciates you." Tracy reached over to the passenger seat and squeezed her friend's arm.

They had a great time at David's, and finding a dress was easier than either of them had expected. "I'm really surprised that they had such a nice selection for maternity wedding dresses," Susi said. She looked at the back seat where her gown in a huge white plastic bag was lying on the back seat. "Are you sure it looks good?"

"Of course," Tracy comforted her. "You make that dress look stunning. Lance will seriously cry when he sees you. By the way, who's gonna walk you down the aisle?"

"Do you think I need anyone?" Susi asked. "I was just going to wing it by myself."

"I just know how nervous you can get." Tracy padded Susi on the shoulder. "If you are sure you don't need someone to hold you up, by all means."

"Honestly, that is the last thing I am sure about." Susi just stared out the window. "I just don't know who I could ask." She couldn't wait; the next two weeks surely would drag on.

****

Tracy had made the room reservation at the Wyndham in Oceanside, but the location of the wedding was a secret until the morning of the wedding. The girls got up early. Susi and Tracy had shared a room and so did Lance and Tony. Tracy had told the guys about her special plans, and both of them were in awe over Tracy's commitment as a friend. She had told Lance that she witnessed Susi with so much pain and it was long overdue that she got the elaborate treatment. Lance was so grateful; things had been rough for both of them and he could not have ever hoped for a better wife and a better friend. He said that he felt he had finally found a family that made him feel that he belonged.

Tracy had told Susi that a limo would be waiting for them at seven thirty in the morning to take them to the wedding venue. They drove for a little while and made their way to Wilshire Road. Eventually they arrived a lush green garden. The sign read, "Paradise Falls–Wedding and Special Events." Susi's mouth dropped open. There were flowering bushes and beautiful palm trees. They pulled into the parking lot, and the coordinator Tracy had talked to was waiting for them. Tracy had delivered Susi's dress the day before while Lance and Susi were getting ready for dinner.

Moments after they got out of the limo, Susi began to cry.

"What's wrong?" Tracy asked.

"I can't believe you did all this," Susi smiled despite her tears, "how can I ever repay you for this?"

Tracy smiled and took Susi's hand. "I have witnessed your tears of pain; you have been my best friend for most of my life and there were plenty of times you were there for me in any way possible. It is now time for me to repay my debt." They hugged.

Paradise Falls could not have been more beautiful. They walked along a palm-lined path to the beautiful white building where Susi was led to her bridal suite. As they entered the building, they met Buffy and Brandy, the two furry branch managers. Susi knelt down to rub their bellies and scratch behind their ears. The next few hours were spent laughing, getting hair and make-up done, having a light lunch and getting dressed. Susi had called Dr. Carl before they left Arizona and told him that she wanted Anna and Casey to be bridesmaids and asked if he would please let them have a few days off. He'd told her he would think about it, and they were in the bridal suite when Susi arrived. The way the day was folding out, Susi knew it was going to be the most beautiful day of her life so far.

The time came for Susi to go to the ceremony. She looked stunning in her pink blush ivory off-shoulder maternity gown. Her hair up in a playful messy bun with little white flowers and a long vail attached. She looked at herself in the floor-length mirror and tried really hard not to cry. She did not want to ruin the amazing make-up job.

"Are you ready?" Susi heard a voice ask behind her. She'd been standing by the window staring out at the gardens and had forgotten about time. In a few minutes she would be face to face with the love of her life. She was familiar with the requirements of being a military spouse. Gene had been in the Army when they met, but this was different. She had no idea what she needed to do when he needed to be gone. There was so much unknown ahead of her, ahead of both of them, but one thing she knew without a shadow of a doubt was that she loved this man more than she could ever love another human being. There was nothing she wouldn't do for him. His touch made her feel at home. It gave her a feeling of security that she had never known before.

Susi spun around hearing the familiar voice of Dr. Carl. "What are you doing here?"

"Your friend Tracy had come by the office and asked me to do this," Dr. Carl said with a smile, "and if I remember correctly, you did ask the missus and me to come to the wedding if we could."

"That is very true." Susi gave Dr. Carl as much of a big hug as she could with her protruding belly. "That gal thinks of everything. I'm not sure what I'm gonna do when I don't have her around every day."

"That's how I felt the first week after you were gone, but you taught Casey well." The doctor suggested, "Shall we?"

Tracy came back in the room and instantly had a huge grin on her face.

"When did you do this?" Susi inquired.

"When we got back to Mesa. You had laid down to take a nap and while you were resting, I went to propose to Dr. Carl that he be the one to walk you down the aisle. He was thrilled about the idea. I let Lance and Tony in on the secret, and Lance thought that it was a great idea, especially after the gift he had given you." Tracy was beaming with pride over managing yet another great surprise. She directed Susi and the doctor on where to go and then walked in ahead of them. Susi paused when they arrived at the ceremony site. She had to take it all in. She had no idea where all these people came from, she didn't know that many. The canopy of the trees almost created a tunnel. Each tree wrapped in lights, the waterfall at the end of the aisle, sitting in a small pond surrounded by waterlily leaves, sounded like music and a violinist played along with it. Each row of brown wooden chairs had an old-fashioned milk canister full of white roses and baby's breath.

Lance and Tony were standing up front with the chaplain, waiting for the bride, both in their dress whites. Susi felt the butterflies becoming very active in her stomach. As the doctor and Susi had reached the front, Susi could see how nervous Lance looked. She smiled at him and whispered, "I love you."

"You okay, man?" Tony asked. "I can hear your heart pounding." Lance returned a nervous smile. "Yeah, I'm fine, just really excited." Lance felt a little teary-eyed from the sight of the beautiful woman who was about to become his wife.

"Who gives this woman to this man?" the chaplain stated officially.

"I do," answered the doctor, who gave her hand to Lance.

Lance stole a moment to whisper, "You are so beautiful."

Susi smiled. She didn't want to cry.

They kept the ceremony short. Neither of them cared for all the fanfare of a long ceremony. The newlyweds left with their attendants to take the obligatory pictures while their guest enjoyed drinks and appetizers at the pavilion. When Susi and Lance arrived and were announced for the first time, Susi found herself near tears. There were rows of beautifully decorated tables with crisp white linens, tall pillars holding up amazing floral arrangements with countless white roses. A huge floral chandelier hanging over the dance floor with countless white roses took her breath away.

After Susi and Lance had their first dance as husband and wife, she had to find Tracy. She found her at the bar with her brother. She didn't want to interrupt them, so she looked at her and simply moved her lips, "Thank you?" Tracy nodded.

"You're crazy, this must have cost a fortune!" Susi scolded her when she finally got a chance to talk to her several minutes later.

Susi knew that Tracy never did anything without putting her whole heart into making everything the best possible, and to her the best possible usually meant a high price tag as well. She did not just do this for her dear friend on her wedding day but with most everything she did.

"It wasn't too bad, and it gives me great joy to have been able to do this for you." Tracy squeezed Susi's hand. "You are worth this and so much more."

"Agreed!" Lance came up behind Susi and gave his new wife a gentle hug. "I want to give you the world, my love," he whispered in her ear.

They ate, had the traditional speeches, cut the cake, and danced. When the evening came to a close, the guests said their good nights. Tracy got a cab to her new apartment in Hillcrest. Lance and Susi went back to the Wyndham where Tracy had rented a room for them for the night. Lance was able to get leave for a week for his wedding and transfer to Camp Pendleton.

They had a wonderful wedding night and enjoyed breakfast in bed the next morning before making their way to Bluegrass Way in Oceanside where their new home was located. Neither of them was surprised to see Tony and Tracy at the house, but seeing that the moving truck was half empty already shocked them both. Apparently, the movers were able to work quicker since there were people in the house arranging furniture and emptying boxes.

"When did you guys get here?" Lance yelled at Tony, who had just walked out of the house.

"About seven I think; Baker and Snail are here to help, but they just left a few minutes ago to grab sandwiches for an early lunch." Tony patted Lance on the back. "You can give me a hand with these boxes if you don't have anything else to do."

Susi laughed and went inside; they had gotten a lot of work done. "You guys didn't have to do all this, you're making me feel bad." Susi frowned.

Tracy stopped unpacking a box, put both hands on her hips, and looked at Susi. "Look, little missy, you know you're not supposed to do anything, so just let us help and don't worry about it." Her tone was serious, so Susi raised her hands in defeat and laughed.

By dinner time the truck was empty, the furniture arranged, and most of the boxes had been emptied. "Wanna go get pizza or go out and eat?" Baker, a friend of Lance's at Pendleton, wanted to know. "I'm starving."

"Let's go out," Lance replied. "You guys went above and beyond today. It's our treat."

They locked up the house and headed for their cars. "Hey, there's a new place downtown, think it's called Flying Pig Pub. You guys up for checking it out?" Snail shouted. "Heard it's pretty good."

"You know how to get there?" Lance asked.

Snail nodded. "Just follow me."

"Tracy, are you guys gonna stay the night?" Susi asked. Tracy quickly talked to Tony and then nodded. "Then ride with us." Tracy locked her car and the two of them got into the back seat of Lance's.

They joked about the hardship of moving and had a few good laughs along the way. At some point Susi lowered the visor on the passenger side to check her face in the mirror. She glanced at Tracy, who was smiling at her. She smiled back. This was something they had developed over the years just to let each other know that right now life could not be any better.

****

Lance was near the end of FMF school, and the new couple enjoyed life. Tracy and Tony came up to visit whenever his duty schedule and her time allowed. Susi had settled in with her new doctor at the naval hospital, and her previous condition was no longer an issue and well contained with the medication. She had her hospital bag ready to go, her emergency numbers hanging on the fridge, and the nursery was ready. Susi and Tracy had painted the nursery and it was a white-and-pink paradise for a little princess. Lance had painted the ceiling blue with puffy white clouds, and Susi had hung glow-in-the-dark stars from the ceiling. They had bought a beautiful white crib, changing table and rocking chair with a white-and-pink plaid cushion. They were ready for their daughter. Susi had small contractions here and there but nothing significant.

One night in mid-March, she woke up around three in the morning to go to the restroom. On her way back to bed, her water broke.

"Lance!" she spoke loudly to wake him. "Honey, wake up." She walked to the bed and gently shook his arm.

"Is everything okay?" he asked her while trying to wake up.

"It's time," she told him.

Lance jumped out of bed and grabbed his jeans from a nearby chair. With one leg in the jeans, he stopped and looked at Susi, who laughed.

"Honey, everything will be fine. I just need you to get dressed and I'll call Tracy, then we can head to the hospital," Lance told her with still just one leg in his jeans.

"Do you want me to get your bag from the nursery?" he questioned.

"Yes, please." Susi stopped and grabbed the door frame; a strong contraction nearly made her double over. She remembered the breathing techniques she had learned and applied them.

"What do you need me to do?" Lance gently laid his hand on her lower back and she grabbed his other one with her free hand. When the contraction had passed, she kissed him on the cheek. "Are you ready for this?"

"Do I have a choice?" he joked.

They were already checked in and in a bed when Tracy and Tony got there. The labor and delivery rooms at the Camp Pendleton Navy Hospital were absolutely beautiful. A large window on the right side of the bed would display a beautiful view in the morning, but for now there was darkness. Plenty of room for all of Susi's support team, a crib, the monitors, and bathroom. The room was decorated in blues and browns, giving it a warm and welcoming feel.

"You got here rather quick," Lance noted.

"I may have been speeding a little." Tony glanced at the ceiling. "With this one in the car, I would have liked to be able to just teleport." He pointed at Tracy, who stood next to him with a huge grin on her face. Moments after their arrival, a nurse came in and asked Susi if she wanted all of them to stay for the birth. Susi told her yes just before she had another contraction.

When the time came for the actual delivery, Tony decided he'd rather wait in the family waiting area. On his way out, he announced he was not sure if he'd ever wanted to see anyone else go through that.

An hour later Tracy went out to get him and bring him back to the room. Susi was sitting up smiling, the hours of labor behind her, hair stuck to her face. She looked tired, but her blue eyes were beaming with pride. Lance held his brand-new baby girl, her tiny arm laying across her little chest and a pink beanie keeping her tiny head warm. The new daddy was grinning at Tony as if he'd just won the jackpot in the lottery.

"You're not proud at all, are you?" Tony gently slapped Lance's back.

"Can I see her?" Lance nodded and slowly turned so Tony could get a good look at the little girl.

"Hi, sweetie," Tony said with tears in his eyes. "Can I hold her?"

Susi nodded but stated she would like him to sit down first. Lance gently handed the sleeping baby to his friend.

"She's beautiful!" Tony declared. "Do you have a name yet?"

"Yes, she's Samantha Rose," Lance announced.

"Welcome to the world, Samantha Rose." Tony kissed the little girl's head and then handed her back to her mother.

The friends visited a little bit longer. Tracy and Tony promised they would be over the next evening, after work, and bring dinner. The nurse came in to check on the new arrival and her mom before dimming the lights, so the little family could get some rest.

By the next evening, little Sammi was resting in her basinet, and multiple visitors had come by to greet her and drop off welcoming gifts. Susi was amazed by the outpouring of kindness of other military wives, even though she had met very few of them since they had moved to Oceanside. The news of a new baby seemed to travel fast and it seemed the Navy Mom's looked out for each other.

Life began to settle down for the three of them. Lance gladly got up once a night to feed his daughter despite his early mornings at work. By August she was sleeping through the night and growing as she should. The three of them had moved to San Diego, and Lance had started his duties at the hospital for the time being. Sammi was making her first small efforts of crawling, and her parents had fun with her. Weekends were often spent going to the mountains to hike or spend at the beach.

In early August Lance brought Tony home for dinner as he did every other week with Tracy joining them when she got off work. On this particular Thursday, both guys seemed preoccupied with something. "Is everything okay?" Susi asked.

"There's some trouble brewing in the Middle East. Iraq invaded Kuwait today," Lance replied.

"I saw something about that on the news earlier. Is that going to affect you guys?" Susi was concerned.

"Let's hope not." Lance kissed her cheek and hugged her. "Time will tell."

EIGHT

Deploying to Desert Storm

"A thing is mighty big when time and distance cannot shrink it."

B Y LATE AUGUST THE conflict in the Middle East had been officially labeled Operation Desert Shield, and American troops were
being sent. Susi followed the news as much as she could during the day
while Lance was on duty, and she grew more and more worried, fearing
that he would be deployed. She had no idea how to deal with this, how to
be supportive, and how to hide her fear. Halloween arrived to temporarily
break the uneasiness. Lance and Susi enjoyed dressing up their little one
as a little pumpkin and taking her around their neighborhood in her
stroller. As for most events at the time, Tracy and Tony joined them.

Lance had become as close to Tony and his sister as Susi had been all
her life. Though none of them were very religious, it went without saying
that if anything should ever happen to Lance and Susi, they'd want Tracy
to take care of their little girl. Susi made sure it was legally recorded.

By mid-November Susi started making plans for Thanksgiving. Though
their place was rather small, she figured they could set up a bigger table
outside and invite a few single guys who did not get the chance to spend
the holidays with family or other friends. Lance was well-liked by his
Marines and it didn't take him long to find a few guys to invite.

Most of them came down from Pendleton. Susi enjoyed cooking for
a crowd. The fear of Lance having to deploy had subsided and she was
focused on other things. She knew Lance was bias about her cooking,

SABINE CHENNAULT

but they'd had several dinner parties, and everyone would tell Susi what a phenomenal cook she was and that she should consider cooking professionally. A few days before Thanksgiving, he came home but was not as cheerful as usual.

"Is everything okay, honey?" Susi asked him. He looked at her and she instantly knew that what he was about to tell her was something she was not prepared to hear.

"When?" She felt the color drain from her face and a knot in her stomach making her feel as if she wanted to throw up.

"In ten days," Lance replied in a low, trembling voice.

Susi tried all she could to hold back the tears, but they made their way down her cheeks.

"We won't even get our first Christmas together?"

"I'm sorry, baby," he whispered as he took her in his arms. Hugging him with all her strength, she whispered, "I will always be here waiting for you. I do not want to be unreasonable and make you promise that you will come home to me, but I need you to promise that you will do everything within your power to stay safe."

"Of course, baby. You will be with me every step of the way and I will write you whenever I can." Lance sighed, "It's just going to take a few weeks for mail to get back and forth." He loosened his hug, and Susi took a step back. He looked into her eyes and noticed that she was trying hard not to cry again.

"You don't have to be tough, honey; I know this will be hard…for both of us."

"I was just thinking that you won't be here for Sammi's first Christmas and, most likely not her first birthday either." A tear rolled down Susi's face.

Lance hugged her again. "Don't think about that right now. Let's enjoy Thanksgiving and then we will take it one day at a time, okay?" Susi reluctantly nodded; deep inside she was trembling. Life could not be this cruel. All those years of abuse from Gene and she'd finally found the one that made her world complete. Now he had to go to war? This was just not fair.

Thanksgiving had come and gone. Though they shared a great meal that

87

Susi and Tracy spent two days preparing, there seemed to be a faint shadow overcasting the celebration. Not just Lance and Susi but Tracy and Tony, as well as two of their dinner guests, were facing the same dilemma.

****

The day came when Susi had to take Lance to the ship. He held her hand the whole way and everything in him told him that letting go would be the hardest thing he'd ever do. He knew what he was about to get into, at least in theory. He was assigned to a platoon with forty Marines. It would be his job to make sure if anyone of them got injured to patch them up. He would have to be at the front lines with them, and his risk of injury and death was as high as any of theirs. This was not something he shared with his wife, but he was sure she'd familiarized herself with the duties of an FMF Corpsman.

"Honey, will you promise me something?" He spoke very softly and squeezed her hand.

"What is it?"

"Promise me that despite what you may see on the news, you do not give up hope." He took a deep breath. "Unless someone comes knocking on the door and tells you otherwise, you have to believe I'm alive and will come home."

"I promise," Susi said, forcing a smile, "with every fiber of my being, I promise."

They parked near the pier and while Lance was getting his gear out of his trunk, Susi got Sam out of the car seat and sat her in the stroller. She was still so small. Susi felt as if every step got harder the closer they got to the ship. She was glad that Tracy had promised to come over that evening. It would not have been possible to find each other amongst all these people, and she knew she'd have to come with Tony. The announcement was made that the guys had to get into formation. Susi quickly pulled a shoe box from the diaper bag and handed it to Lance.

"What is this?" he asked with curiosity.

"Just a little card for each day of the nine months you're supposed to be gone."

Lance grabbed his wife and hugged her like he never had before. He kissed her forehead and then her lips. He knelt down to kiss his sleeping little girl and again looked at his wife. Without a sound he moved his lips to tell her he loved her.

She fought with everything in her to not cry but failed as she held on to Sam's stroller.

"I love you so very much," she softly whispered. "Please come back to me, you are my whole world." He turned around, hearing her plea, and nodded. It seemed like hours before all the men were lined up on deck and the ship slowly started to move away.

"I'd thought I'd find you standing here until you could no longer see the ship," Tracy announced herself. "Are you okay, sweetie?"

"I will have to be," Susi admitted. "It's not like I have much of a choice. You know, honestly I know that somewhere in me I have the strength to get through this. My life with Gene made me stronger than I knew I was, but this is… I don't know." She took a deep breath along with one last look at the departing ship. All of its occupants had left the deck and there was nothing more than a grey vessel.

"Why don't we head to your place and figure out what to do about dinner?" Tracy suggested.

"Sounds like a plan. Actually, I need to stop by the commissary and get some things. I take it you are more or less stranded here."

Tracy laughed and added, "Yeah, I have his keys, but the car is going to stay here. Wanna stop by the liquor store and get us something good?"

The two women smiled. Tracy knew that for right now a laugh may be too much to expect.

****

Tracy had every intention of talking Susi into coming to stay with her, at least part of the time and especially for Christmas, New Year's, and little peanut's birthday. Tracy didn't care much for Logan Heights. It really only had two things going for it: lots of Navy families and cheap rent. Lance knew that Susi had saved a lot, but together they had decided to invest some of their money and keep the rest in savings. At one point they'd want to buy a house and the invested money and savings would help. There was no need to buy a house now when they would be moving every three years; that was if Lance decided to make a career of the Navy.

Tracy, Susie, and Sammi arrived at the small house just after five, and Susi had dinner ready quickly. She was surprised just how long it took to watch the guys do their thing on the ship, watch them depart, and then all of the running around she'd done. Sammi had been such a good little trooper all day. Susi had really taken a liking to Mexican food since they'd moved here, more so than when she lived in Arizona.

"I really think you need to go to culinary school," Tracy recommended while laughing and stuffing more nachos in her mouth.

Susi ignored the comment about school. "I promised Lance that I would not pay attention to the news, but how can I not? There is really no other way for me to know what's going on."

"I know, sweetie," Tracy acknowledged, barely audible with a mouthful of food. "I'm sure he didn't mean not to watch it at all, just don't trust everything on the news and wait to hear what he tells you."

"Aren't you worried about Tony at all?"

"I am, but it's not the same as worrying about a husband and the father of your child. Besides, he's not up front with the Marines."

The two friends enjoyed their dinner and had a few good laughs watching little Sam in her high chair trying to pick up little pieces of baby snacks. Susi started clearing the table when she heard, "Dada," behind her. She spun around. "Tracy, did you hear that?" Tracy stared at the little girl and nodded.

Susi set the dishes down by the sink, returned to the table, and pulled her chair closer to Sammi. "What did you say, sweetie?"

The spunky girl pointed at the chair where her father would normally sit during dinner and, again, she babbled, "Dada." This time it seemed to be more of a question. Susi pulled her out of her high chair and kissed her face multiple times.

"Oh, my God, this is so amazing, and, of course, he had to miss it."
Susi's joy disappeared in an instant.

"You can't look at it like that," Tracy argued. "You need to get a
journal and write all these special things down with the dates and what
happened." Tracy told her that she would take care of the dishes, so
Susi could give the little one her evening bath and get her ready for bed.

"I'm not sure how I'm supposed to get through these nights without
him," Susie wondered.

"You'll have to do this one day at a time," Tracy advised. "I think it
may not be a bad idea to find something to keep yourself busy with, that
should help make the time go by faster." Tracy scratched her head. "I
think there was something on the job announcement board for the day
care. I can check on it for you if you want."

"That may not be a bad idea at all. I would just honestly be worried
missing a call or something."

"Sounds like excuses to me, dear." Tracy gave her friend a conde-
scending look.

Susi knew Tracy was right. "I just can't even think straight right now."

"Honey, he just left today. You can't do this to yourself for the next
nine months."

"Two hundred and seventy days," Susi responded and grinned. "Wanna
stay here tonight?"

"Sure, let me run home and grab some things and I'll be back within
an hour. I may stop by Best Buy really quick."

"What for?" Susi was curious.

"Thinking about getting a video camera. It would be nice to have one,
so we can record all of Sammi's milestones and then her daddy can see it
all when he gets home. It'll be like he gets to see it in person." Tracy
smiled, "When I get back, I'll make a pitcher of margaritas."

The idea was greeted with excitement, not just the one about the video
camera. Tracy headed out, and Susi headed to the bathroom with her
little one to get her ready for the night. More than once she paused,
waiting for the familiar voice of her husband and his scent that gave her
so much comfort. She wondered how far they were and if he missed her

as much as she missed him. Tracy was right, keeping herself busy would make the time pass faster.

She played with Sammi during bath time, dried her off, put lotion on her, and Samantha started rubbing her eyes. She put her jammies on and then got her baby tucked in. When she lowered her daughter down into her crib, she noticed a picture that had been placed on the headboard. Lance must have put it there earlier that day. It was Susi's favorite picture of him and Sammi.

It only took seconds for her little girl to drift off. Tracy wasn't back yet, so Susi sat at the kitchen table to write the first, of what she knew would be hundreds, of letters to her husband.

Tracy got back a little after nine, made the drinks, and then spent the next thirty minutes getting the huge camera set up. The women agreed that it would be fun for Lance to watch everything when he returned. Susi had just poured another margarita when there was a soft knock at the front door. Tracy looked at Susi and then at her watch. Both women wondered who was knocking this late in the evening. Susi went to the front door; her neighbor Katy was standing there.

"Is everything okay?" she asked as she motioned Katy to come in.

"The house is so quiet, and I don't know what to do. I'm sorry to intrude so late, I saw your lights were still on." Katy seemed relieved by the invitation and followed Susi to the kitchen. Tracy got up and introduced herself.

"Margarita?" Tracy inquired.

Katy nodded. "Just a little one."

"Have a seat," Susi offered, pulling out a chair. "How long have you guys been married?"

"We got married right after Josh was done with boot camp, so almost two years ago," Katy shared. "We've been together, more or less, since sixth grade, so we kinda have been making all the decisions together. When we were juniors, he said that he wanted to join the Marines. In his family the men for the last three generations have all been Marines, and he didn't want to break that chain."

"I haven't seen any kids, so I bet being totally alone makes this even worse," Susi guessed.

"Actually, I found out last week that I'm two months along, so the baby will come while Josh is gone." Her eyes became glassy. "That's why I asked for a little drink." Susi and Tracy looked at each other, both thinking the same thing. They had to make Katy part of their little family. Susi remembered what an important part Tracy had been to her own pregnancy; she couldn't even imagine what it would be like to be totally alone through all of that.

Susi got up and hugged Katy. "I'm so sorry. Here we have been living next to each other for a few months and I never took the time to come say hi and invite you for coffee or something." She reached for Tracy's hand. "Tracy and I will both be here for you. You can come over and have dinners with us and we can do things together. There is no need for any of us to be alone through this." She looked at Tracy.

"We will be happy to help you prepare for the arrival of your baby. We are all in this together," Tracy affirmed.

"Is your husband in the service as well?" Katy asked Tracy.

"I'm not married. It's my baby brother who is sticking his neck out. He's a hospital corpsman, shipped out with Lance this morning."

"Your house is so much brighter than ours," Katy noted.

"It was remodeled right before we rented it," Susi responded. "I wish it had more of a yard, but it'll make do for the couple years we are here. I love the wood flooring throughout, it's so much easier to clean. For me the main attraction was the kitchen. I'm not a big fan of the turquoise stove, but the white cabinets are beautiful."

"She is a phenomenal cook," Tracy announced. "Wait till you have some of her food."

Susi laughed and shook her head.The girls sat at the kitchen table, sipping margaritas and sharing stories. Before long Tracy announced that she needed to get to sleep since she had to work in the morning. Katy bid her new friends good night and headed to her house next door. Susi felt a knot in her stomach. She didn't want to think how terribly lonely it must be to be completely alone. She waited until Katy was safely inside and then turned off the lights, heading down the hall and checking on her sleeping baby before getting herself ready for bed.

She noticed that Lance had placed a wedding picture on her nightstand. There was a small envelope lying in front of it. How had she not noticed that before? She pulled the flap open:

> *My Dearest Susi,*
>
> *It's hard to express how I feel, I have so many thoughts rushing through my head. We had to wait so long to be together and now this. There seems to be no certainty, nothing that gives us the guarantee of things to come. No matter what happens you are in my thoughts every moment of every hour of every day. I cannot wait to wrap my arms around you again and kiss your soft lips. You are my everything, now and always.*
>
> *Lance*

When she was done reading, she pressed the note against her chest. Why did missing someone have to hurt so bad? Sleep did not come easy that night. Every time she closed her eyes, she saw his face smiling at her.

****

Somewhere in the Pacific Ocean, Lance had gotten into his rack. While he never had issues falling asleep, he did tonight. He had taped Susi's picture on the wall and despite the dim red light, he could see her face. He touched her lips in the photo and thought, *You are what is going to get me through this. You are my every breath. I love you, Susi.*

He'd heard some stories; they were hard to avoid while on duty. This conflict was going to be tough; no one could deny that.

They arrived on Hawaii on December 6 and stayed for Pearl Harbor Day the next day to reload supplies. Lance took the opportunity to mail the first three letters home. He knew it would be a while until they would get mail delivered, but he didn't have to wait to get his out.

"Hey, Doc, wanna make a call home?" one of the guys shouted to Lance.

"Are you serious?" Lance was surprised.

The guys had been given a couple hours for anyone who wanted to call home to do so. Time was tight since they would only be on the island for a couple days. He got to the phones in time to miss long lines. Everyone's time was limited so they'd all get a chance. After today he had no idea when he'd be able to call again.

He picked up the receiver and dialed the number. It rang multiple times and then disconnected. He tried again. Finally, after a few rings, there was a panting "Hello?" at the other end.

"Honey, it's me," Lance said, excited to hear her voice.

"Babe? Where are you? How can you call?" Susi seemed really surprised. "I miss you so very much."

"I only have a few minutes," Lance said quickly. "We are on Hawaii to get supplies, we'll be moving on tomorrow. Who's there?"

"Tracy and Katy from next door. Katy is alone and almost just over two months pregnant. Her husband should be on your ship," Susi told him. "I want to kiss you, touch you, hold you." He could tell from her shaky voice that she was near tears.

Then she suddenly informed him, "Hey, I got a little part-time job at the child-care center at Boeing. Tracy arranged it for me. It gives me something to do other than just miss you, and it makes time go by faster, plus it's a little extra income to put into savings."

"That's awesome, honey." Lance felt good that she was being strong. "I really love the cards. I want to read them all now, but I'm being patient. I miss you so much."

"I miss you too." Susi paused and took a deep breath. "Thank you for putting the picture in Sammi's crib and on my nightstand." She didn't wait for a response. "Oh, guess what? Sammi said, 'Dada.' Well, she's been saying it every night at dinner and when I put her to bed."

"Shit." Lance was upset. "Of course, I have to miss such an important event."

"Don't worry, honey. Tracy got a video camera, so she's running behind Sammi every chance she has so you can see everything when you come home."

"That's awesome. Tell her thanks for me and kiss my little princess. Honey, I have to go. I miss you and love you so very much." So many of his feeling were still new and unfamiliar. For years he had hidden his feelings and now he wanted to cry; this was unusual for Lance. This woman had fixed everything wrong in his life with nothing more than a touch of his hand.

"I love you too. Please take good care of yourself," Susi said, and he could hear her swallow hard. "I'll see you soon, my love."

With that they both hung up. For a moment he felt like they were right back where they had been when she was in Arizona and he was still at Great Lakes. The only difference was this time he had no idea what was waiting for him at the other end of his journey. They spend Christmas and New Year's in the Philippines and though it was interesting, Lance missed his family, especially Sammi's first Christmas.

The war officially started on January 17, 1991, with Operation Desert Storm. Though it lasted only forty-three days, the United States lost 383 service members, and many more came home with invisible wounds that would haunt them for years to come. Lance's training was put to the test multiple times, but his confidence grew with each life he saved.

By Lance's birthday in April, they were somewhere off the coast of Somalia. The USS *Germantown* went to Abu Dhabi, Dubai, and Bahrain, and at each port Lance purchased a small gift for his girls back home. Just after the eruption of Mount Pinatubo, they were back in the Philippines. It looked nothing like it had a few months earlier. On August 2, 1991, Lance crossed the equator for the first time and earned his Shellback status—a tradition dating back four hundred years or more; no one is really sure how or even when the ritual started. The ceremony changes a sailor from a mere slimy Pollywog to a worthy seaman who has crossed the equator and is henceforth known as a trusty Shellback, also known as son or daughter of Neptune.

NINE

Life Is Not Supposed to Hurt This Much!

"I hold you in my heart until I can hold you in my arms."

T HE FIRST CHRISTMAS THAT should have been spent together with their little girl had come and gone. Samantha was growing and moving along by all means possible, and she kept her mom busy. Susi enjoyed the work at the day-care center, and it was nice that she could have Sammi there with her. Lance had called when they got to the Philippines but sadly, she'd been at work. That was the one thing she hated about the job. He did leave her a very nice message on the recorder. She'd listened to it so many times when she was sad, over-whelmed, at night before going to sleep, and especially if being without him was just too much. His voice always brought her inner peace, and she was able to refocus her mind.

He had mailed a couple of letters from Hawaii and again from the Philippines, and she was surprised how much he had to talk about. Susi had started a scrapbook with the letters and some newspaper clippings. No matter where she went, people were talking about the war. Schools had begun to encourage students to write letters to the military personnel so far away from home. The news was harder and harder to avoid.

The first air attacks on Iraq were launched on January 17 after Iraq ignored a UN resolution to withdraw its military forces from Kuwait.

To worsen the situation, the next day Iraq attacked Israel, which was not part of the U.S.-led coalition. More and more conflict led to more and more deaths. It had been nearly a month since Lance's last letter. Susi was worried and checked with the base ombudsman. She was told that the massive amounts of mail the guys lovingly referred to as "fan mail" slowed down the process of getting mail to the troops and mail out to family back home. Susi knew that everyone meant well, and she was sure that there were many who had no close family who must have appreciated the letters and drawings.

Susi spent time each evening reading stories to Sammi, who had learned to add "mama" to her little vocabulary collection. Susi had added another picture to the crib, and each night when she put Sammi down for the night, the little girl would kiss the picture. Susi captured it and placed the photograph in one of the letters she'd sent to Lance.

Katy's belly was getting bigger. The morning sickness had subsided, and the cravings had set in. Each evening Susi and Katy took a nice long walk; the weather was amazing despite it being February. Susi went with Katy when she had her first ultrasound, and she'd found out that she was going to have a little boy. The technician had said nothing was more obvious. She even circled it on the picture, so Katy could send it to Josh.

Despite how busy Susi got during the day, she always made sure she'd write a few paragraphs in the evenings so she could send two letters a week to her honey. She was blown away by the number of military wives who would go out on weekends and bring guys home. One of them from down the street stopped by one day to invite Susi and Katy to go out, but Susi politely turned her down.

"I don't exactly have old world values, but I'll be damned if some woman who doesn't give a shit about her husband shows up at my door wanting us to go man-hunting," she said. Both Katy and Tracy burst out in laughter. "Tell us how you really feel," Tracy joked.

The ombudsman had told Susi that there was always that one bunch at each base. Jodies were plenty and every single guy deployed and in a relationship worried when it was going to be his turn to be cheated on. Susi was amazed by the reasoning to cheat. Some actually claimed that they did it because he was gone and left her alone.

In late February the women were out on their evening walk. Tracy had joined them this time. She'd brought a pizza for dinner for the three of them, so they were done quickly. They had gone around the block and decided to keep the walk a little shorter since clouds were rolling in. Even though walking around the block generally did not take more than twenty minutes when it was just Susi and Katy, they'd stop and chat with other Navy wives along the way. The clouds promised rain that would be welcomed. A few houses down, a car pulled up in front of a house.

"One of these days I'd just like to bring the video camera and video-tape these cheating bitches," Tracy said to no one in particular. They were just about back in front of Katy's house when a car pulled up in front of her house and two men in full uniform got out. Susi and Katy froze as they watched the men walk up to Katy's front door. Katy screamed and dropped to her knees. Sammi in her stroller pointed out the lalus (flowers) she was next to when Susi ran the few steps and asked the Marines who they were looking for. Neither of them said anything.

"If you are looking for Katy Giles she's right there, I'm Susi Wells." Susi pointed to where Tracy was standing. Tracy had helped Katy back on her feet, and they took the last few steps to the walkway of Katy's house. Both Susi and Katy noticed that one of them was a chaplain.

"Mrs. Giles?" the chaplain inquired, and Katy identified herself, her voice trembling. "The commandant of the Marine Corps has entrusted me to express his deepest regret that your husband, Sergeant Joshua Giles, was killed in action on February twenty-seventh in Kuwait City. From what we know, your husband did not suffer. The commandant extends his deepest sympathy to you and your family in your loss." Susi felt numb. This all sounded so rehearsed, but she understood that this had to be a horrible job. Katy dropped to her knees on the step by her front door, and the chaplain knelt down to console her and share a prayer with her.

Susi looked at the notification officer. "She's six months pregnant." She had no idea why she felt the need to share that and looked away. Down the street several women and families had come out to the street. News like this traveled like wildfire. Women stood crying, crying both in sadness for the one who had been notified and in gratitude that it was not them.

"Ma'am is there anyone else we should notify?" the chaplain gently asked Katy. She shook her head.

"I'm her neighbor," Susi explained. "I'll stay with her and help her with phone calls and arrangements. Right now, I'm more concerned with her not going into labor."

The two men briefly spoke with Susi before they departed.

"Katy, honey, let's go inside." Susi gently helped her friend to her feet. "Tracy, would you mind getting us a bottle of wine?"

"Can we just please go to your house?" Katy interjected between sobs, "I can't go in there right now and see all of his things."

Susi agreed, and they walked across the yard. Tracy took Sammi out of the stroller and sat her on the floor by her toys in the living room.

"Do you want to call your mother?" Susi asked Katy as she was pouring a glass of wine. Katy nodded, got up, and walked to the phone on the wall. As she reached for the receiver, she cringed in pain.

"No, no, that can't happen," Susi yelled in a panic. "Contractions?" Katy nodded.

"We need to get you to the hospital. I'm gonna call nine-one-one." Susi asked Tracy to help Katy sit down while Susi got on the phone.

"*Nine-one-one, what's your emergency?*"

"My name is Susi Wells, I assume you have my address. I have a young woman here; she is twenty-seven years old and six months pregnant. She just has been notified of her husband passing in action and has gone into premature labor."

"*Has her water broken or is she bleeding?*" Susi repeated the question to Katy, who shook her head.

"*I have paramedics on the way, they should be there momentarily, please stay on the phone with me until they have arrived.*"

"Thank you, I will." Susi turned to Katy. "They are on their way and will be here momentarily." Susi asked Tracy to put Sammi in her high chair, open the front door, and give Sammi some crackers to occupy her with. No sooner had Tracy opened the door and they could hear the sirens. It seemed as only seconds passed before the paramedics loaded Katy into the ambulance. Somewhere in the process, Susi thanked the 911 operator and hung up.

Susi asked if Tracy could stay with Sammi and make sure she had her dinner and bath. Tracy was happy to help anyway she could.

"That is one thing I have always admired about you," Tracy stated solemnly. "You stay so calm and collected and know just how to manage a crisis situation."

Susi met Katy at the naval hospital emergency room where a doctor was checking on her.

"We'll be able to stop the labor, and the baby seems fine," the female doctor spoke in a monotone voice, no expression in her brown eyes. "We will do an ultrasound, and I want to keep you here for the night to keep an eye on you, just to be on the safe side."

Katy cried but nodded. "Susi?"

"Yes, dear?" Susi took Katy's hand.

"Can you please help me call my mom? I want to have her come out?" The tears just flowed, and Susi could see that Katy was on the verge of a complete breakdown. Susi wondered how Kate had kept it together this long. She looked so lost and scared.

"Of course, her number is in your little book in your purse, right?"

Katy nodded. "I don't think I can tell her about Josh."

"Sweetheart, you will need to. I cannot imagine the pain you are feeling right now, and I will be here to help you through that, but right now you need to be strong, for Josh, for that little boy in there and for you, can you do that?" Susi asked. Katy wiped her tears, took a deep breath, and nodded.

"Your parents as well as Josh's have to know." Susi squeezed Katy's hand and gave her a gentle kiss on the forehead.

Katy agreed and let Susi know that all the necessary numbers were in her little book. Susi dialed the first number and waited for the ringtone, then handed the receiver to Katy.

"Mom?" Katy spoke quietly while crying.

"Katy? Honey? What's wrong?" Susi could hear the woman at the other end.

"Josh is dead. He was killed in action; he's not going to see his baby boy." That was all she managed before she laid the receiver in her lap and started sobbing. Susi felt as if saying the words made everything really set in.

"Mrs. Schuster, this is Susi. I'm a friend and neighbor of Katy's," Susi spoke softly after picking up the receiver.

"Is she okay? Is the baby okay?" Susi could hear the worry in her voice.

"Ma'am, she's in the hospital and both her and the baby are fine. She'd gone into premature labor, and they are keeping her at least overnight." Susi took a deep breath. "The doctor said she has to avoid stress and excitement, not sure how they expect that under these circumstances."

"Oh, dear God!" The woman at the other end began sobbing, trying to explain to her husband what was going on. Katy's dad took the phone. "Did they say how?"

"Not really, sir, just something about an ambush. I don't envy those guys and I'm sure they have a certain protocol to follow. Katy said she needs you here, is that possible?"

"We will be on the first flight out." Mr. Schuster sounded stern. "May we call you when we arrive?"

"Of course, sir." Susi gave him her phone number, assured him that she would be right by Katy's side and bid him a good night. She sat back at the edge of the bed and let Katy drop her head on her shoulder. Susi wrapped her arm around her, she felt sick to her stomach and had to take a couple deep breaths to push away the light-headedness which was trying to creep in. All she wanted to do was sit and hold Katy, sob with her, mourn the loss of her wonderful husband, and forget that there was anything but pain. Susi had not been raised that way, her father had been a paramedic for twenty-five years and he had raised her to stay calm in a crisis. He had always told her if she needed to fall apart when everything was taken care of and the crisis was over she could fall apart and cry, but while someone else was suffering she had to stay calm.

"Let's get it over with and call his parents, then you'll need to try and rest."

A nurse had come in, saying, "I will add a light sedative to her IV once we have her moved to a room. Would you want to wait to make the other call until you are moved?" Katy nodded. In less than thirty minutes, she had been transferred to a room. Katy had asked the nurse to wait until after the call to be given the sedative.

Susi picked up the receiver and again dialed a number. It only rang twice before a man answered, and Susi quickly handed Katy the receiver.

"Hello? Anyone there?" the male voice asked.

"It's me, Richard," Katy managed having calmed down a little.

"Katy? What's going on?"

"Josh was killed in action," Katy stated. Susi knew that Josh's dad was a retired Marine. She could hear the shift in his voice from caring father to a Marine commander. "When?"

"On the twenty-seventh. They believe he was killed in an ambush." Katy tried to control her tears but couldn't.

"That's what they always say, along with he didn't suffer. Is everything okay with my grandson?" Richard asked.

"Yes, sir, that's what the doctor told me. They still want to do another ultrasound to be sure. I was brought in due to premature labor set on by stress. The doctor was able to stop the labor, but they are keeping me at least overnight, just for observation."

"We will be on our first flight out," Richard stated. "I will inform his mother."

"I'm sorry, Dad." Katy was sobbing again and barely managed to be audible.

"You just calm down, little lady, you need to be strong and make sure my grandson stays put," Mr. Giles said. "Get some rest and we will see you tomorrow. Good night, my dear, we love you." Without waiting for the response, he hung up the phone.

Susi pushed the call button, and moments later the nurse came in. "She's done making phone calls," Susi said.

The nurse disappeared and came back moments later. "They want to get your ultrasound done before you go to sleep, so we'll hold off a few more minutes on the medication."

As the nurse left an orderly came and took Katy for the ultrasound. Susi waited in the room. Her mind drifted, she stared out of the window. It had gotten dark but she could see the city lights in the distance. The room seemed cold; the grey tile floor matched the plain white walls. Grey curtains on the window added to the iciness of the room. Susi began feeling the adrenaline subside, it was too soon. The orderly brought Katy back to the room and the nurse followed immediately with the sedative.

"You need to get some rest now. I will be back in the morning. You have my number and if you need to call, please do," Susi said. "I will wait for you to fall asleep though."

Susi sat with Katy for a little while. She stroked her friend's hair and listened to Katy talk about Josh. She talked about how he had hoped that their little boy would love football as much as his father, how Josh had cried when she found out about the pregnancy. As Katy was softly talking she didn't notice that tears had started falling down Susi's face. Once Katy had drifted off Susi gently laid her head on the pillow, wiped her own tears and made her way to the parking lot.

When Susi got in her car and stuck the key in the ignition, she paused. Maybe, just maybe, some of these women cheated as a way of dealing with their fear. Not that it made it any less wrong, but that was a possibility. When she got home, Tracy was waiting. "I took tomorrow off. Figured you'd need me to stay with the little monster. I told my assistant to let the day care know that you won't be coming in for a couple days."

"His parents are gonna be here, and I guess they are staying at Katy's house." Susi squeezed the back of her neck. "Not sure if I'd want to deal with an old Marine in a situation like this."

"At least he won't be driven by emotions and will be able to keep a clear head like you," Tracy added.

The women had a glass of wine and then headed to bed. Susi tried sleeping, but when she was still awake after half an hour, she sat up and began writing a letter to Lance. Katy called twice during the night and Susi managed to calm her down enough to go back to sleep. By the time she got the letter done, it was nearly one in the morning and she'd written eight pages. She took the picture off the dresser and kissed it. "Please be careful, baby, come home." With the picture in her hand, she slid under the covers and cried herself to sleep.

****

Late the next day, Katy was back home. Both her and the baby were physically fine. Both her parents and Josh's had convinced her to move back east, and Josh's parents had packed up most of his things. They would have the funeral at Arlington, and Katy didn't have to push much to get Susi to agree to come to Virginia to attend the service. Even though it would still be a few days, Richard insisted that Katy come stay with them until Josh's remains were delivered at Arlington. He would have to be sent to Wiesbaden in Germany and then on to Dover.

"May I have a word with you?" Richard asked.

"What can I do for you, sir?" Susi replied. She noticed that someone had hung a gold star ribbon in the window by the front door. This signified that Katy had lost her husband in combat.

"I wanted to thank you for your strength. As the wife of a corpsman, I can understand your compassion." Richard took a deep breath. "It was a corpsman who saved my ass in Vietnam. Please tell your husband we truly appreciate him and thank you so much for acting so fast to make sure Katy and our little grandson would be fine."

"Thank you, sir." Susi smiled and hugged the old Marine.

Josh's father made arrangements for all of Katy and Josh's possessions to be moved to a storage facility while Katy got the funeral behind her. Her parents were in North Carolina while Josh's parents lived in D.C. When the funeral arrangements had been made, Katy let Susi know and Susi flew to D.C. Tracy kept Sammi and took her to work with her for those few days her mother was gone.

The experience was hard for Susi. The formal procession, the pall-bearers in their uniforms moving in precise unison. Seven old guard soldiers lined up for the twenty-one-gun salute. It sent chills down Susi's spine and she couldn't help but cry. The flag was folded and handed to Katy by the senior member of the unit with crisp white gloves. Katy stared at the coffin holding her husband's body. She took the flag without making eye-contact, she seemed to be off in her own mind somewhere. It had been recommended that Katy and her family not have an open casket. Richard had insisted on seeing his son and so had Katy; neither of them had spoken a word about it. It was the beginning of March and a beautiful spring day but rain would have been more fitting for the occasion. Susi had been to a couple of funerals. One of her grandmothers died when Susi was twelve, her grandfather passed away a couple weeks before Gene and she left for the States, but nothing had the effect as this one. Something had changed within her after witnessing the funeral.

****

When Susi was back home, she and Katy would talk on a regular basis, and Susi was thrilled that Katy had decided to name her son after his father. Katy had also decided to stay with Josh's parents for a while. It felt good being in the place where he had grown up and where they had gone to school together. In mid-May Susi got a call from Katy's mom that little Josh had been born, and both he and his mama were doing well. About the same time, Susi got a letter from Lance letting her know that he'd be home in June. She was to call the base ombudsman for the exact day and time.

Finally, these long months were over. Sammi was walking and had learned so much since Lance had left. Susi felt excited for him to see the videotapes of her growth, and Tracy went to work to make a reasonably edited version.

Susi flew back to D.C. to meet little Josh. Katy's parents came up to visit, and Richard enjoyed playing tour guide at the National Mall and

around D.C. The two women visited Josh alone the day before Susi
had to head back to San Diego. They stood arm in arm in front of the
white headstone marking Josh's grave, and Susi had her arm around
Katy while she cried. It would be years before Katy could visit the
grave without crying.

"I don't know what I would have done without your support. Well,
yours and Tracy's." Katy squeezed Susi tighter. "The only people who
have known what I'm about to tell you are my parents and Josh. I was
on anti-depressants until I got pregnant, and it was Josh who encouraged
me to come knock on your door." She had to take a deep breath. "I'm
honestly not sure if I would have survived his death if it hadn't been
for you and Tracy. Since little Josh has been born, I haven't had to go
back on the meds, and I'm in counseling, not just for the loss of my
husband but for the depression as well. I sincerely hope we can stay in
touch, and next time little Josh and I can come visit you."

"That would be awesome." Susi was excited for her friend. "I know
Lance is kind of hoping to be stationed at Lejeune after San Diego, but
we'll have to see." The next day Tracy and Sammi picked Susi up at
the San Diego airport. She was happy to be home and made it a priority
to call the base ombudsman the next morning to find out the exact day
the ship would return.

"Hi, Susi, I was just about to call you." Liz, the base ombudsman,
was such a cheerful person. Susi had never met her face to face, but they
had talked on the phone a few times. "Oh, what's up?" Susi was a bit
confused. Why would Liz call her? "Is everything okay with the guys
coming home?" She didn't wait for an answer to her first question.

"Oh, yes, yes. I didn't mean to frighten you. I'm just calling everyone
to let them know that the ship will actually be here day after tomorrow."
Liz paused. "They are actually getting in ten days early. They'll be
docked outside the harbor for a week, and then they'll come in to dock
in the harbor."

"Woo-hoo!" Susi shouted. "I'm so happy."

"I figured you would be." Susi could feel Liz smiling at the other
end. "The ship is supposed to dock around 1300 next week Thursday.

You want to make sure you get there early to get parking and a good spot."

"We'll do, thank you so much."

"Of course." Liz chuckled. "I will see you down there."

"Sounds good." Susi knew that this would be the best day in nine months. "Oh, hey, by the way, Katy sends her regards and wanted me to convey her thanks for all your help."

"Did you talk to her?"

"I was actually just on the East Coast to visit her. She had a little boy. We went to Arlington and visited D.C.; it was nice. She's adjusted well, but it's easy to see how much she misses him."

"It's never easy to lose someone you love," Liz said, getting serious. "Especially in combat. She was very lucky to have you there to help her. So many women are alone when they get the terrible news. I heard how you helped, and I'd like you to think about joining our support team."

"I would be honored, Liz, when you have time, I'd like to talk to you about something." Susi wanted to address the "Jodie" problem with Liz.

"What is it?"

"Nothing urgent, I'm just concerned with the number of wives who have another guy in their bed, sometimes the day their husbands are deployed. I know it's really none of my business but…" Susi hoped she had not pushed a button.

"I absolutely understand what you mean," Liz responded. "You are not the only one angered by this, it is really the majority of wives who are angered by this, but this is really not something I can discuss on the phone while at my job. We should get together and have coffee sometime soon. There are actually nice little groups who feel the same as you do and spend their time honoring their husband's duty rather than not."

"Thank you, Liz. Hopefully, I will see you Thursday."

Susi went to the living room where Tracy was sitting on the floor playing with Sammi.

"Sammi." She waited for the little girl to turn towards her. "Do you know who is coming home?"

"Daddy?" This had only been the second time she'd said "Daddy" instead of "Dada." Susi picked up her little girl and twirled around with her. "Yes, Daddy. I bet he is as excited as you are."

Tracy jumped up and joined the dancing. "Wonderful news, now we can finally celebrate Miss Samantha's birthday." Tracy brought them all to a sudden stop.

"I thought we already had a nice little party for her birthday," Susi protested.

"Yes, she did, but we should have another one... one with her daddy here. I have the absolutely best idea." She had the biggest grin on her face. "We should all go to Disneyland for a late birthday celebration and for her daddy coming home."

"That's a great idea but expensive." Susi didn't want to be the killjoy, but she tended to be more realistic sometimes. She knew that they could afford the trip, but Sammi being only one, she wouldn't remember the whole thing anyway.

"But..." Tracy grinned, "she will see the videos when she's older and I will cover the cost," Tracy stated happily, bouncing with Sammi, who was giggling up a storm. With each bounce the little girl started laughing all over again. "I got my bonus last week and I was saving it for something special." Tracy stopped bouncing. "There is nothing more special than this little girl, her daddy, and her Uncle Tony."

"Well, then I guess it's settled." Susi laughed. "Why don't you get that little monster bathed and to bed so we can plan some awesome homecoming posters."

The next morning Tracy took all her things back to her own place. She found it amazing how much stuff she had accumulated at Susi's in the last nine months. She had also learned that Logan Heights was not a bad place. There were some friends and camaraderie she didn't have where she lived.

"Has it really been nine months already?" She stopped stuffing clothes into a duffle bag.

"If there is one thing I know about you, my dear friend," Susi said, laughing and grabbing some of Tracy's things. "You're a lousy packer. Besides, you could really stay the couple days." The next day the three girls shopped for craft materials to make coming-home posters, and in the evening they were busy embellishing poster board with glitter and welcoming messages. Sammi sat in her high chair covered in glitter and glue, crayons in both hands, drawing her own poster for her daddy.

Susi barely slept that night and was up before the sun. She felt the same as she had when she first met him. Breakfast was done in no time and was kept warm in the oven. She stole a few moments before waking Tracy and the baby to sit out on the front step to have a quiet cup of coffee. The "For Rent" sign was gone from the lawn where Katy and Josh used to live. So much had changed since Lance had left. Sammi had grown and learned a lot. Susi had witnessed the horror of that car pulling up with the notification officer and chaplain.

She was thankful that Lance was coming home without injuries. The conflict had been over rather quickly, but troops were still being left in country, especially since Saddam Hussein had ordered all the oil fields to be set on fire. Lance had even stated in his last letter that the air was horrible. It was nearly impossible to breathe, and the air was black and heavy from the smoke.

"Mommy?" Susi heard the little voice calling from the kitchen. She got up and went inside.

"Good morning, my little sweetie pie." Susi sat down her coffee cup and picked up her daughter. "Are you excited that Daddy is coming home today?"

Sammi stuck her index finger in her mouth and smiled.

"I know you love your daddy." She kissed Sammi on the cheek. "He loves you very much too, and he is excited to see his little honey as well. You want to go wake up Aunt Tracy?"

Sammi nodded and Susi put her down. As she had done multiple times in the last few months, Sammi went into the spare room and climbed on the bed to wake up her auntie. Only moments later the three of them sat at the kitchen table for breakfast. Tracy was surprised that even she felt some excitement about her annoying little brother being back.

Before long the small group was on their way to the naval base. The drive was short, less than ten minutes. There were already some families there but not too many.

Susi strapped Sammi in her stroller and let her hold onto the colorful sign she had made. Tracy carried the other two so Susi could push the stroller.

"Susi?" a voice called from just behind them. They turned around.

"Liz?" Susi asked, and the lady nodded. "It's nice to meet you." Susi introduced Tracy, and the three women chatted a few minutes, then made their way closer to the pier. Within an hour there seemed to be hundreds of women, children, and even parents assembled, waiting for their loved ones. There was an ocean of welcome-home signs among crowds of anxious spouses and children. Susi thought, This is not something you can convey to another person; this is amazing.

It seemed like only moments later, the ship came into the harbor. Everyone cheered. Just as they had been when they left, they lined the deck of the ship. Susi searched frantically to find Lance, but at that distance is was impossible to discern who was who.

The time came for the ship to dock, and finally Susi saw Lance about the same time he saw her. His facial expression went from worried to excited. Susi jumped up and down. She waved and shouted despite the fact that she knew he couldn't hear her. It only seemed like minutes before she saw him walking towards her. She took Sammi out of the stroller and let her run to her dad. Lance dropped his duffle bag and knelt on the ground. He scooped up the little girl and kissed her face over and over. Susi waited her turn; she could see the tears of joy running down his face. When he reached her, he took her in his empty arm and the two of them cried together.

"Mama?" Sammi questioned. Lance was amazed at hearing his daughter speak, and he realized that he'd been gone for a huge time of growth in her life.

"I love you, sweetheart." Susi gently pinched Sammi's nose. "Mommy is crying happy tears 'cause Daddy is home and I missed him so much."

The two of them kissed their little girl and each other and laughed.

"I cannot describe how happy I am to have you back," Susi said, staring at her husband.

"Sometimes it blows my mind how much you love me," he stated. "I can literally see it in your eyes. I love you so much." He looked at her and kissed her forehead. "It's as if the last nine months were just washed away by what I see in your eyes."

Moments later Tony and Tracy joined them, and all of them made plans to have dinner together. When dinner time came, they made plans for a weekend at Disneyland and to have a nice barbecue the following weekend.

Lance had one more short deployment but was back in time for Christmas. Now they could officially celebrate their first Christmas together. Tracy had bought a house, and they celebrated Thanksgiving, Christmas, and New Year's at the beautiful waterfront home. Sammi loved the beach. She enjoyed running in and out of the water, and the friends spent many weekends having fires on the beach and reminiscing.

TEN

NAS Whidbey Island and Culinary School

"The two most important days in your life are the day you are born...
and the day you find out why."

L ANCE WENT BACK TO work at the hospital. Susi had gone back to her part-time job in the day-care center at Boeing, and life was all around good. Towards the end of the third year in San Diego, Lance got his orders. He could choose between Cherry Point and Whidbey Island. They decided, for the time being, they'd like to stay on the West Coast as long as possible. Susi and Lance flew to Seattle and drove up to Whidbey to find a house and check on schools. They looked at several houses, but there seemed nothing that they both liked. The next day they decided that if nothing turned up, they would check base housing.

They found a house on Beeksma Drive in Oak Harbor; they had looked at countless houses and nothing felt right. When they walked into this house, they looked at each other and nodded. At 1,330 square feet, it was small, but the hardwood floor throughout and the shades of blue and brown were very inviting and warm. With three bedrooms it was just right for their small family and the occasional visits from Tracy. The kitchen was modern but needed an upgrade on the stove, which Lance was sure they could arrange since it had a gas hook up.

The house itself was amazing but the fact that it was only several steps to the beach was the main selling point. The public beach was literally right next to them.

Sammi stayed with Tracy. She spoiled her rotten and Susi had to, more than once, scold Tracy about the amount of money she spent on the little girl. The area was beautiful; there would be lots for them to do outdoors.

"This would be a great place to kayak with Sammi when she gets a little older and, maybe, you can get back into trail running," Lance pondered. "I could play a bit more golf up here as well with the Gallery Golf Course less than ten minutes away, and the Whidbey Island golf Club is even closer." Susi grinned and shook her head.

"I'd love to kayak," she announced. "Maybe that's something we could all do together, but golf is all you, my love."

Six months later they had settled in; Sammi started at Kinderhuis Montessori in Oak Harbor, and Susi found herself with several hours a day with nothing to do. Though rather expensive they found Montessori to be the best option for Sammi. It helped that Susi had few expenses while having a decent income working for Dr. Carl and she'd saved a lot. Otherwise they would not have been able to afford some of the things they did. They'd chosen Montessori to prepare her for school, learn to socialize, and interact with others her age. Once Susi had Lance off to work in the morning, she would get Sammi ready and dropped off, then she'd go for a run. She loved running across the Deception Pass Bridge. Though she had an issue with heights, she would always stop halfway across the bridge and enjoy the view. The whole area had so much history and beautiful views. The bridge itself was built in 1935 with an open a view to the beaches below and lush pine forests. At a height of 180 feet, it had sadly had its fair share of suicide jumpers. Usually by nine thirty she'd be back home and showered with not much to do.

"I'm looking into the culinary program at Sno-Isle tech in Everett," she told Lance at dinner one night.

"Oh? Finally getting serious about that culinary degree?" he replied.

"Well, everyone has been saying I should, so why not? I enjoy cooking and I could do something with an education like that."

"That is true." Lance squeezed her hand. "Don't want to go back to be an optician?" Susi shook her head. "No thanks, I bet I could not get a good boss like Dr. Carl had been."

"Have you heard from his wife anymore after he passed away?" Lance asked.

"Not really. I'd called a couple of times but only got their oldest son. Apparently, his mom had decided to take an extended cruise with her sister. I honestly had a feeling that once he retired, he wouldn't last much longer. His job was his life, and I don't think he had a purpose without it."

The following evening, she told Lance that she'd have to wait until Sammi started kindergarten, since she would not have enough time to do classes and get back in time to pick her up.

"We could get a baby sitter to pick her up and bring her home, maybe someone who could do some light cleaning as well, so you're not stressing," Lance said. "I know how particular you are, but it's something to think about. I know you want to cook, but just some of the daily cleaning could be done by a nanny."

"Honey, are you sure we can afford Montessori and a nanny? It's not like we have a bottomless pit of money." Susi sounded concerned.

"I looked over our finances the other day," Lance remarked. "Remember the savings we converted to a mutual fund? We made quite a bit on that, but it has to be our decision."

"I'd like if we could start doing the finances together, create a budget for necessary expenses, investments and the stuff we like to do."

"Absolutely." Lance smiled. "Why don't we take a little time Saturday afternoon and go over everything?"

Susi agreed. "I really think you have an absolutely good point. Having gone to school in Germany, I am really not a big fan of public education here. Teachers are not paid enough and are way too limited with the curriculum. I think Montessori is the best choice, at least as long as we are here." Susi hugged her husband. She loved hugging him; he was taller than her and her head fit comfortably on his chest. Every time he hugged her, he told her that she was tiny and it made her feel incredibly happy.

The following day after dropping Sammi off, Susi skipped her run. She'd seen a flyer at the commissary that had been posted by someone who was looking for a nanny job. Susi did some shopping and then wrote the number down to call the lady once she got home.

"Hello?" the woman greeted.

"Hi, my name is Susi Wells," Susi said. "I saw you ad for a nanny position. Are you still available?"

"Yes, ma'am, did you have specific days in mind? By the way, my name is Ronnie."

"I will be in school in Everett Monday through Friday, so my daughter would need to be picked up on those days. Would you be able to come over and meet with my husband and I as well as our daughter, Sammi?" Susi inquired.

"Where do you live?"

"We are on Beeksma Drive. When would you be able to come over?"

"What time would be good for you?" Ronnie responded.

"Would five thirty work? My husband will be home then and so will our kiddo."

"That works for me," Ronnie said. "I will be happy to bring references for you with numbers you can call."

"That's awesome." Susi was thrilled. She provided the exact address for Ronnie. "See you later."

Susi was happy that Ronnie had offered to bring references, otherwise she would have had to ask and that would have been difficult for her. Something like that was more Tracy's thing; she had always been the one who was more outgoing and aggressive.

That evening Susi anxiously awaited Ronnie. Lance took care of the dinner dishes so she could focus on talking to their guest. Ronnie looked at least ten years younger than she was, her brown hair pulled back into a ponytail and blue eyes that had a shine that Susi thought her mother would have now. She was in great shape, and Susi found out that she was an avid runner. She told Susi about the Deception Pass marathon which she had done the last few years. Susi told her she would look into it.

Ronnie had been a military spouse as well, but her husband had been killed by a drunk driver some years earlier. She had stayed on Whidbey Island so she could care for his grave, and she really liked it here. She had been an elementary school teacher for several years when they were stationed on the East Coast, and since they had purchased a bigger house with a nice yard in Oak Harbor, she opened a day-care center. After her husband died, she went into seclusion for a year, trying to figure out what she wanted to do. She had worked as a nanny for a few years now and her references were impeccable.

Ronnie excused herself to go to the bathroom, and Lance took the chance to tell Susi what he thought. "She seems perfect... and... Sammi seems to like her." He had a point there. Sammi had been smiling at her and chatting with her since she had arrived at the house.

When Ronnie came back from the bathroom, she asked, "Do you have any other questions? Would you like to think about it for a day or two, check the references, and get back to me?"

"That's not necessary," Susi and Lance stated at the same time and laughed. "We'd love to have you take care of our peanut," Susi said. It was settled. Susi asked Ronnie to meet her at Montessori the next day so she could introduce her to Sammi's teacher. Ronnie laughed and told Susi that her oldest daughter, Carrie, was a teacher at Montessori, and she was very familiar. It turned out that Ronnie's daughter was Sammi's teacher. This all turned out almost too perfect.

Susi had requested information from the school and had scheduled an appointment with admission for the following week. Ronnie had picked up Sammi a couple of times to help out. They all thought it would be good to establish a routine for Sammi to get used to.

A week later Ronnie brought Sammi home. They had been at the beach and the playground, and Sammi was as happy as a child could be. Lance invited Ronnie to stay for dinner, but she had to excuse herself as she generally had dinner with her daughter on Wednesdays.

The small family had just finished dinner when Lance had an idea. "I've actually been thinking about getting Sammi into golf when she's three or four." Lance waited for a response. He knew how Susi felt. To her, golf just wasn't a sport for anyone under sixty.

But she surprised him. "That's a great idea. Just please make sure that she likes it. I want us to be parents who make suggestions on activities but don't force, you know what I mean?"

"Of course," Lance assured her. "On a more serious note, I've been meaning to tell you something." He knelt down in front of her and took her hands. "You've done so much for our family; I'd like to see you do something you are interested in. I'm glad you are doing school and I'm very proud of you."

Susi got teary-eyed. Sometimes she really hated that she was so emotionally driven, but Lance had told her many times that he liked that about her. She wore her heart on her sleeve, which he found amazing given the abuse she had been through at the hands of her ex-husband. She always put one hundred percent of herself into whatever she did and that included being his wife.

The next day Susi skipped her run again and went straight to Everett after dropping Sammi at school. The admissions counselor was very nice and extremely helpful. She would be starting classes in just a couple of weeks and there was a lot to be done. One thing she could be sure of was that Lance would support her every step of the way. The drive would be hard, over an hour, and a ferry ride between Clinton and Everett.

****

By the time Christmas came around, Lance, Sammi, and Ronnie had eaten wonderful experiments, and the family decided to have an early New Year's celebration to show off some of Susi's new talents. Ronnie had become an irreplaceable member of their family.

Susi had prepared a fantastic shrimp fettuccini dish and they were all stuffed. "What do you guys say we drive to the beach by Gallery Golf Club and take a walk after I get the dishes put away?" she asked.

"How about you let me do the dishes," Lance smiled, "my little chef."

"You two remind me so much of the way my husband and I were when we were your age," Ronnie noted.

Susi blushed and kissed Lance on the cheek. "I bet your husband was an amazing man and father."

"Yes, he was." Ronnie seemed to drift away in her thoughts. "I still miss him so much."

"I'm sorry." Susi felt bad. "I shouldn't have mentioned that."

"Oh, honey," Ronnie told her, "please don't feel bad. I treasure his memory, and there will never be another man for me."

"Let's go to the beach, ladies." Lance interrupted the serious moment.

They agreed and within an hour they were strolling along the beach near Gallery Golf Club. The course itself was a soggy mess, but that was the norm for this time of year.

"I'm kinda playing with the idea of joining you in golf this spring," Susi told Lance as they were walking. "What are your thoughts?" Lance looked at Susi and gently shook his head as he grinned from ear to ear.

"You are something, my love," he whispered to her. "If you think you can make time for it, maybe you can take some lessons. I just don't want you to overdo it with Sammi, school, your running schedule, and then golf".

Sammi ran ahead in an effort to find shells. Despite the cold water, she had taken her shoes and socks off and handed them to her mother, so she could walk right along the edge and let the water wash sand across her feet. She seemed to be in her own little world.

Susi took Lance's hand. "Are you glad we decided to not have another one?"

"I am," he stated and squeezed Susi's hand. "If we'd had another child, you wouldn't be able to follow your dream yet and Sammi wouldn't be able to go to Montessori, and we wouldn't be able to have Ronnie. I could go on, but I think I made my point."

They walked as far as the shoreline allowed them and then turned around. By the time they got home, Sammi was asleep in her car seat. Lance scooped her up and took her in.

"I really wanted her to take a bath to get all the sand washed off." Susi looked at her daughter's dirty feet as Lance laid her on the bed.

"Why don't we just let her sleep? I'll change her bed tomorrow, so you don't have to," he convinced her and gave her a hug. "Why don't we relax on the couch, watch a movie, and have a glass of wine? We had such a great day. Let's keep it going for a bit."

Susi got on her tiptoes and gently kissed Lance. "Why don't you open a bottle for us? I'll go change."

"Sounds promising." Lance grinned and headed for the kitchen.

Moments later they were both sitting on the couch. Susi was focused on a baking competition airing on the Food Network, and Lance wasn't paying attention to anything but his wife. Susi noticed him staring at her out of the corner of her eye.

"Is everything okay?" she asked.

"I love you and I think you are beautiful," Lance stated directly.

Susi blushed. "Well, thank you. I love you too."

Lance sat his wine glass on the coffee table and moved closer to his wife. He took the glass out of her hand and placed it next to his. Susi started to say something, but he placed a finger on her mouth so she wouldn't speak. Slowly he replaced his finger with his lips and while kissing her, he picked her up and carried her to the bedroom. He undressed her all the while keeping his eyes locked on hers. She loved when he seduced her like this.

After they made love, she laid in his arms. "No matter what happens in our lives, I hope you never stop doing that," she said. "It is so amazing." He pulled her closer with his right arm and kissed her on the forehead. Moments later they were both deeply asleep.

****

Nearly two years later, Susi had worked herself to the top in her class, and instructors often asked her to assist them in private catering events. She had also worked in a basic baking class as a teaching assistant, and a couple of her chef instructors had told her that they were not looking forward to her graduating. Lance was beyond thrilled and proud that she was doing so well, and he had taken over a lot of the household chores as well as entertaining their daughter when Susi was busy. He purchased a two-seater kayak, and on weekends when Susi was busy at a catering event, he would have Ronnie take care of Sammi in the morning while he played a round of golf, and in the afternoon, he would take the little one out in the kayak.

The time came when Lance had to pick orders as their last year on Whidbey Island approached. Susi was getting nervous about her graduation. She'd gone to high school in Germany, and over there they didn't make a big deal about graduation. You just finished; it was part of life. She had no idea that Lance had planned a big graduation celebration at the Whidbey Island Golf and Country Club. He had told her that they would have dinner there after her ceremony, but she had no idea what he had planned.

She graduated with honors and while happy to be done, she was also a bit sad.

"I am so proud of you," Lance told her and squeezed her hand in the car on their way to the restaurant. When they arrived, Lance took Sammi out of her car seat and the three made their way inside. Susi did not notice that Lance stayed slightly behind her. She was stunned at the group of people standing up clapping when she walked into the reserved room. Huge windows overlooked the first hole and lush greens. Flowering shrubs framed the picture. The tables were draped in white linens, the chairs covered in white covers, and an arrangement of red and white roses made the red napkins at each place pop. Susi scanned the crowd. Co-workers of Lance's, two of her instructors, Ronnie and her daughter, and, this could not be true, Tracy. She turned, tears of gratitude running down her face and whispered thank you to Lance. As she turned to go hug Tracy, she was already behind her. They had not seen each other in more than eighteen months. Tracy had gotten another promotion at Boeing and her travel time was limited.

"I can't believe you actually made it." Susi hugged her tightly.

"I would not have missed this for the world," Tracy beamed. "I'm so proud of you. This is so amazing."

Sammi was just as excited to see her Auntie Tracy, and the two stayed together until it was time to end the evening and head home. "I hope you didn't get a hotel," Lance said to Tracy.

"No, sir, I followed your instructions, drove straight up, hid in the background at the ceremony, and then came here," Tracy replied, smirking.

Susi and her family said their good-byes to their guests and then made their way to their car. Both of her attending instructors told her that they'd have plenty of work for her in the very near future. Tracy followed them home. Though it was early fall, it was beautiful outside, and the three friends sat on the deck with a bottle of wine to catch up, and just simply watch the tide come in.

"I can't believe you get to see sunsets like this every night." Tracy was in awe. The sky was shades of orange and red which reflected in the calm water, and one could not see where the sky ended and the water began, the horizon nothing but a faint blur between the two.

"Where is Tony at these days?" Lance wanted to know. "Haven't heard from him in a while."

"He went to Norfolk just a little while after you guys came up here," Tracy told him. "He doesn't like it. Actually, he is hoping to get leave approved for Christmas, and then he plans to come over and spend Christmas with me."

"You should both come up here. We get orders soon and we will be leaving before the end of next year," Lance told her.

"That sounds like a great idea." Tracy was excited. "Susi, there was something I wanted to ask you." She seemed to get shy, which was something very out of character for Tracy.

"What's going on?" Susi questioned.

"Would you be my maid of honor?" Neither Susi nor Lance believed what they had just heard.

"Excuse me, your what?" Susi stared at Tracy and without thinking pulled her left hand out of her lap. She couldn't believe that there was a ring on her ring finger, and a sizeable one at that. How did she not see that earlier? If anyone would have asked Susi if she thought Tracy would ever get married, she would have said not for all the money in the world.

"What? When? How, and most importantly, who?" Susi had no words. Tracy laughed. "Wait, why have you not told me anything about this? I have been your best friend for a hundred years." Susi was stern.

"I would have told you, but I didn't want you to take your focus away from school. Lance knew, actually for some time." Tracy smiled and Lance blushed.

Susi glared at her husband and then at Tracy. "I can't believe you two. Keeping important secrets like that."

"I know," Lance confessed, chuckling. "By the way, Tracy arranged the whole shindig tonight as well."

"I'm not surprised." Susi shook her head. "Thank you both bunches, it truly was amazing, but I detect an attempt to change the subject."

Over the next hour and another bottle of wine, Tracy filled Susi in on all the details. Tracy had met Max at a company dinner. He was there as the date for his sister, who had just broken up with her boyfriend. Tracy told Susi that he was an executive at Amazon and had as many odd habits as she herself did. They were really a perfect match. Lance already knew most of the details, so he made sure Sammi had her bath and was put to bed.

****

Tony, Tracy, and Max had come up for Christmas, and Lance poked fun at Tony that it was going to be his turn now, as the impossible had happened and his sister was getting married. Max towered over Tracy at just over six feet tall with salt-and-pepper hair. Susi could tell he was a runner by his thin but athletic form. His eyes were a deep grey, something Susi had never seen. When he put his arm around Tracy, he could easily lay his armpit on top of her head.

The friends had a peaceful Christmas and New Year's, and just after the new year started, Susi and Tracy spoke nearly every day in the process of making wedding plans. Susi got Max to help her with the contact information of co-workers Tracy was particularly fond of as well as other friends who she might like to join her bridal shower.

After Tracy and Max had been to multiple bakeries in Seattle, Bellevue, and the surrounding area, they decided to have Susi make their wedding cake. Susi was honored that they both trusted her that way.

The following May Tracy married Max in the Chihuly Glass Garden by the Space Needle. This was generally not done, but apparently Max had connections and the money to make it happen. While Tracy had made sure years ago that Susi had the wedding she'd always wanted, Tracy wanted hers small and simple but elegant. That's exactly what she had.

The ceremony took place in the glass pavilion, hundreds of orange glass flowers hanging above them and the yellow-orange glass sunburst outside providing the perfect backdrop for their altar. Max had no siblings, so he had asked Tony to be his best man and Lance to be a groomsman. Susi was the matron of honor and Shelly, one of Tracy's coworkers, was a bridesmaid. Both Tony and Lance wore their dress whites as Tracy had requested. She loved the formality of the uniforms.

The reception took place at the Space Needle, just across the walkway from the glass gardens. Susi knew that Tracy would have liked to have the reception in the revolving restaurant, Sky City, but Tracy also wanted her guests to dance, so they had to rent a private room in the Space Needle. They still had an amazing view of everything from the Cascade Mountain range, the Puget Sound with the ferries running back and forth to Bremerton and Bainbridge Island, Bellevue, and the Olympic Mountain range, which even in May still displayed its beautiful snowcapped peaks.

As Susi so often did at the end of a beautiful event, she thought about the changes they had all gone through in the last few years. As she watched Tracy dance her first dance with her new husband, she thought about the fun she and Tracy used to have, Tracy being a devoted bachelorette and feisty as hell. Susi thought she'd never see the day

that she'd see her best friend dance with her new husband and look
lovingly into his eyes. She smiled and looked at Lance. She was thankful
that she had found him. He seemed to remain strong no matter what.
He'd gotten a little quieter, but that was about it. She deeply hoped he
would not have to go through anything else that might alter who he
was and who she had fallen in love with and still loved very deeply.

ELEVEN

Guam – I'm Always Here for You

"You were given this life 'cause you were strong enough to live it."

T HE LAST THREE YEARS had almost felt like a honeymoon. They had spent so much time together, not just as a couple but as a family. Life could not have been more perfect. Though Desert Storm had taken a slight toll on Lance a few years ago, he seemed to have recovered well. Susi and Lance felt closer than ever, and their little one was about to start first grade. She had done well in kindergarten and loved all her friends. She had her mother's red hair, her father's amazing blue eyes, and more freckles than the sky had stars, and the spunk to match.

They always seemed to have several little girls in the house on weekends, and Lance never failed to entertain the girls by building a fort from boxes and blankets, or providing the movies and snacks for a movie night. With Tracy and Max just two and a half hours away, they could visit often for the weekend and each time they got together, it was as if no time had passed at all. Max loved golf as much as Lance did, and on occasion they would play when Lance's duty schedule allowed.

It was an evening in late May 1996 when the little family sat down to dinner, and Sam was going on and on how much fun she had with her friends that day. Lance seemed distant minded, and Susi was a little concerned that he may be going through a bout of depression.

"Hey, honey?" She tapped his shoulder. "Everything okay?"

Her question startled him back to reality, and he took her hand and kissed it.

"Got offered to pick what's available for orders today," he stated frankly while loading spaghetti onto his plate.

"Oh? Care to share?" Susi pulled out her chair and sat down when Sam jumped in.

"Daddy, what are orders? Are we moving?"

"I'm afraid so, baby girl," Lance responded with a sad face.

"Oh, wow, where are we going?" Sammi continued eating her spaghetti and didn't seem upset about the news at all. Susi smiled at the conversation between the two and was amazed how this little girl just seemed to accept things; sometimes she really seemed more like a little adult than a child.

"Well, little lady," Lance replied, smiling and winking at Susi, "we have the opportunity to be stationed on an island in the Pacific Ocean. The island is called Guam and there are a lot of Navy people there."

Sammi dropped her fork full of noodles and sauce, her mouth hung open. "An island? Really?"

"Yes, and you know the best part?" Lance did not wait for a response. "Crissy and her family are moving there as well!" Sammi's excitement seemed to be influencing his own mood.

Sammi stood on her chair and cheered, her freshly loaded fork waving in all directions and depositing spaghetti on the kitchen floor. Susi got up, took the fork out of her daughter's hand, and picked up what had landed on the floor. "Okay, little one, how about you sit back down and finish your dinner?"

"Yes, Mama," Sammi reacted. "Can I call Crissy after I'm done eating?"

"Why don't you wait till her daddy tells her and lets her call you," Lance answered. "He's not off duty yet, so he probably hasn't had a chance to tell his family yet."

Sammi frowned but agreed.

"When would we be leaving?" Susi asked quietly when she finally had a chance to ask.

"Looks like mid-August," Lance replied. "It would probably be best to enroll Peanut in school at the base there. I'll see if I can find out the exact date so we can prepare for her school. I'd rather we didn't have her start here and then take her out after a week to go to Guam."

"Good point." Susi smiled at him, and he again took her hand and kissed it. He had told Susi some time ago that he liked that kind of show of affection.

He smiled back at her and whispered, "How did I ever get so lucky to have you as my wife?" He stayed focused on her eyes. "I love you so much. I'll happily go anywhere in the world with you." With that it was decided that Lance would choose orders to go to Guam.

"Mommm!" Sammi's voice was getting more insistent when Susi finally heard her.

"Oh goodness, I'm sorry, sweetheart, what?" she responded, laughing.

"Am I not going to go back to school here?" the little lady wanted to know.

"Most likely not," Susi and Lance stated almost at the same time.

"Okay!" Sammi shrugged her shoulders and continued eating. Just like that the whole thing had been settled. No tears, no arguments. Lance told Susi that he felt lucky. Many of the guys dealt with family drama about kids leaving friends, and often it wasn't much different for the wives.

"Aren't you upset to leave your friends?" Lance inquired with Sammi.

"Crissy is moving too because her daddy is in the Navy too," Sammi stated with a slight attitude. "Teacher explained to the other students that when you are in the military sometimes you have to leave your friends, but it's fun to write letters and keep in touch. So, I'll do that. Nothing to cry about."

Lance and Susi looked at each other and almost burst out in laughter. This little girl was something else. They must have done something right for their daughter to see things that way at such an early age.

Of all the times they'd had to move, Susi had never complained and always managed to keep in touch with the few friends she had made at various duty stations. Lance told her that he was very happy his home life had no stress and that he was lucky enough to have an understanding, supportive wife.

Towards the end of June, the movers came; one thing Susi was thankful for, she hated packing. The second week of July they arrived on Guam, which was beautiful. Coming from the cool Pacific Northwest to a tropical island was a huge change, but the beaches and turquoise water made up for it. Until their belongings arrived, they stayed at the Navy Gateway Inn and Suites. They rented a suite so Susi could provide meals and they wouldn't have to eat out every day. They were only four hours from New Zealand and Australia, and before their first week was over, they had made plans to visit. They both agreed that it would be perfect for Sammi to be exposed to as many different cultures as possible.

Their household items arrived in the usual manner. Finding a house was another matter. Lance didn't care for base housing, and neither of them wanted to live in a condo or apartment after the wonderful house they'd had on Whidbey Island. What had been fairly easy on Whidbey Island turned into a nightmare on Guam. After all their belongings were in storage for three weeks and Lance having been at work for nearly a month, living at the Gateway Inn had become nearly unbearable. While Sammi was at school and Lance at work, Susi took the time to run each morning, exploring new neighborhoods.

"I really think I need to pull some money from my account in Germany so we can rent a house that will suit us for the next three years," Susi remarked after she'd gotten Sammi to bed. "You can forget anything near the water the way we had it on Whidbey. If we're lucky we'll have a glimpse of ocean out of one of the windows."

"You know, I've been thinking about this for a few days." Lance approached what he wanted to say with care. Susi was very budget minded and she might not like his idea. "What do you think about us buying a house, and when we leave here we can either sell it or get a property manager and rent it out, you know, use it as an investment property."

"Actually," she replied, pouring a glass of wine and motioning Lance to see if he wanted one as well, "that sounds like a good idea. With all the running I've been doing in various neighborhoods, I've seen a lot of for sale signs on some amazing properties. I could call the real estate agent I've seen on most of them."

He'd really expected more of a struggle but was happy she agreed. "Did you expect me to argue that point with you?" Susi smiled and handed him his wine.

"A little, but I think you've about had it with living in this little space." He kissed her cheek as she sat next to him on the small blue couch.

****

"Ellen's Reality, this is Richard, how may I help you?" The voice at the end of the line sounded very cheerful.

"Yes, hi, this is Susi Wells and we have been on the Island for nearly six weeks, trying to find a rental near the water, but have struck out." Susi knew she had provided unnecessary information. "We, that being my husband, Lance, and I along with our daughter, decided we'd like to buy and I've seen a lot of signs on various properties with your agency's name on it."

"We are the number one agency on the island," Richard stated with the same enthusiasm as before. "What is your budget if you don't mind me asking?"

"I'd say about four hundred fifty thousand," Susi responded.

"That will get you a lot of house." Richard's excitement seemed to grow.

"Very true." Susi was thankful that she had been smart financially so they could do this. "My husband is in the Navy, so we will only be here for three years, but we were thinking we could use this as a rental property once we leave."

"We can help you with that as well," he announced, and Susi felt she could hear the smile on his face. "Ellen likes to take care of buyers in that price range herself. Would you mind holding for a second?"

"Not at all," Susi replied.

"Hello, Mrs. Wells, this is Ellen Wilkinson, I'm the broker for this agency," Ellen stated. "Richard tells me you are looking for an investment property for four hundred fifty thousand?"

"Yes, Ellen, that is correct." Susi tried to sound more businesslike. "When I went for my run this morning, I saw one of your signs on Talo Verde Way."

"Oh, you run out there?" Ellen wanted to know.

"I've been running all over the island just to get an idea of the real estate available." Susi smiled. "We have literally lived at the Navy Gateway Inn on base for the six weeks we have been here."

"That house has not been on the market for long and has had a lot of interest." Ellen's voice was serious. "We'd have to move quick if you are interested."

Here comes the pressure, Susi thought but said, "I could meet you there in thirty minutes if that works for you."

"Sounds great, I will see you there," Ellen confirmed. "Just one more question, will you be using a VA loan?"

"No, ma'am," Susi stated rather proudly. "We won't need to finance."

"Wonderful, I'll see you in half an hour," Ellen told her and hung up. All Susi could think about was how grateful she was that the exchange rate between the German mark and the American dollar had been so amazing in the eighties. "Thank you, President Reagan," she said to herself.

At precisely eleven a.m., Susi pulled up at 209 Talo Verde Way. The navy-blue Mercedes that had been behind her for the last few minutes pulled in next to her. Lance would have a less than twenty-minute drive to the naval hospital.

"Hello, Mrs. Wells, it is truly a pleasure to meet you," Ellen greeted her, extending her hand.

"The pleasure is all mine," Susi responded and shook her hand. Susi thought she had gone through a lot and saved a lot of money to finally be able to buy something that would provide the people she loved a beautiful home and a long-term investment income.

"Shall we?" Ellen pointed towards the front door. Ellen's Asian brown eyes were warm and her facial expression welcoming but elegant. She was Susi's height and slender. Ellen told Susi that she appreciated fellow runners. It was her favorite way to let the stress of the realty business slide off her shoulders. Susi told her that she would enjoy having a running and occasional coffee friend. Ellen told her that would be fun and they could talk later.

They walked up to white double doors. The grass in the front yard looked unkept, but Ellen explained that with the recent rain and no on living on the property that was not unusual. Susi liked the small palm trees lining the driveway, reminding her of the desert. The house could have been picked out of the Spanish countryside with its white exterior and red roof tiles. Spanish tile lay throughout, broken only by the black tile designs in the hallways.

The kitchen was modern and beautiful with a double-door refrigerator and freezer, a five-burner gas range, and a wine rack, basically a chef's dream. Susi began to dream about cooking classes she could teach for other Navy wives and catering she could do. Three dropped lights enhanced the curved glass exhaust vent over the range and provided warmth to the walnut brown cabinets. Susi felt she had found her dream kitchen; she knew from culinary school that a good chef could make any kitchen work, but why when you had this?

The whole house had high ceilings with warm off-white walls and crown molding that Susi liked a lot. She wasn't sure about the floor tile going up to the ceiling in the guest bathroom, but it could grow on her and it would be easy to clean.

The stairs to the second floor had the same walnut brown color on the banister that she had found in the kitchen, and it was supported with wrought iron design. The master bedroom had double doors and a beautiful recessed ceiling. His and hers closets with mirror doors lined the way to the master bathroom. The large corner soaking tub took Susi's breath away. A double sink with walnut brown cabinets led to a door that opened to a private balcony. Susi could only imagine her and Lance sitting out there enjoying a glass of wine after making love.

The guest room and guest bathroom were just what she would want for Tracy and Max. She knew Tracy's taste, and this was right up her alley. A nice soaking tub, a class encased shower, and dark cherry cabinetry with double sinks.

Susi thought they could use the loft at the top of the stairs as an office or family play area. It was bright but also needed the carpet replaced with the white-wash wood that she envisioned. There were some nice built-in shelves in the bedrooms.

While she missed being so close to the water, Susi liked that there was a community pool and a tennis court. She hadn't played since she was fourteen back in Germany.

"Do you play tennis?" Susi asked Ellen.

"A little, I'm still learning and don't have a lot of time," Ellen responded. "I'm sure you won't have any trouble finding a partner here."

"Were there any other properties you'd like to see?" Ellen asked.

"I don't think so." Susi felt good about this place. "I'll talk to my husband this evening, and I will get back to you first thing tomorrow."

Ellen shared a few pointers about great running areas and told Susi that she'd like to go for a run together some time or just have coffee. Susi liked the idea and told her that she was looking forward to having her over for dinner.

With the house being purchased outright and no financing to deal with, they were moved in within three weeks. Lance and Sammi didn't get a chance to see the house until after Susi signed the paperwork and the sale was final. They were both ecstatic. By the end of August, the family had settled in nicely, and Sam had already started making friends in the neighborhood and at the base school. They spent every possible moment at the beach, and when Sammi declared she wanted to learn how to surf, no one objected. Life was once again–perfect.

Christmas came and though spending it on a tropical island was not Susi's first choice, it was too soon to request leave and go to Washington State. Susi called Tracy and asked if she and Max would like to come spend Christmas with them on the beach, and she didn't have to ask twice. They arrived four days before Christmas. Tracy was in awe of the house and told Susi that she made the perfect choice. Max and Lance played golf every chance they had. Max loved the weather and teased Tracy that they would have to come back a few more times before the opportunity was gone.

The first week of January, the guests flew home, and the little family resumed their island life. From January until August 6, 1997, life was as blissful as it had been on Whidbey Island. They had no complaints. Lance was getting much better at golf, Sammi had fun at her surfing lessons, and Susi was making a good amount of money with her cooking lessons, which now covered four afternoons a week with six people each time.

****

On August 6 Lance had duty at the hospital at night. He didn't mind the overnight hospital shifts unless they were on weekends. There was always someone who'd come in after getting into a drunken fight. The middle of the week seemed to be bringing an uneventful night, and he thought he might be able to catch up on his reading. He headed to the naval hospital at nine thirty; his shift started at ten. Everything was quiet, and he shared a cup of coffee with the corpsman going off duty. By midnight the hospital was so quiet it was eerie. The white walls and grey doors with their little windows could have been something out of a horror film. Red signs on the doors reading Authorized Personnel Only. Lance could see faint light through the little windows in the doors. Something felt off. He'd been alone in that part of the hospital before. In an office near the ER with the door open, he could always hear other people, but tonight, despite the muffled sounds from the ER, something was not right. Around midnight it started pouring. Lance didn't like nights like this. No one was aware of the storm that was about to hit.

Not long after one in the morning, Korean Air Flight 801 had started its descent to Guam international airport. On board were 237 passengers and a crew of 17. Most of the travelers were Koreans coming in for vacation, some honeymoon couples, three children and three infants, and thirteen Americans. Reports would later state that at 1:21 a.m., the first officer told the flight captain that the conditions at Guam were not good. It was pouring rain, dark, and no runway lights were visible. The first officer requested a slight course deviation, which was approved by ground control to Guam. Visibility became so bad that the crew had to rely mostly on their instruments rather than visual guides.

The Guam airport appeared out of nowhere, and the first officer requested landing clearance for runway six left. The controller instructed the flight crew with a heading, and the crew performed its checklist as they had done countless times before. At 1:41 the tower controller cleared the flight to land and the crew began its landing checklist, but by 1:42 the first officer called for a missed approach.

At 2:08 a phone rang at the hospital near Lance's office, with a call from the naval security office, and within minutes emergency personnel were on standby. Guam Fire Department communications would later reveal that a call had been received from the Guam ramp control at 2:07 about a downed airliner. Everyone went into autopilot mode as did Lance. Within minutes two Jeeps with personnel and equipment were assembled and they headed out. They could see the bright glow of the crashed plane over Nimitz Hill. Engine Company 7 of the Guam Fire Department was dispatched, but it was reported that they could not leave until they recharged the truck's brake fluid, which was drained on a daily basis to prevent overnight condensation buildup. Twelve minutes after being notified of the crash, the engine finally left. Naval personnel arrived at the gate to the pipeline/VOR access road, the only road leading to the crash site, at 2:34.

Later reports revealed that the Federal Fire Department Station No. 5, located on Nimitz Hill, was only a mile away from the crash site, but Engine No. 5 did not arrive at the gate until 2:39. The first responders dispatched by the Navy arrived to a chaotic scene at the only access. A damaged oil pipe blocked a section of the road, and as the crew in one fire truck attempted to make their way around the damaged pipe they got stuck in the mud. It took an hour for the truck to be pulled out.

The dispatched naval personnel there took matters into their own hands.

Master Chief Charleston, an older man with hunched-over shoulders who hated nothing more than rain, signaled the men together: "We need to get down there. If there are any survivors, they won't have much time, not in a crash that size." Senior Chief Laremy told the men to grab everything they could carry and leave the vehicles behind. Laremy didn't let anything bother him. He'd been in the Navy for fifteen years and there was no other life for him. His wife had walked out with their kids four years ago. He spent two weeks each summer with the kids and other than that, there was little communication. At six-foot-four, he was one of the tallest guys. Lance had told Susi multiple times it seemed odd that Laremy didn't even date.

They took flashlights, ropes, and the only trauma kit they had and made their way on foot through shoulder-high, razor-sharp, elephant grass. They didn't have to go far before they saw the fires and heard the screams. Bodies had been thrown about and the few survivors, some stumbling, were hard to see. The extreme dark made visibility harder; the rain did not help the matter. There seemed to be smoke screens everywhere created from the heavy rain and fire. The plane with its magnificent blue and white fuselage had broken into several pieces, each one engulfed in flames.

Master Chief Charleston separated the guys into two groups to find as many survivors as possible. Senior Chief Miller, HM1 Specks, and HM3 Fulton made their way to the front section of the plane.

"There has to be a lot of people still in there," noted Specks, a skinny Irish guy with red hair and a million freckles. He feared for the people trapped near the front of the plane. The cockpit, galley, and first-class section had broken off and the men could hear the excruciating screams from the inside of what was left of the section.

Lance screamed, "Too many are trapped, we have to find a way in." Master Chief Charleston, Lance, and HM3 Kaiser circled the mid-section of the plane for any possible way in. Even wrapped in protective gear, there was no way to get inside, the fires were too hot. All they could do was wait and listen as the screams grew silent. There was just no break in the flames for anyone to get through. They would need the fires put out, but the fire trucks had not made their way down.

Not much later the Seabees were able to clear a small area for a helicopter to land and set up lighting in the triage area, but all of this took time in this tropical terrain. Time that cost many of those who might have been saved.

Each stretcher that was carried to the chopper required four men to hold it along the muddy path. Communication was patchy at best since the civilians and the Navy used different radios frequencies. Between the men from the hospital and the Guam Naval Activities Station, also located on the hill, two triage stations were quickly set up. In small groups the men approached survivors, and those in shock and frightened were approached with care and a reassuring Neoleul dobgi wihae was-eo (I am here to help you). Lance and Specks worked together. They found a small group and checked each person for vital signs.

"I don't think I will ever get used to the smell of burning flesh," Specks almost whispered.

"If you find yourself used to it, you need to find a different job," Lance replied.

"The worst are the children," Specks added. "I don't care what the situation is, but if there is a child involved, it hits me hard." Specks checked a little girl sitting next to the body of what might have been her mother. Tears were running down her ash-covered face.

"She seems to have nothing more than minor burns on her hands and legs. Her heart sounded strong and so did her lungs. "*Naega deliloe gal su-iss-eo* (Can I pick you up)?" Specks asked the little girl and held out his arms. She sobbed and held on to the torn shirt of the dead woman next to her.

"I didn't know you speak Korean," Lance said, surprised.

"Yeah." Specks kept eye contact with the little girl, attempting to win her trust by smiling at her. "My mother speaks six languages and insisted that my sister and I learn at least four." He pulled a Kit Kat bar out of his chest pocket, opened it, and handed a piece to the girl who reluctantly accepted it.

"I always carry a few things of candy; you never know when you might need it." They watched as the little girl ate the piece of chocolate, and Specks held out another piece but did not let her take it. He told her that she had to let him pick her up. She let go of her mother and reached out her arms.

"Wells!"

Lance whirled around. "Right here, Senior," he replied.

"I need you here," Senior Chief Laremy yelled.

"You got this?" Lance inquired with Specks. He nodded and continued to focus on the little girl. Lance made his way to a section of the back of the plane.

"Yes, Senior?" he addressed Laremy.

"We have two right here in very critical condition. We need help getting the stretchers in and moved." Laremy seemed to have aged just in the last few hours.

"I got it, Senior." Lance started to walk to one of the triage stations. He got no further than eight feet or so when a hand reached up from a small group of bodies and gripped his leg. He thought he had stumbled over something. "What the hell?" He turned and saw the hand reaching up between two bodies.

"I need help here!" he yelled. Specks, who had taken the little girl to triage, and HM3 Snider ran to help him.

"There is someone buried alive under these bodies." His voice had an extreme sense of urgency. They gently moved the bodies off the survivor, a young woman, late twenties maybe, who was lying on her side. It was impossible to see what injuries she had, but they needed to get her to triage.

"I'll get a stretcher and neck stabilizer." Snider ran off, and the senior chief took his place. Lance had kneeled down to check her pulse and vitals. "She's barely there, Senior."

"Stay with her," Laremy instructed and walked off. No sooner was the senior chief gone, the young woman grabbed Lance's hand. She was saying something he couldn't understand. "Specks, listen, what is she saying?"

"*Nae agineun eodi issni?*" she whispered. Lance looked at Specks, waiting for the translation. "She wants to know where her baby is." They had found the charred bodies of two infants, and Lance hoped that neither of them was hers. He told her that they would find her baby and that they needed to get her to the hospital.

Seventeen of the survivors were taken to the naval hospital and twelve to Guam Memorial, most of them treated for second- or third-degree burns. Witnesses would later say that they saw a bright burst of light, but no one was sure where it came from. No one could understand how anyone had survived given the breakup of the fuselage and the fires.

The woman was processed through triage and placed on a helicopter, holding onto Lance's hand the whole time. The senior chief had instructed Lance to go with her. She was injured beyond help. At the hospital they cleaned her up as much as possible, and another doctor tended to her only to confirm what they all knew. She would not survive...no one was left in the assigned emergency room but the nameless woman wanting her baby and Lance. He wondered how she was still alive; nothing in her was still functioning properly. He stood, fighting tears, and gently wiped away the black, bloodied hair that had fallen into her face, her dark brown eyes barely hanging on to life, her skin looked so pale. She smiled, and her lips moved. Lance bent over with his ear as close to her mouth as he could.

"Did you find my baby?" Her English was very poor, but he managed to make out what she said in a faint whisper. He knew she only had minutes left. Why should he tell her the truth? At this point the truth would do more harm and cause more agony in her final moments. "Yes, we found her," he lied. He realized he'd made a mistake not knowing if the baby was a boy or a girl. He was hoping she didn't understand him that well. "The baby is doing very well. When you feel better, we can bring it in for you to hold." He knew he went against policy, but he did what he felt right. She smiled and squeezed his hand. He could see that she wanted to say something else and he leaned in again.

"I will sleep a little, then I see her?" He felt relieved that his hunch about the baby girl was correct. Tears welled up in his eyes and he hoped she wouldn't see. The last infant body they had found was a girl about eight months old. "Of course," he lied again, and she responded with the hand squeeze.

The door opened. "We're here to take her to the morgue!" one of the two guys standing in the door announced. Lance glared at them. "Get out, just get out." They backed up and the door swung shut behind them.

"Damn, that guy's got issues," he heard one of them say. Had this been any other time, he would have gone after them to set them straight, but not now. He didn't care about their comment. He turned his attention back to the young woman.

He must have stood there for what felt like an hour or more before her heart rate slowly decreased and the inevitable tone of the monitor announced her death.

For a moment Lance stared at the machine, the sound piercing the silence. He reached over to turn it off. Time seemed to stand still when he slowly sank back into the chair he had sat on. He noticed all the bloody rags on the grey floor, how cold the room was, and some small part of him wished he hadn't chosen FMF. He thought of Susi and Sammi, and in a matter of seconds the whole night came crashing down on him. He had seen horrible things in the desert during his first two deployments but nothing like this. He fought with all he had in him but could not hold back the tears. A tremendous wave of guilt swept over him. He should have been able to save her, he should have stayed at the site, he should have done more. He looked at the small hand in his and repeated over and over how sorry he was.

He had no idea how long he had been sitting there when he felt someone taking the dead woman's hand out of his.

"Your wife is out in the lobby, why don't you let us take over?" suggested one of the other corpsmen, who had come in to prepare the body for transfer to the morgue.

The rain- and blood-drenched uniform had dried along with all the mud on his boots. He could not take his eyes off the woman and walked out of the room backwards. It was not until he was in the hall and the doors had closed that reality made its way back to him. His shift had ended hours ago, and he knew by now Susi would have heard about the crash and been worried.

He made his way through the ER waiting room and stopped dead in his tracks when he saw his wife sitting in one of the chairs. He knew she was that one small island of escape and serenity that he had come to so many times when his mind just couldn't process anything else. Even when he was deployed, all he had to do was hold a picture of her and he'd get the same comfort.

Susi stood up and rushed to her husband, wrapping her arms around him, she whispered, "I'm so sorry." She began to cry. "Nate told me about the young woman and her baby."

"Are you ready to go home?" His voice was tired.

She kissed his cheek and nodded.

"Did you drive?" Lance asked her. "No, Snider's wife dropped me off when she came to get him."

Lance took Susi's hand and they walked silently outside. The clouds and rain from the night before had vanished, and the bright sunlight was an unwelcome sight. They found Lance's white Jeep and got in. "Do you want me to drive?" Susi asked. "I know you haven't slept."

"I'm all right." He forced a smile, took her hand and kissed it. She had learned a long time ago that at stressful times like this, it was best not to contradict him but to allow him to process everything without interruption. Their house was no more than twenty minutes away, but they had barely made it off base when Lance pulled over, stopped the car, and leaned over the steering wheel. Susi could see by the rise and fall of his shoulders that he was crying. She got out, walked to the driver's side, and opened the door. She stepped up and leaned over him; she kissed his head and stroked his muddy, sticky hair. "I'm here for you, baby. I am so sorry you had to experience such a horrible thing." She spoke very gently all the while stroking his head and gently kissing it.

"You take all the time you need, I'm here for you. There is no need for you to say anything. I know you are hurting, not just for all those who perished but especially for that young woman and her child."

He took one hand off the steering wheel so he could take his wife's hand. He couldn't speak; he silently cried. Several minutes passed.

"Would you like me to drive?" Susi gently asked, and he nodded. A few minutes later he had pulled himself together enough to step out of the car and trade places with his wife. When both of them were back in the car, they continued home in silence, just holding hands.

****

At the house, Alexis, who was jokingly referred to as Cookie by all her friends, greeted them in the kitchen with hot coffee. Lance took the cup and went to the kitchen window. The two women exchanged glances that let Cookie know this was not the time for questions. Crissy and Sammi were playing on the swing in the yard. Lance had built an elaborate swing set with slide and climbing wall over two weekends. The slide ended in a small embedded pool. That was the hardest part, getting that in the ground and making sure the pump worked, but he'd pulled it off and was proud of it.

Lance walked outside on the deck to watch the girls play. Sammi saw her dad and brought her swing to a sudden stop with both feet, sending a dust cloud around her. Just for a moment she observed her father and then walked up to him. She stood right in front of him, looked up at his dirty face, and said, "I love you, Daddy."

He rustled her hair and smiled. "Do you need a hug?" she asked.

"Yes, please!" he replied. He leaned down and picked up his little girl, and she wrapped her arms around his neck and squeezed. He remembered how tiny she had been when she was born, a head full of dark hair and just so little.

He held her and laid his head on her small shoulder and cried, "I love you so much, Peanut." She looked at the kitchen window and saw her mom crying as well. "Today is not a good day, huh, Daddy?" Lance shook his head. "It's a really sad day, baby girl."

"Are you crying cause your heart hurts?" Sammi inquired and Lance nodded. She squeezed his neck. "You just cry, Daddy, sometimes it really helps to just cry. If it doesn't Mommy can kiss it. That will help for sure." He had to smile at the wisdom of his daughter.

Lance chuckled. "You are so smart, you know that?" She giggled and nodded, her deep blue eyes sparkled.

"You should take a shower, you stink!" Sammi changed the subject. He laughed and put her down; she hugged his hand and ran back to the swing. Lance watched the girls for a few minutes while he finished his coffee and then went back inside. "I was told to shower because I apparently stink." He sat down the coffee cup.

Susi looked at him as if to say, I'm here if you need me. He smiled at her, walked over to her, and kissed her forehead. "Thank you," he whispered before he headed upstairs to the shower.

"Did you hear that Dr. Ferrell's sister was on that flight?" Cookie asked Susi.

"Holy crap, are you serious?" Susi stopped in shock. "Did she survive?"

Cookie shook her head and Susi laid her hand over her mouth. Doc Ferrell was one of Lance's favorite doctors. They often played golf together, and she debated if she should tell him now or wait. She decided to wait; he'd been through enough. The thought did not leave her mind, and when they went to bed that night, Susi told Lance about the doctor's sister. He told her that he had heard at the hospital that morning that she had been on the plane and had not survived.

****

Life returned to normal, as normal as it could be after a disaster like that. Of course, there was the investigation and a scandal about the governor making access to the crash site more difficult for first responders. Those who had been there, those who worked at the naval hospital, had their military trained minds back on their daily duties.

Lance had finally talked Nate into trying his hand at golf, and they had gone out to the Nimitz Golf Course several times. Nate told Susi and Lance over dinner one night that he was still on the fence about getting his own clubs. For the time being he was fine with the rentals. At the end of a fun day on the course, they both walked into the house where they found Cookie and Susi chatting while the girls played in the yard.

"Lance, can I steal you for a moment?" Cookie asked, looking at him and smiling. Susi knew what she was up to and had to bite her lip not to chuckle out loud. Lance looked at his wife and could see the two women were up to something. "Sure, what do you need?" he replied to Cookie. She got up, slid her arm around his, and pulled him into the garage.

"I got these today for Nate, do you think these are good?" she asked as she pulled a beach towel off a golf bag full of clubs.

"Holy shit, woman, these are great." Lance pulled some of the clubs out and examined them. "Well done, but I would have helped you if you'd let me know you were planning this."

"Well I am counting on you and Susi helping to surprise him Saturday for our anniversary. I thought you could invite him to play, and we can meet you at the club where I will present him with this present."

"Great idea, consider it done. We should do this at the country club though since they have a restaurant." Lance was happy, he liked surprises like this.

Later over dinner Lance made the suggestion to play Saturday afternoon.

"Man, I'm not sure, it's our anniversary." Nate looked at his wife as if he were needing approval.

"It's fine, honey. It would be nice to have dinner at the club. Susi and Lance could join us."

"Done," Lance proclaimed. "I'll make a tee-time first thing in the morning, and Susi can call and make the dinner reservation."

It was not unusual for the four of them to have dinner together, and Cookie suggested that she would take care of the babysitter for the girls.

****

Saturday morning came and Nate got a call that they needed him at work for a few hours to fill in for one of the guys whose wife had gone into labor a couple of days early.

"Can't they live without you just one day? Especially today," Cookie growled. "If you take the car, Susi or Lance will have to come pick me up."

"Don't worry, doll." Nate squeezed his wife and kissed her on the forehead. "I'll take the bike and meet you guys there. I'm sure it'll be fine to leave the bike at the club till tomorrow morning."

"You're not going to play and then have dinner in your uniform!" Cookie was still a little grouchy. "No, honey, I'll take stuff with me," Nate assured her. "I'll meet Lance at 1400 for our round and I'll see you ladies at the club house at 1830." He snapped his fingers. "This actually works out better anyway. This way Lance doesn't have to come get me. I'll meet him there and if Susi doesn't mind getting you, neither of us will have to drive home." He winked at his wife and gave her a slight pat on her bottom. Cookie playfully smacked his hand and cautioned him to get to work. He kissed her deeply and winked again as he walked out the door.

Cookie called Susi and arranged for her to pick her up. She knew Nate would call Lance when he got to the hospital. She continued with her day and made sure she had plenty of time to do her hair and makeup. It was their tenth anniversary and she wanted to look extra pretty. She had gotten a pretty new pink-and-yellow summer dress a few days ago that she knew Nate would love, her being of Middle Eastern decent, those colors worked well with her dark skin. Susi had often told her that she envied her exotic looks. Susi loved both those colors, but her bright red hair did not work with pink, and her pale freckle-invested skin wanted nothing to do with yellow.

Just after two that afternoon, she got into the shower. She heard the phone ring and figured whoever it was would call back if it was important. Not an hour had passed when the doorbell rang. Susi arrived with Sam. "Don't you look stunning!"

The little girls ran outside to play in the small pool. The two women settled at the picnic table with a cup of coffee. Cookie was excited and asked Susi if she'd help her with her hair. Only moments later the phone rang again, and Cookie went inside to answer it.

What seemed like seconds later, she stepped back out. The color had completely drained from her face, her lips were quivering, and she was shaking.

Susi knew something horrible had happened. She stood up and took her friend's hand.

"What is it, Cookie?" she asked gently.

"Nate... he's been in a bad accident. I need to go to the hospital."

"Do you want me to take you?" Susi was already wondering what they would do with the girls and if Lance knew. Cookie nodded. "I'll call Lisa and have her come over right away." No more than five minutes later, they were on their way and it didn't take long from Mendiola Drive to the naval hospital where Nate had been taken. "Do you want me to let you out by the door and I'll go park?" Susi gently asked Cookie, who had been eerily quiet the whole way. That was her personality though. In a crisis she kept everything in. Nothing more than tears rolling down her face. Cookie shook her head in response to the question. "I'm not going in there alone."

Susi parked as close to the emergency room door as she could, and the two women got out. Susi took Cookie's hand and laid her other arm around her. The door slid open and they approached the reception desk. "This is Nate Cooper's wife, Alexis. He has been brought here." The receptionist responded, "One moment please." She picked up the phone, pushed a button, and said something neither of the women could hear. A door opened and a solemn looking doctor approached them.

"Mrs. Cooper?" Cookie nodded and Susi felt as if her friend was getting weak. "Would you come with me, please!" He didn't wait for a response and walked back towards the door he had emerged from just seconds ago, one of those with signs that said authorized personnel only. Cookie and Susi followed him; he didn't stop until they stood in front of a room with a sign on the door reading 'Trauma 1.'

Cookie stared at the doctor while Susi looked through the small window in the grey door. Nate lay motionless on the table, more tubes and hoses attached to him than she had ever seen on anyone before. "Mrs. Cooper, I am very sorry but your husband did not survive his injuries, he..." Cookie began to say, "No," over and over and slowly sank to the floor.

"Ma'am, do you need us to call anyone?" Cookie looked at Susi with a tear-stained face. "Please call Lance." She couldn't say anything else.

"I will, sweetheart. Can you stand up for me? I need you to listen to the doctor. I will just go right there to the nurse's station and call Lance. You won't be out of my sight. I promise." Cookie got up with the help of Susi who led her to a chair nearby. "Mrs. Cooper..." the doctor began, and Susi walked to the nurse's station.

"Please wait for her to come back," Susi heard Cookie tell the doctor.

"Lance is on his way," Susi stated and sat next to Cookie, taking her hand.

"Mrs. Cooper," the doctor said again, taking a deep breath, "your husband had left the hospital about 1300 and was apparently on his way to the golf club. The delivery driver from the Crown bakery at the corner of Highway eight and ten lost control of his brakes and hit your husband."

"I don't want to hear anything else. I just want to know if he..." Cookie paused.

"I promise you, he did not suffer," the doctor assured her and squeezed her hand. For a moment Susi's mind wandered back to San Diego when Katy had been told that her husband didn't suffer. All Cookie could do was nod. How the hell could he possibly know that? "Would you like to see him?" She nodded again. "Can I wait for Lance, please?" The doctor nodded. Neither Cookie nor Susi knew that both of the men had worked with this doctor on occasion.

Moments later Lance came running in. Susi had only told him that Nate had been in an accident. She couldn't tell him on the phone that his best friend was dead.

"How is he?" Seeing Cookie's face and the expression on Susi's answered the question for him. Susi looked at the floor and shook her head. "He's gone."

In a split-second Lance's demeanor changed. "What? How?" He grabbed his wife's hand. The doctor explained to Lance what he had just told Cookie minutes earlier and then led the three of them into the trauma room where every effort had been made to revive the young husband and father. Susi covered her mouth to keep from gasping. While his face barely had a scratch, the floor was covered in bloody towels. The effect of the blood seemed to be emphasized by the grey floor. Cookie reached beneath the sheet and pulled out the ice cold, limp hand. She held onto it with both hands and leaned forward to kiss her husband's lips. Faint sobs passed her lips as the realization became stronger that her husband, her best friend and partner, was gone.

While Cookie took the time to absorb the reality of the situation with the help of her best friend, Lance quietly left the trauma room to find the doctor.

"Doc?" The doctor was at the nurse's station finishing paperwork. When Lance addressed him, he looked up. "I'm so sorry, man, he was a good guy."

"Thanks, Doc. Can you tell me what happened? I didn't want to ask his wife right now."

"It's quite all right." The doctor came out from behind the desk and walked slowly down the hall with Lance, out of earshot of everyone else. "The truck that hit him, the driver had lost control of the brakes and flew into the street in excess of over eighty miles per hour. Nate never knew what hit him. When EMTs got there, he barely had a pulse, never regained consciousness. We pronounced him dead just minutes after he arrived here." Lance had to sit down, "I don't even understand how he hung on as long as he did," the Doctor continued. "His liver was torn, his lower spine shattered, broken ribs had punctured his lungs. There was literally no way on earth to save him."

Lance felt blindsided. They were supposed to play golf. "Today is his tenth anniversary," he muttered.

"Damn!" the doctor observed. There really was nothing left for the two men to talk about. Lance knew the routine; he'd worked in this environment long enough. Nate's parents had to be notified. Cookie would have to tell Crissy. The one thought that sat in the back of his mind grew stronger, what could he and Susi do to prevent Cookie from blaming herself?

****

Life still had not given them enough to deal with. They had gotten used to intense storms in the time they had been there, but in December 1997 they would have to deal with the storm of their lives, a super-typhoon. In late November, near the end of the official Pacific hurricane season, a tropical depression began to build in the central Pacific Ocean. An equatorial western wind burst southwest of Hawaii and created a twin tropical cyclone, Paka to the north and Pam to the south. Paka formed on November 28 and was officially declared a tropical storm by the hurricane center. As Paka moved along the ocean and crossed the dateline on December 6, it began to strengthen, then weaken as it made its way to the Marshall Islands, over 650 nautical miles east-southeast of Guam. By December 15, however, it had regained its strength and the storm watch had been upgraded to a super typhoon. Lance and Susi kept a close watch on the nightly news and special weather reports. Warnings were issued for Guam and Rota with wind gusts predicted to exceed 230 mph. While there were no deaths reported, power to nearly the entire island was lost. The drastic change in barometric pressure caused nine women to go into labor and give birth.

The news would later report that if the windspeeds could be confirmed, Paka would have the new highest windspeed on record, and damages were estimated to exceed two hundred million dollars.

Once the storm was over, Susi told Lance that she never wanted to live on or near a tropical island ever again. When they had power restored, Susi called Tracy to tell her about the storm, and she said that nothing she had ever experienced had ever been that scary. Of course, Sammi had announced multiple times it was kind of cool. Well, at least till it got really bad. Susi was, once again, beyond thankful for Lance who did his best to keep them both safe and calm. They were some of the lucky ones living in a cinder-block house. The naval hospital sustained severe damage, and the home of the hospital's commanding officer was completely destroyed.

****

The following year Lance had to choose orders again, and this time they opted for Cherry Point in North Carolina. Ellen's real estate office took over the sale of the house. When they made the decision to either rent it out or sell it, Susi told him that she was never setting foot on the island again. They'd made some improvements on the house and those resulted in a nice profit. As soon as they got to Cherry point, Susi found another realtor to start the process over again. She had told Lance that she really would like to be back at the water the way they had been at Whidbey. Sadly, being that close to the beach again would mean an hour and a half commute twice a day for Lance, and that was out of the question.

"Tyson Group, this is Becky, how may I help you?"

Susi explained what they were looking for and where. She wanted modern, waterfront, not too big and not too small. Two hours later she met Becky on Shoreview Drive in New Bern. Susi fell in love with the house as soon as she stepped out of her car.

"This just came on the market last week," Becky told her.

"This is exactly what I want," Susi beamed.

"Don't you want to see the inside first?" Becky laughed.

The front lawn was kept immaculate. A flowerbed around a huge shade tree was home to orange marigolds and a white clematis climbing up a wire support. Two steps led to a pale green front door, which had narrow windows on either side and above it. To the left of the door sat a small wooden bench and to the right some planters in different sizes. The siding on the front of the house was brick, and it gave the house a strong appearance. To the right of the front door a two-car garage. As they stepped inside, Susi gasped with joy. Light-brown wood flooring led to a wooden staircase with a black wrought-iron banister. The walls and ceiling were soft beige broken up by white crown molding. Behind the stairs a small nook revealed a small wine fridge and wine rack above a marble counter.

"This is perfect," Susi stated.

"Did you notice here underneath the rack you can hang wineglasses?" Becky pointed out. Susi nodded. Directly opposite the wine bar was a coat closet. A little further the living room opened up, the coloring the same as in the hall. The sunlight streaming in through the large windows on either side of a rock fireplace with a beautiful whitewash wood mantel gave a welcoming feel to the room. To the right lay the dining room with floor-to-ceiling window, and just behind it the kitchen. White cabinets with black hardware gave the kitchen a modern look along with the beige-and-brown marble countertop. Susi was very happy that she would have a five-burner gas range.

They walked through the kitchen to the laundry room hidden by a pocket door, and from there they moved on down to a small staircase that led to the garage.

"There's not really a pantry, is there?" Susi asked.

"Sadly, not," Becky noted, "but you could put shelving here in the garage."

They went back to the kitchen, and Susi noticed a porch swing just outside the dining room windows as well as a nice enclosed gazebo set right by Brice Creek. The master bedroom, a beautiful large room with an amazing view, was on the ground floor next to the living room. The walls were pale grey and the recessed ceiling held a large ceiling fan. A whitewashed barn door led to the master bathroom. Two brown cabinets opposite each other provided his and her sinks and a very large walk-in shower. They walked through the bathroom into one of the largest closets Susi had ever seen.

"This is big enough to be another bedroom," she joked. She loved that the closet had a tall window but didn't care for the carpet. She figured that would be an easy fix.

A small room to the right of the front door revealed itself to be a great location for an office or reading room. They made their way up the stairs to a large loft, two more bedrooms, and another full bath. The entire second floor was carpeted. Susi told Becky that she would want to pull the carpet out before they moved in and have it replaced with hardwood. It would be easier to do that before they had furniture in the room, Beck agreed. The larger of the two rooms had a nice walk-in closet and a window seat that looked out the creek. They would set up the second bedroom as a guest room.

They walked out to look at the gazebo and the back yard. Susi took twenty or more pictures while she was walking through the house and sent them to Lance. They'd both gotten their first cell phone the summer before and both felt that they made life much easier. When she sent him a few pictures of the outside, she got a text back, "TAKE IT."

"Guess my husband loves it as much as I do," Susi announced. "Can we meet you this evening for the paperwork?"

"Will you be using a VA loan or conventional?" Becky wanted to know.

"Neither," Susi replied. "We sold our house on Guam and will buy this one outright."

Becky suggested that they meet back at the property so Lance could personally see the house. Susi agreed, and they scheduled for her to be back at five with Lance and their daughter.

"Is this gonna be our new house?" Sammi asked with a happy face.

"Yes, peanut, if you and daddy like it as much as I do," Susi said and took Lance's hand as they walked out onto the deck after Lance looked at the whole house.

Before they left Lance told Sammi to pick a room, and he went upstairs with her to show her which ones she could choose from. She chose one that was about the same size as the master bedroom; she loved the window seat.

"Did I see some boat slips just a couple hundred feet away?" Lance asked Becky.

"Yes, I can find out what the monthly rent is on those if you are interested," Becky replied.

****

Ten days later they moved in. Susi was glad they didn't have to stay at the Devil Dog Inn in Havelock as long as they were at the Gateway Inn on Guam. Becky had gotten them in touch with a fantastic contractor, who had the carpet out and replaced it with hardwood that matched the floors in the rest of the house. Sammi was registered at Creekside Elementary School, a twelve-minute drive from their house.

Within a month Susi had turned the gazebo into a garden paradise. The planter boxes around the small building were filled with a large variety of flowers and herbs. She had placed large terra cotta pots at various locations and filled them with tomato plants, lettuce, and cucumbers. On the water side of the gazebo, a small deck had been added where Susi liked to sit, enjoy a glass of wine, and watch Lance teach Sammi how to maneuver her new paddleboard.

It didn't take any of them long to make new friends. For Lance one of them was Bob Abbott, a tough Marine and four years older than Lance. They came to know each other through an ad Lance had seen in the Camp Lejeune paper in November 1999. Bob was looking for interested people to train for a triathlon.

"I'd really like to give this a try," he told Susi and handed her the ad after dinner.

"Triathlons? Really?" Susi looked at him. "Sounds tough."

"I'm gonna call him to get more details. I know he's looking to put together a team." He kissed her on her head. "I just wanted to know what you think about it."

"I say go for it. You know I will help you in whatever way I can," she said.

After dinner Lance grabbed his phone and dialed the number in the ad.

When someone answered, he said, "Hi, my name is Lance. I'm looking for Gunny Abbott." Lance felt odd.

"Speaking," Abbott replied.

"Hey, I saw your ad in the base paper. Can you tell me anymore about what you're doing?" Lance really didn't like trying to introduce himself over the phone. He preferred eye-to-eye contact and a firm handshake.

"What do you know about triathlons?" Abbott wanted to know.

"I can bike, run, and swim," Lance told him.

"I'm looking for serious people to train," Abbott stated.

"I am serious, sir," Lance stated formally.

"You have a bike?"

"Yes, sir," Lance lied. Susi overheard and threw him a look from the kitchen that made him cringe.

"You don't have a bike, what the hell are you doing?" she mouthed as he shrugged his shoulders.

"Meet me Monday morning at 0500 by the Hancock fitness center entrance." Abbott chuckled. "And bring your bike."

Lance confirmed the location and they bid each other good night.

It was Wednesday, which meant he had four days to find a bike if he was going to meet the gunny Monday morning.

"Guess I'll have to get a bike. Wanna go shopping with me?" Lance asked, smiling.

"I cannot believe you told the gunny you have a bike. Where are you gonna get a bike?" Susi scolded. "You have duty this weekend."

Lance scratched his head. "We can go to Havelock tomorrow after I get home. We'll take Peanut, get a bike, and have dinner?"

Susi laughed, set down her dish towel, and hugged her husband. Propping her chin on his chest, she looked up at him and said, "You know you are impossible, and I love you to the moon and back." He leaned down and kissed her nose.

"I want a new bike," Sammi announced behind them. Lance let go of Susi and picked up his daughter.

"What's wrong with your old bike, Peanut?" He kissed his daughter's nose. "I'm afraid you will have to take that up with the financial director." They both looked at Susi.

"Why do I always have to be the bully?" she replied to Lance. "Sammi, you just got your bike at the end of summer last year, right?" Sammi nodded and leaned her head against her dad's. She knew when the two of them looked at her all sappy, she didn't stand a chance.

"I'll make you a deal, my sweet little girl." Susi thought of a quick plan. "It's still three months till your birthday, and I know you don't want to wait that long. I want you to talk to your teacher tomorrow and find out if there is someone in your class whose parents don't have a lot of money, and if we can find someone to give your bike to, someone whose parents can't afford one, then we can get you a new one when we get Daddy's bike."

Sammi and Lance touched noses and smiled at each other. "You know your mom is awesome, right?" Their noses were touching again.

"Yup, she's the bestess mom out of everyone I know."

Getting Lance's bike was easier than Susi imagined, and Sammi had done well also. At lunchtime on Thursday, Susi got a call from Sammi's homeroom teacher. There was a little girl in the third grade who had just lost her dad in a car accident the year before and he had no life insurance. By Saturday night she had a nicely cleaned bike. Lance and Sammi cleaned it and delivered it to Sammi's teacher, who in turn delivered it to the little girl anonymously. When the two of them returned from the delivery, Lance thought about the lesson Susi had taught their daughter. She was sitting on the couch reading when they walked in. He knelt in front of her and told that she was such an amazing human being and he hoped Sammi would be just like her when she grew up. He'd never known anyone who so freely and easily gave of herself without expecting anything in return.

She told him that all she had ever needed in life was him and Sammi; anything more than that were leftovers she could give away to nice people.

Monday at four in the morning, Lance peeled himself out of bed. For whatever reason Susi was already up. He found her in the kitchen with some cut-up fruit and coffee. She informed him that she'd read a little about what he needed nutritionally for a triathlon, and this was the start of it. She gave him a kiss on the cheek, patted his butt as she often did, and told him that she was going back to bed.

Lance looked at her as if she'd lost her mind and thought to himself what else this woman was capable of.

****

He made it to the meeting spot with his safety vest, helmet, and pretty little reflectors in the spokes of his bike. Gunny Abbott walked up to the only guy with a bike, took one look at him, and burst out in laughter.

"What…the…fuck?" He laughed again. "Do me a favor and lose the vest and reflectors. You aren't in fucking grade school." Lance felt embarrassed that he was the reason for Gunny being unable to contain his laughter. Even while telling Lance the rules, he still chuckled a bit. "If I swim half a mile, you have to do a quarter. If I run ten miles, you have to do five." That day Gunny left Lance in the dust; he went home that night feeling truly humble. He told Susi it was her doing because she always built him up to be this awesome guy. In her eyes he was just that. It may not have translated into superman endurance with everyone else, but for her he was everything.

****

A month later Susi had spent time at the library to learn about proper nutrition for triathletes. She knew she could have found all the same information on the computer, but this way she got out of the house for a bit as well. She wanted this to be a great experience for Lance and she liked the physical changes.

"It is amazing how dedicated he is to his training," she told Tracy, who called for Susi's birthday. "I love it. He's up at four in the morning to meet with his coach at five for two hours, an hour at lunch, and another two hours in the evening. He's losing weight, he's super motivated, and his stamina, holy shit."

"I'm sure he needs more energy in that department," Tracy said, laughing. "Are you going to join him?"

"Nope, I'll stick to running. Besides, it is just for the Marine and Navy guys. We run together now and then, and I tell you one thing, there are times when sweat doesn't matter, you know what I mean?"

"Oh gross, did you have to go there?" Tracy made gagging sounds at the other end and they both laughed.

As soon as Susi hung up, the phone rang again.

"Hello?" she asked.

"Hey, honey, what are you up to, birthday girl?" She could hear the smile on his face.

"Not much, just got off the phone with Tracy," Susi replied.

"I don't want you to make dinner, I want to take you out," he informed her. "Can you see if Charlotte from next door can stay with Peanut and I will bring something home for her when I get you?"

"Of course." Her mind already wandered to what she should wear.

"I will pick you up at 1730, okay?"

"Sure thing, my love. Oh and by the way, thank you for the beautiful roses." She felt embarrassed that she didn't mention that first.

"They are not nearly as beautiful as my wife!" he told her. She knew he meant it. He had a way of making her see herself the way he did, and she blushed. Sammi would be ten that year, and he was still as playful and romantic as he had been in the beginning. When she laid down the receiver, she twirled around like a young girl and smiled from ear to ear.

She quickly called Charlotte next door to make sure she was available and ask that she be over around five o'clock. At five fifteen, Lance was home to get her and, as expected, she was ready. They headed down to Morehead City where Lance had made a reservation at the Crab Shack in the Outer Banks. Susi loved that area and she often made the twenty-minute drive to run along the beach. There was already someone at their table. Lance introduced Gunny Bob Abbott and his wife, Bobbie. Bob had ordered a bottle of champagne, and the four of them toasted to new friends and great birthdays with many more to come.

In March Lance and the team completed their first sprint triathlon with the second to follow in early April. Susi invited the Abbotts and the rest of the team over for a barbecue for Lance's birthday. Little by little she'd gotten to know all of them and their significant others if they had one. Some of them had kids who were Sammi's age, and all of them together made a great extended family. It quickly became known that Susi had attended culinary school and that she made portable foods that sustained Lance during long runs and rides.

"Would you be willing to make them for the whole team if everyone pitched in?" Gunny suggested.

"Sure," Susi replied, "why not!"

"I have a fantastic idea!" Lance announced, and the small group grew quiet. "We should do an Ironman."

"Are you serious?" Gunny responded. "I'm game if the rest of you are, but I will tell you now, that is going to take intense training."

Susi had already gotten used to his five-hour-a-day training schedule, and she was more than willing to deal with it given the benefits she got out of it. In June 2000 Susi and Lance drove to Panama City for Lance to do a half Ironman. It was a way for him to try things out. Tracy had flown Sammi to Seattle to spend a couple of weeks with Uncle Max and Tracy. Both Susi and Lance knew she'd be spoiled rotten. The night before Susi and Lance drove to Panama City, Sammi had called to tell them that she had eaten a lobster at Ivar's, and the next day Tracy was taking her to Victoria in Canada to have tea at the Empress Hotel.

On race day Lance was in good spirits, and he saw Susi as his motivational support. Susi enjoyed how he counted on her to be his wingman.

He didn't have to worry about anything. The swim was first, the weather was beautiful. Lance lined up, his bib number 722 marked on his arms and calves. He went into the water with confidence and three hundred yards from shore, he began to panic. It was hard to catch a breath with the waves filling his mouth with salt water every other breath. He had two choices, either keep going and give it his all or turn around and get pelted by everyone who was still getting into the water. He stuck it out and finished the race in six hours, six minutes, and twenty-six seconds. Susi had been at each transition station with snacks and liquids for the next section. When he crossed the finish line, she couldn't say if she had ever been prouder of him at any time.

Over the next few months, his training intensified. Susi had asked him if he had a goal time for the full Ironman and he'd told her that he just wanted to finish. Susi, Bobbie, Gunny Bob, Lance, and Christian drove back to Panama City the Sunday before the race and stayed at the Sand Dollar Inn. Christian's pregnant wife stayed home and babysat Sammi. The two of them had bonded over Disney Princesses, and

Sammi was excited for the baby to arrive soon. Susi had made enough portable snacks for all three of the guys, and she was so proud of Lance. She'd done marathons and they took a lot out of her; she couldn't even imagine doing a race like this.

November 4 arrived, and the team had a nice dinner early the night before; no alcohol except for Susi and Bobbie. They arranged their meeting time in the morning for breakfast and then headed to the starting line. The air at the start line had a chill, but it was warm enough to not require the athletes to wear a wetsuit. Lance's bib number was 377. The signal went off for all of the athletes to start swimming. Susi had no idea how long it would take him for the 2.4-mile swim, but she made her way to the swim/bike transition point with Bobbie.

He finished the swim in one hour, eight minutes, and six seconds. Susi had never seen a more determined look on anyone's face than what she saw in Lance's eyes when he got to the transition point. She had his snacks ready. He dried off the best he could and put his bike shoes on. His breathing slowed down, he was hyper focused.

"You got this, my love," Susi whispered and kissed his cheek. Seconds later he was on his bike speeding away. All Susi could think about once again was how it was possible to love someone that much.

"Well, we may as well move on to the next transition. Lance is not that far behind Bob." Bobbie took Susi's arm and guided her along.

"How are they doing this? I mean, really, they still have to do a marathon at the end of all this!" Susi was winded just thinking about what her husband was going through at this very moment. Lance finished the 112-mile bike ride in five hours, thirty-three minutes, and fifty-six seconds.

"This is just not possible. I can't do a marathon in under four hours and you're doing this?" Susi asked at the next transition station.

"Must be your awesome portable snacks." He laughed and kissed her. Seconds later he was on his way to complete the last leg, a full marathon. Susi was sure that he would not be doing that in any record time, but she was wrong. She'd been proud of her marathon times but had never managed one in less than four and a half hours. After all the physical hardship he had already been through that day, he finished the run in four hours, twenty-four minutes, and thirteen seconds. She had his finish line picture as the wallpaper on her cell phone from that day on. There would be no better physical achievement than this.

TWELVE

September 11, 2001 –
The World Changed

"Coming together is a beginning, staying together is a progress,
and working together is success." —Henry Ford

T HE TIME AT CHERRY POINT seemed to fly by and their next
duty station was Washington D.C. Lance would be working at the
U.S. Capitol. He had requested the assignment and had to go through
three interviews to get in. Soon after getting to the new duty station,
they realized how much they had been spoiled in San Diego, on Guam,
and New Bern. Trying to find a house that would be within reasonable
driving distance for Lance seemed to be a huge undertaking.

They kept the house in New Bern as a rental property for extra
income and would now use their VA benefits to get a home loan. They
both had great credit, and their income-to-debt ratio was better than
they could have hoped for since they paid cash for most everything.

They both realized for the time they we here they would need to
accept living in the suburbs or an apartment in the city. Neither of them
wanted that restriction, especially for Sammi. They found a nice place
on Coventry Road in Alexandria. Though Susi would miss the gas
range, there were some good tradeoffs. She'd have a nice pantry and a
soaking tub. And though the house had been built in the seventies, it
had recently been renovated. The outside did not lead on to what lay

behind the front door. There was hardwood floor on the main floor and while the kitchen was a little outdated, it was big and had a breakfast nook, which would be useful rather than using the dining room all the time. Susi could finally have her formal dining room. Behind the kitchen they found a beautiful space with lots of windows. It could easily be turned into an atrium and an area where they could spend time in nature without being outside when the weather was bad. The living room itself was rather small and would work better as a TV room. A bedroom on the main floor with a bathroom would work well as the guest room. The master and second bedroom were on the top floor, and they would have to share a bathroom with Sammi.

"We'll make it work," Susi assured Lance. "It could be worse, and it is fun to experience something new."

"Yup," Lance said but looked doubtful. "I'm sure you don't mind if we rip the carpet out upstairs?"

"Not at all," Susi agreed. "And while we're at it, let's get the basement done as well and maybe add a bathroom down there if possible. We could put a bar and pool table down there or turn it into a gym with a stationary bike and treadmill."

"I think it's big enough down there that we could do both," Lance told her.

Susi got a job at Voila Bakery and Cafe in Alexandria but kept it to mornings so she could be home when Sammi got home from school. She had established a solid fan base for her portable snacks, and Gunny Bob and Bobbie were sad to see them go. They were still close enough to visit, but it would have to be timed around duty and time off.

Both Lance and Susi were proud of the young woman their daughter had grown into. At just eleven years old, she was in advanced classes and her teachers had nothing but good things to say about her. She was one of the popular kids but always made it a point to stick up for those who ran the risk of being bullied. She was thrilled to find out that her dad would be working at the Capitol Building, and she had hundreds of questions lined up for him every night at dinner.

"I really think she likes my job more than I do," Lance told Susi while Sammi had run to the restroom before dinner.

"I heard that," Sammi yelled in the direction of the kitchen. "I'm sure you working at the Capitol will help me in some class. Maybe history or something." Susi laughed, but before she or Lance had a chance to respond, the phone interrupted them, and Lance answered.

"Hey, Lance, it's Charlie," the caller said. Charlie was one of Lance's good friends and neighbors. Susi and Lance had been at Charlie's wedding two months ago in July. She had baked their wedding cake, and they had asked Sammi to be the flower girl despite her age. Charlie's new wife, Kristen, loved Sammi and since there were no other little girls in their circle of friends and family, they knew Sammi was the obvious choice.

"Sorry to bother you, bet you're in the middle of dinner," Charlie stated.

"No worries, my friend, we were just about to start," Lance reassured him. "What's up?"

"The car overheated on Kristen today and she had to take it in to the dealership," Charlie told him.

"Didn't you just get that car right after the wedding?" Lance wanted to know.

"Yeah, we sure did, that's what doesn't make sense," Charlie continued. "She was on her way to work this morning and the damn thing overheated. She sat on the 495 for almost two hours before the tow truck got there."

"Shit, are you serious?" Lance was shocked.

"She called a friend at the NASA Goddard Center, and she came and stayed with her till the tow truck came and then took her to work and brought her home. I was gonna let her take my car in the morning if I could catch a ride with you."

"Are you still at the Pentagon?" Lance asked.

"Yeah, for the time being," Charlie told him.

"No problem, brother, I'll pick you up at six," Lance said.

"Thanks, man." Charlie sounded relieved. "I owe you one."

"You got it, brother, beer and pizza this weekend?" Lance suggested.

"As long as Susi's making the pizza, sure thing."

The guys shared some more small talk and then Lance told Charlie he had to go since the burning looks of his wife were digging holes into his back. He hung up and joined Susi and Sammi at the dinner table.

"I take it you are picking Charlie up in the morning?" Susi stated. Lance nodded and gave her a quick run-down of the conversation he'd just had. He told Susi he would have to leave about half an hour earlier.

The commute to the Capitol could be nasty some days, but they liked were they were. This night, like many others during the summer, Lance and Susi sat on their deck and shared a little time alone after Sammi went to bed. Susi would have a glass of wine, but Lance stuck to water since he had duty the next day.

****

The next morning Susi got up before Lance as she always did to make his breakfast sandwich and coffee. That was one thing he could count on no matter what time he had to get up. On the morning of September 11, 2001, she made two sandwiches, so Lance could give one to Charlie. Susi had taken the day off since she had to attend parent-teacher conferences at Montessori of Alexandria School, which Sammi attended.

Lance left, breakfasts in hand, at five thirty. Susi told him to let her know when he got to work, and he thought it was odd that she would ask that. She had told him that she had a feeling that wouldn't go away but she couldn't put her finger on it. She kissed her husband good-bye for the day after she found out what he wanted for dinner.

Once Lance left, she got in the shower to get herself ready for the day and then got breakfast ready for herself and Sammi.

"Hey, Mom, can I go to school with Jenn this morning?" Sammi had just hung up the phone. "Sure, honey, that actually works out well." Susi was glad she didn't have to drive to school. She had to meet a wedding cake client and she'd be pressed for time. Half an hour later, Sammi was out the door and Susi had some time for herself. It was almost eight o'clock and she was glad to have some peace and quiet. Sammi liked Jenn and her mom, Gabby, a single mom who lost her husband to cancer three years ago. He was a scientist at NASA's God-dard Space Flight Center. They had met at Charlie and Kristen's wedding and were instant friends.

Susi got her cup of coffee, sat on the couch, and flipped on the TV before she tended to the morning dishes. Just minutes after 8:50, the normal morning program was interrupted for a special report. She had two hours before she had to meet her client. When the pictures appeared on the screen, Susi's hand lost control and her coffee slowly spilled on the floor in front of the coffee table as she raised her left hand to cover her mouth.

The news anchor stated that at 8:46, American Airlines Flight 11 crashed into the North Tower of the World Trade Center in New York. Susi was watching when minutes later, at 9:03, United Airlines Flight 175 crashed into the South Tower. Everyone on the plane and countless of those inside the building were killed. Susi would later learn that just moments before, the White House chief of staff alerted the president that a small plane had crashed into the North Tower, and it was assumed that the whole thing was a tragic accident.

The anchor announced that the men and women in the South Tower were told that they did not need to evacuate, as the building was secure. They were told that if they were in the process of evacuating, they could go back to their offices without worry. But soon people left the building screaming, some even jumping from the windows.

An announcement was made that the FAA banned all departing flights going to New York City or the surrounding air space. Susi glanced at her watch; it was 9:08. At 9:21 the Port Authority closed all bridges and tunnels in the New York City area.

Susi tried to call her client to cancel their meeting, but there was no signal on her cell phone. She tried using her landline but only had her client's cell number, so she couldn't get through.

Susi went back to the TV. An announcement was in progress that yet another flight was in trouble. Apparently, passengers and crew members were able to contact family members on the ground. Mere moments after the announcement that same flight, American Airlines Flight 77, crashed into the Pentagon.

Susi's mind instantly went to Lance. He would have dropped off Charlie and had moved on to the Capitol. He should have been there by now. She went to the bedroom and got her phone off the charger. Multiple attempts to reach Lance failed; there still was no service, no connection. She had the main number somewhere but had no idea where she had written it down. *Why didn't you put this in your phone? This is important*, she told herself. Her hands were shaking.

While wondering where she might have the number to reach Lance on a landline at the Capitol, she heard yet another announcement on TV. The FAA grounded all flights over or bound for the United States, and over the next few hours all flights would be re-routed to Canada. They kept talking and replaying the events of the morning. Susi had lost track of time. The anchors stopped talking when the horror of the South Tower collapse occurred. People could be seen running and screaming, some with bloody or ash-covered faces.

Shortly after ten the news came that yet another plane had crashed. The passengers of United Airlines Flight 93 had gotten in touch with family on the ground. They had made an attempt to overtake the hijackers and caused the plane to crash in a field in Somerset County, Pennsylvania. Pictures where shown, transmitted by helicopters over the scene.

"How did the passengers get a hold of family on the ground, but I can't get through to my husband"? Susi stated at the TV as if it would answer her. She hated herself for that selfish statement. They announced that all 40 passengers and crew as well as the hijackers of Flight 93 had been killed.

There was just no end. Susi glanced at her watch again: 10:15. The Pentagon's E Ring, the west outer ring, collapsed. What seemed like seconds later, Susi stared at the TV as the North Tower collapsed. The news anchor stated it had been 102 minutes after American Airlines flight 11 crashed into it.

Susi knew she should have been at the parent-teacher conference by now, and she'd need to pick Sammi up in a little while. She felt the nagging voice in the back of her head telling her to find a way to get in touch with Lance, but some part of her was scared to death. She could deal with anything life dished out but not losing her husband, not losing the father of her child, the one man who meant everything in the world to her. Susi checked her phone, maybe there'd be a signal by now. There was a missed call from Jenn's mom and a message stating that she would take Sammi home with her, and she could come by and pick her up when she was ready. Susi was relieved. She needed to get a hold of Lance. She had no idea whether he had made it to the Capitol Building after he'd dropped off Charlie.

"Oh my God, Kristen!" she screamed. She tried calling Kristen but there was no way of getting through. In a panic she ran next door, leaving her front door wide open.

Kristen's front door was unlocked, and she opened the front door and started calling out her friend's name. "Kristen?" She found Kristen on the floor between the couch and coffee table, the horrific events of the day repeating on the TV, her jeans wet with blood and soaking into the white furry rug Kristen loved so much. Kristen was unresponsive, cold, and clammy. Susi called nine-one-one. Calls luckily went through on a landline, at least most of them. Kristen was rushed to the hospital. An hour later Susi found out that she had a miscarriage. The shock of the day's events and the fear for her husband had set the event into motion. The hospital had sketchy information.

With all the events of the day and now this, everything was spinning, but she was able to get a hold of Sammi.

"Hi, sweetheart, I'm so sorry I wasn't there to pick you up." Susi was near tears.

"It's okay, Mama, I'm still at Jenn's, and her mom said you should take all the time you need. She was going to drop me off but figured I should stay since I hadn't heard anything." Sammi was worried. "Have you heard from Daddy?"

"No, honey." It took all Susi could do to not start sobbing. "All of the phone lines are jammed, and I know he had to drop off Charlie this morning. I know that was long before all that happened, so he should have made it to work on time." Susi took several deep breaths to control herself. She didn't want to appear weak, she needed to be strong, she needed to hear from Lance.

At that moment she came to realize how much strength she drew from her husband, how much she loved him, and how much she needed him. She began to wonder if she had told him enough how much she loved him. Did he know how much she felt for him? How was she supposed to go on if anything had happened to him? Did he know he saved her soul?

Sometime in the late afternoon, the Seven World Trade Center's forty-seven-story building collapsed after burning for hours. There was no more specific news that day, just everything that had happened during the day with more updates and new death toll numbers. At eight thirty that evening, the president addressed the nation and called the events of the day "evil, despicable acts of terror," stating that America and its friends would "stand together to win the war against terror."

Earlier that evening Susi had gone to pick up her daughter. She knew Sammi was safe where she was, but she wanted—no, needed—her at home. She was the only link to Lance; she had nothing else that connected them.

"I'm sorry, honey, I know you probably wanted to stay at Jenn's," Susi stated on the way home.

"It's okay, Mom, I'd rather be with you and wait to hear from Daddy." She smiled at her mom. "It's difficult to be with people who can't really understand what it feels like to not know whether or not he's alive and okay."

"Gabby did lose her husband and for three years she hoped he would survive. She had a lot of hope, so I do think she knows what we are going through," Susi stated. "However, she was able to hold her husband's hand when he passed away, not really a comparison, but you know what I mean." Sammi nodded. "Would you mind if we went and got Five Guys or pizza?" Susi asked, "I really don't feel like cooking."

"It's okay, Mom, I didn't mean to seem disrespectful to Gabby," Sammi said. "I had a burger for lunch, so let's get a pizza."

Susi took her daughter's hand and squeezed. She and Lance must have done something right for this kid to be so smart and grown up. Not that they pushed her to grow up, rather the opposite, but she was a very unique and awesome kid.

Susie continued to try making calls multiple times but was still unable to reach Lance. They kept themselves busy by getting a pizza and driving home.

No sooner had they walked into the house, the landline rang. Susi dropped the pizza on the table and yanked the receiver off the cradle.

"Lance?" she screamed.

"Oh my God, honey, I am so sorry; the phones have been down all day." Lance let out a huge sigh, Susi knew he was relieved to hear her voice. "Are you and Peanut okay?"

Susi was now crying. She had held it in all day, and hearing his voice took such a load off her mind that there was no holding it back.

"Baby, is everything okay?" Lance repeated.

"I'm sorry, my love," Susi said while gaining strength. "We're fine. I was so scared. All day I tried not to cry... I couldn't get a hold of you...I felt like I haven't told you enough how much I love you... you are my whole life."

"Honey... baby," Lance started to chuckle. "Babe, I know how much you love me; I know because that's how much I love you. It doesn't matter what I have to deal with, what I have to face, it's your love that gets me through everything. You are always with me."

"When can you come home?" Susi had slid down the wall and sat there, her head on the shoulder of her daughter who was also crying tears of relief. Susi kissed her forehead.

"We are at a secure location at the moment. As soon as they let us go, I'll be home," he assured her. "It was nuts this morning. As soon as the first tower got hit, the alarm in the building went off and we had to evacuate the building. We grabbed our medical gear and made our way to our ambulance. Honey, I have never seen so many snipers. Just moments after we got outside, the plane that hit the second tower flew right overhead. All I could think about was you two, wanting nothing more than for you guys to be safe."

"Babe, Kristen is in the hospital." The tears changed to sadness. "She had a miscarriage and there still is no word from Charlie. She was in shock when I found her and drenched in blood."

"I'm so sorry, honey, I wish there was something I could have done." She could tell that he truly felt bad.

"Are you going to be home soon?" Susi wiped her nose on her sleeve and realized she had already asked that question.

"Mom, really?" Sammi was shocked and got up to get a tissue for her mother. She shook her head and under her breath muttered, "If I did that, she'd have a cow."

Susi laughed. "I heard that, young lady, and you are absolutely correct. Given the events of today, I have a legitimate excuse."

"I'll get home as soon as I can. I love you, babe."

"I love you too, please be careful." For as long as they had known each other, they knew the precise moment that they should both hang up.

Sammi had two slices of the almost-cold pizza while Susi barely managed to eat one. By nine that evening, Lance walked in the door, and Susi could do nothing more than to hold him as tight as she could. He let her take all the time she needed; so did Sammi. Thousands had lost their lives that day; thousands more were wondering if their loved ones made it out alive. Right then at that moment, they had each other. They held on, not just for each other but for Kristen and Charlie and all of those thousands of people who lost loved ones that horrible day, for those who perished in Shanksville, Pennsylvania, in Manhattan, and at the Pentagon.

****

Lance was back at the Capitol by seven in the morning. There was no one there but the medical staff; it was eerie. Normally the halls were buzzing with people, not today. Susi had found out early in the morning that two of her friends from culinary school perished while at work at Windows on the World in the North Tower of the World Trade Center.

There was still more personal tragedy. Not long after Lance got to work, he called Susi to let her know that Charlie was one of the casualties at the Pentagon.

"I don't know how much more loss I can handle," Susie said. "Katy lost Josh, Cookie lost Nate, and now this? Kristen is still unconscious; she has no idea that she'd not only lost her baby but her husband as well."

"I know, babe, this is so much to handle." Lance knew how difficult this was for her. After Nate died she had told him that she was starting to feel guilty that her friends were hit so hard and she had the love of her life by her side.

"We'll get through this, baby." Lance wished he could hold her. "I love you!"

****

"I need to go next door and see if I can find a number for her parents," Susi told Sammi. School had been cancelled for the day, and Susi asked her daughter to stay by the phone while she went to Kristen's. It didn't take long, and Susi was back with the information she'd needed.

She reluctantly dialed the number and waited for the someone to answer.

"Hello?," a woman said. It was Lois. They had met at the wedding. Susi wondered how she was going to tell this woman that her daughter had been unconscious since the day before, lost her baby, and that her son-in-law had died in the attack on the Pentagon.

"Ma'am, my name is Susi Wells. I don't know if you remember me from the wedding, I'm a friend of Kristen's and her neighbor." Susi swallowed hard.

"Oh yes, I remember. Is Kristen okay? What about Charlie? We haven't been able to get a hold of either one of them." Susi could tell how worried Lois was.

"I'm so sorry. Kristen has been in the hospital since yesterday. I found her unconscious. She was pregnant but lost the baby. Sadly, she's still not awake and I think you need to come up here as quickly as possible." Lois gasped for air. Only seconds later she asked the inevitable question. "What about Charlie?"

"Ma'am, I am so very sorry." Susi tried to stay calm. "Charlie was killed in the attack on the Pentagon."

"Russ!" Lois yelled. Seconds later a man was on the line and Susi had to repeat what she had just told Kristen's mom. Russ told Susi that they would be there as quickly as possible and thanked her for letting them know. He asked for her number so they could be in touch as soon as they got there.

"I'm sorry, sir, that the hospital hasn't called you, but I don't think anyone took her purse or anything that would have allowed the hospital to contact you." Susi felt guilty. "I just wanted to make sure she got medical attention as quickly as possible. My husband was at the Capitol and I was worried about him."

"Susi, you do not need to apologize," Russ assured her. "Yesterday changed this country, and I am so thankful that you got my little girl to the hospital and she's alive because of your actions." Those words should have made Susi feel better, but they didn't. She let Kristen's parents know which hospital their daughter was at.

****

Within twenty-four hours the country had united in a way not seen since the bombing of Pearl Harbor seventy years earlier. On the negative side, the president and others had to call out to the public to not take action against Muslim-Americans as an act of retaliation.

Days after the attack, Susi got a call from one of her former co-workers.

"Remember Balbir Singh Sodhi from the Chevron station up the road?" Casey asked her.

"Yes!" Susi had fond memories of Balbir.

"Well some jackass went into the gas station last night and shot him; he's dead." Casey's voice seemed to echo.

"What?" Susi couldn't believe what she'd heard. "Guess the president asking people not to judge didn't mean anything."

Susi had known Balbir for most of the time she lived in Arizona. He had checked her out multiple times when she got gas and snacks there. The station was just down the street from the office where she had worked. His death would later become known as the first hate crime that took place in response to the attacks of September 11. Frank Roque, the man who shot and killed Balbir, claimed to be a patriot and that he stood for the American way. Two years later he found out that the American way was a trial by jury. That same jury found him guilty of first-degree murder on September 30, 2003. They also found him guilty of five other charges, including drive-by shootings aimed at Middle Eastern people in the Mesa area. He was sentenced to death.

In August 2011 Balbir's name was removed from a 9/11 memorial because he was not a direct victim of the terrorist attack. Community advocacy groups convinced Gov. Jan Brewer of Arizona to veto the bill and continue honoring the memory of Balbir. He was one of the most generous men known to customers in the east Mesa area.

Susi knew if she ever found a reason to go back to Arizona, it would be to visit that gas station at Eightieth Street and University to honor Balbir and, hopefully, get to thank his widow, his brother, and his daughters for their never-ending kindness and their great sacrifice to the country they chose to live in.

When Lance had completed one year at the Capitol, the family decided that North Carolina and Camp Lejeune would be their new home. The next two years for Lance were spent training at work. He and Susi spent more time running together and they completed several half marathon's together. No matter how she tried, she could not get her marathon time under four and a half hours. She didn't care; she enjoyed the races and wasn't looking for record times. The people who rented their New Bern house had to cancel their lease two months early as the couple was going through a divorce. Becky had new tenants within a week.

THIRTEEN

The Battle for Fallujah

*"He knows I'll be here when he gets home, and I'll know
that I'm in his heart wherever he goes."*

T HE NEXT TWO YEARS were spent training with the Marines at
Camp Lejeune. They found the perfect house in North Topsail
beach, right on the water. Sammi was in heaven and at the beach every
chance she had. Tensions in the Middle East grew constantly and with
it the worry in the back of Susi's mind that Lance would eventually
have to go. When he still hadn't been deployed a year later, the worry
decreased. They'd had more than one conversation regarding the matter,
and Susi let Lance know if he had to go, she would accept it. She understood his need to serve.

"Has it ever dawned on you that all of this wears on you as well?"
Tracy had asked her in one of their weekly conversations. "Katy,
Kristen, worrying, all this has an emotional effect on your mental health
as well."

"I'm okay," Susi told her. "I really am. I know there are not that
many more years left that we are going to do this. He said he'd be done
at twenty."

"We'll see!" Tracy stated sharply.

"I promise you; I am fine. You will be the first to know if I'm not, I
promise," Susi said. She was glad to have such a dear friend, someone
to turn to in the time of need when she didn't want to burden Lance.

After the September 11 attacks, tensions across the country were

174

high. Even more so on every military base across the country. Not just the American public but countries across the world wanted some level of revenge. American military focused its power on defeating Al-Qaeda, the militant terrorist group responsible for the attacks, and two months later, Marines were the first major ground forces in Afghanistan. Susi knew it was only a matter of time before Lance would come home to tell her he was being sent to the desert.

Fallujah would come to be known as one of the most intense battles in the Iraq conflict, which began in 2003 by a U.S.-led coalition to overthrow the government of Saddam Hussein. The city was less than an hour away from Baghdad. The Marines could not get near the city without being fired upon. Susi knew what would be waiting for Lance. She'd watched the news every day before Lance got home. While the Marines had their job to take out the enemy and accomplish what they had been sent to do, it was the corpsman's job to help them in any way he could. Where the Marines went, the corpsmen had to go. Lance was, without a doubt, one of them. She had heard it more than once that the corpsman is a jack-of-all-trades when it comes to assignments on the battlefield.

Susi remembered how she had worried about Lance during Desert Storm, but this would be extremely different. Young men and women signed up for every branch of the military. They wanted to go and show them what Americans were made of and what happens when you mess with us. He had told her that he really didn't see it as a big deal. He had been to the desert, Japan, Okinawa. This would be his fifth deployment, and he just saw it as a time with its ups and downs but really nothing out of the norm for someone like him.

In mid-October 2003, the senior chief hospital corpsman at Naval Air Station Brunswick in Maine was looking for volunteers to deploy with the Second Medical Battalion out of Camp Lejeune. Lance had deployed with them before, so he was happy to possibly see familiar faces.

The time they had spent in North Carolina had been fun for the small family. Lance felt he and Susi had really come back together as partners, and Susi had really helped him overcome the trauma of Guam. Whatever he had to face, she always did her research to help him the right way. He valued her more than ever and found it difficult to share with her that he wanted to volunteer, but the last fourteen years had shown him that she supported him no matter what. They were sitting at dinner and Lance was unusually quiet. Susi knew that something was heavy on his mind. Somehow, she knew he was going to tell her that he was leaving again.

"What's going on, babe?" Susi inquired in between bites. "I hope you know you can talk to me."

"Senior Chief ask for volunteers today to deploy to Iraq; I'd really like to go."

Susi paused; she knew what this meant. At least now they had cell phones and computers and didn't have to rely on mail that would take weeks to get back and forth, but at that very moment, it was a small consolation.

"Baby, I know this is not easy for you to agree to and I know it is asking a lot to let me go, but please understand I need to do this." Lance sensed that underneath she was saddened. Unable to speak, she just nodded and whispered, "I know." He got up and walked to her chair. Kneeling next to her, he attempted to turn her chair so he could hold her hands in her lap. She followed his lead and turned. He took her hands and kissed both of them.

"Honey, you are my best friend. You are the amazing ying to my yang, the angel who rescues me whenever I need to be rescued, my one true flame, the one who makes my life whole and worth living. You are the one who has believed in me from the beginning of this journey and you are always with me." Lance looked deeply into her eyes. "I see so much sadness in your eyes. That is not what I want, my love." He laid his hand on her cheek.

"I know, baby," Susi tried to speak. "I'm sorry I'm selfish and want you to myself. I'm scared of what could happen to you. Saying I'm okay with this is like I'm telling you I'm okay with you possibly not coming back."

They both paused.

"I know you need to do this, and I won't keep you from it," she continued. "You do what you need to do, my love. I will wait for you as I have done before." She wrapped her arms around his neck. "This is never going to get any easier."

They held each other for a moment and then cleared the dinner dishes together. Sammi was next door for a sleepover. They would tell her about the decision tomorrow. She had grown into a smart and outgoing teen and faced troubles head-on without too much emotion. Both Lance and Susi were glad that she seemed to have her own support group through other military kids her age. When Sammi came home the next morning, they sat down with her and explained what Dad needed to do.

At almost fourteen years old, she could sometimes act more like an adult than many others her age.

"I can't say I understand why you want to do this, but at the same time I do understand," she said. "I guess you just need to do what you feel in your heart. I know I'm no replacement for you with Mom, but I can help her as much as possible."

"How did you get to be so grown up when you're not even fourteen yet?" Lance asked, laughing, and Sammi shrugged her shoulders. She got up and went to stand in front of her mother.

"We've done this before, Mom, we can do it again." Susi hugged her daughter and wished she had her strength.

"Keep in mind, babe," Lance said as he squeezed Susi's hand, "I will have my cell phone when we ship out and, as far as I know, we will have phones and computers over there. It's not like before."

"I know," Susi whispered, "I know." She searched for something in that statement that would help her feel better but came up blank.

****

The day after New Year's 2004, Lance had to report in. The preparation took nearly three weeks. The closer he was to departure, the harder it was leaving home in the morning. How much would his daughter change this time? How much would he change? He'd tried more and more to be the man Susi had fallen in love with, but this life was taking a toll on him.

The last night home, Sammi said her "See you soon" and went to a sleepover. She hated the sadness and going to a friend's house took the scare out of things. Lance and Susi were glad to have the night alone. They had planned to go out to a nice dinner but decided to just get a pizza and some wine.

They had been parents for nearly fourteen years, but they still enjoyed each other as much as they did the first night. Neither of them found sleep that night. They made love three times and talked in between about everything, including the way they met, the hardship of Guam, and their families.

"Maybe when I get back, we should go to Germany." Lance kissed his wife on the forehead. "I'd like to see where you grew up."

"Maybe we could look up some of my cousins or school friends, or my aunt." Susi turned on her side and snuggled against his chest. She loved the way the hair on his chest tickled against her back ever so lightly. She always missed moments like this the most. The way he would just take her in his arms, kiss her, and gently undress her. No words would ever be spoken. It was as if they could communicate by simply looking at each other. All these years and nothing in the way he touched her felt any different.

She knew he had changed. Over the years he had become quieter, especially after Guam. Sometimes he startled easier than others and at times, his temper seemed a little shorter. Yet everything he had been through had not affected the way he looked at her nor the way he wanted her.

"That's the aunt you call on Christmas, Easter, and a few other times, right?" Lance pulled her closer and kissed the back of her head. "Your hair smells good."

"Thank you, babe. Yes, Aunt Anni, my mom's sister. Maybe she can help me with my parents."

"That's something we haven't really talked about, ever. Well, here and there, but nothing solid. Is there a reason why you haven't spoken to them in so long?" Lance turned his wife toward him. He smiled. "You know one thing I have loved about you from the first night is how tiny you are. Despite having had a child and getting a little older, you keep in shape." He had completely changed the subject and she didn't mind. "I'm glad you love to run. Maybe when I get back, I can get into that again as well and we could do some races together. Anyway, has there been any progress with your parents?"

"Do we need to talk about this now?" Susi was just not in the mood.

"You haven't wanted to talk about it for almost fourteen years, ma'am. It's time to confess." He tickled her. Her history with her parents had come up multiple times since they first met, but she'd always averted any conversation about it.

"We have never really talked about our parents." Susi lost her smile but remained in her husband's arms.

"No, we haven't, never thought there was a need to. I mean, I told you that I was adopted, so there isn't much to tell on my side." Lance felt some irritation growing.

"Hey, sailor, simmer it down." Susi reached down and caressed Lance's penis. He closed his eyes and let out a deep breath.

"That's not fair," he sighed.

"Oh really?" She smiled at him and slid under the covers. Two minutes later she popped back out and ask if he still wanted to talk about her parents. He slightly moaned, shook his head, and playfully pushed her head back down. She laughed. She knew him too well. They both knew each other to the very core of their souls. For a moment she popped back out, wrapped the covers around her face, her hair sticking out here and there. "I love you, Lance."

He opened one eye to look at her. "I love you too, baby." She went back under the covers. She knew what he needed right now, and she loved giving it to him. At that very moment she knew that she would never be as grateful for her blessing of being with Lance and having Sammi than right now. This very moment would carry her through the coming months. She could feel him in every fiber of her being.

When she was done, she came up from under the covers. "Is it normal for two people to be this connected?"

"I could care less how connected others are. I care about how you make me feel and how I feel when we are together." He sat up. "Susi, I need to tell you something." She moved so she could lie in his lap and look at him.

"I know little to nothing about my biological parents and I don't care to know," he said, swallowing hard. "Since you've come into my life, everything changed. I ran from these feelings before, but when I met you, time stopped. You are my salvation; you have fixed everything that was wrong in my life."

Susi stared at him and tears softly rolled down the side of her head. She reached up and touched his lips; he kissed her fingers. "What did I ever do to deserve someone as amazing as you," she whispered.

"I'd give you the moon and the stars 'cause I think you deserve that and so much more." He gently tapped a finger on her nose.

"You've already given me that and so much more," she responded.

Lance wiggled down so her head would lie on his chest. "How so?"

She rolled over and covered his chest with little kisses, and with each kiss she told him one amazing thing he had done or given her. "The way I felt the first time we met, the way you faithfully called me each week, the way I can share everything with you, our daughter, your cards, your letters, the unexpected notes I find here and there, the way you make my coffee on your days off...do I need to go on?"

He smiled and shook his head. "I really had no idea you felt that way."

Susi moved around, sat in front of him, between his legs. "I've never asked you to put me on a pedestal, nor have you ever asked me to do that, but from the moment I met you, I knew that you were the missing piece to my soul. Why would I treat you any better, or different, than myself?"

"Baby, you do so much for me, for this family. Look at our daughter, the way she behaves you would think she's five years older." He leaned over and kissed her. "You are the glue that holds this family, hell, the glue that holds me together." He picked up his phone to check the time: 3:45 a.m.

"We have forty-five minutes until I need to shower, wanna nap or?" He smiled at her in his usual boyish way. He knew she couldn't resist.

"I'll be good with the or." She caressed the inside of his thighs and it only took moments until he was ready again. They made love, the way only two people who felt about each other the way they did could make love. Love in every way it could be perceived in the romantic and sensual way. It was the only way these two people knew how to be.

Forty-five minutes later, they took a shower together. Susi was tired, but she knew for the next few months she would be sleeping without her husband. The man who meant the world to her. Some part of her knew that another piece of him would be gone when he returned from this deployment. The Navy, Middle Eastern conflicts, and Guam had already taken so much. She wondered if there was a way to prepare for the damage. Maybe she would look into counseling, not just to learn but to heal some old scars. Lance had healed so many without even knowing it. Maybe he told her tonight that she had done the same for him.

By six a.m. they were at Camp Lejeune, and once again she had to let him go, not knowing if she would ever see him again. She'd learned not to cry too much; she didn't want to be seen as sappy but in love enough to not be included in the deployment antics of other wives. She felt like an oddball sometimes, and sometimes she felt that she wished she could find just one other woman among the military wives who fought for their marriage, who was as committed as she was. She was sure they were out there; she would just have to find them.

She remembered how much energy she had wasted on worrying about that back in San Diego when they'd first gotten married. Though it still bugged her, it was not nearly as much as it had back then. Maybe if they lived on base she would have more opportunity to meet like-minded women. It was just hard living in town.

Two hours later she was on her way home, and the man she loved more than life itself was on his way to another war zone. A place gripped by hatred against everything the Western world believed in, a place that hated the Western world to the core of every human being there. They were taught the hate from early on; it was their way of life. She would do what she could to learn what she could do to help him if he came back.

****

The troops flew to Kuwait. From there on to Iraq, and from there they drove to Camp Fallujah. Lance was beat by the time they finally were able to get some sleep. All he could think about was getting a phonecard soon to call Susi. He wondered how he had managed deployments before. They had not been like this; you could hear the bombings in the distance and the tension could be felt in the air. This one was different. He was part of a surgical team, call sign Tourniquet. While they had to make do with tents on his first deployment all those years ago, this was, in a sense, better. They had walls, actual buildings, a chow hall, and computer center. Laundry service, phones, showers, and even a PX of sorts.

After being trained on their local jobs and how they were to be performed, they took over as Fallujah Surgical. In a way it was even fun at times because there was constantly something new. While the days and often the nights were busy, he was able to keep his mind on his work. It was the nights he lay in his bunk that seemed unbearable at times. It wasn't long before he had his first phonecard to call home. He knew she was ten hours behind. If he could catch her just after breakfast, that would be great.

The phone rang several times. "Hello?" Sammi answered.

"Hey, Peanut." He was glad she answered the phone. "How are things?"

"Hey, Daddy." He heard joy in her voice. "How are you?"

"I'm great, honey!" It was such a relief to hear that voice. "How is school going?"

"It's good, glad we just have a few more months to go before summer break. Do you want to talk to Mom? Oh, hey, I got an A in math, can you believe that?"

"Of course, I do, I'm proud of you." He was happy, even though phone conversations had never been their thing. In person they could talk for hours, just not on the phone. He was so proud of his daughter; he could not have asked for a more amazing young lady. He thought about how he and Susi had talked about having another child when Sammi was about three but decided they were happy with the one they had.

"Hi, honey," Susi said at the other end. "How are you? I miss you so much."

"I miss you too, baby." Saying he missed her didn't quite cover how he felt. He wanted to hold her and never let go. "How are things at home? Any problems?"

"No, none at all." He knew she was lying. "You're not about to tell me if anything were wrong, would you?"

"Would you want me to tell you that last week I had a blow-out on the freeway and nearly died from the panic of it, or that I had to call a plumber because the water heater leaked?" She waited for a response.

"I'm sorry, my love," he said quietly.

"I don't want you to be sorry. This is why I don't want to tell you things. I don't want you to feel guilty," she said almost too harshly. "I'm thinking about signing up for another half marathon. What do you think?"

He knew she shouldn't ask about things beyond his control at this point, and that was one of the things he admired in her. She was such a strong woman. Sadly, life, or better yet her previous marriage, had taught her that. She could be so soft, cuddly, and needy, and then move a mountain if she needed to.

"That sounds like an awesome idea. You love to run and that would be the best way to improve your time. Have you thought about doing the Marine Corps marathon? I should be home in time for that," he told her.

"Wow, that sounds like fun! Really?" She seemed surprised. "I can't wait for you to be home and maybe we could train together!"

"Sure, why not? There is plenty of time to train." He knew he'd sparked her interest. "It's not till October so you have several months to up your training, and I can start here."

"You have a point, my sweet sailor. I shall look into it," Susi said. "Hey, honey, do you want me to send you anything? A care package, some money?"

"Yes to both if possible." He paused to think. "Can you send me some of those oatmeal cookies you make? Money wise, just send what you can."

"I can send you a hundred and fifty. I've been putting money in savings every other week, so I can send you some when you need it. Sammi and I really don't need that much, and I've been putting the difference into savings."

"What do you mean, the difference?"

"Well, let's say I spend two hundred on groceries every other week when your home and only a hundred twenty-five for Sammi and I. The difference goes into savings. The same with everything else, since we don't spend as much on fuel and dinners out, stuff like that," she explained.

"Oh, that's a great idea." Something else he was amazed about, she just made everything work, he never had to worry about anything. "I'm so proud of you, honey. You are truly an amazing wife. I can't wait for those cookies!"

"I'll bake them this weekend and send them out Monday. I love you, honey. I hope you are enjoying the cards!" The cards were something she had done every deployment, and she'd never been off more than a day or two at guessing when he'd be back.

"I am, sweetheart, they keep me sane and focused. That is the one thing I most look forward to every night." For a moment he closed his eyes and thought about her scent and what she felt like when he hugged her.

"Thank you, baby," she nearly whispered. "I feel you."

"I need to go, honey, my time is up. I'll call again soon." He didn't want to hang up, but there were others waiting.

"Okay, my love." He could hear that she was fighting tears. "Sammi said she'll write you a letter. Honey, please be careful and take good care of yourself."

"I will, babe. I'll do the best I can. I love you." With that they both hung up. He knew she would be standing there for a moment with her hand on the receiver, just as he did.

Even after all the years they had been together, he still wondered how two people could be that close, that much in sync. He needed a minute to bring himself back to reality.

Camp Fallujah had the Second Marine Recon, a SEAL team or two, and all the Marine units any camp could want at that time. This also meant that each and every day they saw a large number of gunshot wounds, burns, explosions, chlorine exposures, and more from Marines, Army, Iraqi Military police and civilians, including children. Even with a ninety-eight percent survival rate for the patients coming through the doors at Fallujah Surgical, it soon became the norm to be numb to the deaths they witnessed.

Several days after the phone call, Lance was standing with a small group just outside the entryway of their surgical unit. It was hot and the sand seemed to reflect the heat; the sun was slowly setting behind the large coiled razor wires on top of the berm walls.They talked about everything from the local camel spiders they had encountered to the crazy weather, especially sandstorms. Lance was glad that he'd been able to avoid smoking. Most of the guys there did, and he'd been tempted to more than once.

The setting sun was a relief, as the temperatures dropped and made being outside bearable. It was just after eight in the evening when a Humvee patrol returned. They had been out for ten hours. The door of the first vehicle opened and Sgt. Robert Baker got out. Lance and he had been friends since Camp Pendleton and got along really well. Baker enjoyed golf, and they had played together a few times. They had begun running together as a way to de-stress since they'd gotten over here and always had good conversation. Lance turned toward his friend; something seemed off. The usually bright eyes looked dark and lost, and Lance didn't like it. The six-foot-two, two-hundred pound high school football star seemed to have shrunk. Lance could almost see the invisible weight pushing him down.

"Hey, Baker, everything okay?" Lance stopped.

Baker had pulled his handgun from its holster.

Within the blink of an eye he looked at Lance, saying, "I can't do this anymore, man."

He raised the gun, set the barrel under his chin, and pulled the trigger. Lance leapt at him screaming, but it was too late. The blood pouring out of the hole in the back of his head ran across Lances hand. Several others came running when they heard the shot, shocked at what they found. The doctor on duty pronounced Sgt. Baker dead moments later. There was nothing anyone could have done to save him. Somebody had pulled Lance up, and he just stood there feeling empty. He must have completely blacked out for nearly an hour when Chief Foster approached him.

"Wells? What's going on?"

"How do I process this, Chief? He just got out of the vehicle and said he was done. There wasn't even a second that any of us could have done anything." Lance was searching for answers where he knew there wouldn't be any. The chief suggested that he get some rest. Things would look different in the morning. That was the first night he would sneak on the roof of the Fallujah surgical building to look at the sky and listen to music. During the day the city looked much different. Square houses with flat roofs all in the same sandstone color as the ground they were built on, beige linen curtains in some of the windows, and the few women rushing through the streets shrouded in their black hijabs. At night they became different sized blocks, no life or light seen anywhere other than helicopters landing now and then to bring wounded. Lance had never been a big fan of classical music but since he'd been here, he'd developed a liking for it. It was what they played in surgery.

That night he lay there listening to Pachelbel's Canon in D and cried. What a beautiful piece of music to listen to in such a shitty place, he thought. Death and destruction were all around him. That night was only the beginning. The following week he called Susi again. He wanted so much to tell her what happened. He knew she'd help him, he knew she would talk him through this, but he didn't want her to worry.

Two months later another incident; they'd gotten a call that someone was bringing in a wounded Marine. Lance was ready, or so he thought. They'd just finished chow and were standing outside. That's where most of the guys hung out and smoked. Lance had not said no to a cigarette the day after Baker died but had not told Susi about his new nasty habit. He would quit before he headed home.

A seven-ton rolled up in a cloud of dust. The first person he saw was a Marine he had known well from Lejeune, and he was excited to see a familiar face. Lance approached him. He looked distressed and filled with sorrow. He was bringing a fellow Marine, a buddy. When Lance saw the Marine's injuries, he knew no matter what they did, he was not going to make it. He died that night on the operating table.

The next six months brought nothing more but the same. The survival rate seemed to shrink as the conflict intensified. A young corporal who had led his squad in attacks against a large enemy force was injured but returned to his unit only days later to lead them in another attack before being killed. A sergeant rolled on top of a wounded Marine to shield him from a blast; he absorbed the brunt of the explosion.

In July 2005 Lance was being rotated out. It was time for him to go home. He went from the Iraq desert to Ramstein, Germany, and then on to Raleigh in North Carolina. He wore his clean and pressed cammies for the flight home. He was stunned by the response of people, offering seats, allowing him to go to the front of the line at a coffee shop. There seemed to be an outpouring of gratitude and appreciation.

He came out of the secure area and scanned the crowd for his wife. When his eyes met hers, he knew he had never seen anything so beautiful in his whole life. He wanted to scream with excitement, cry for joy and, most of all, never leave her side again. They stood right there in the airport and just held each other. Susi felt his warm tears running down her neck. She knew this time he was deeply scared. They got his duffle bag and made their way to the car.

****

"Honey, I cannot imagine the things you have seen," Susie told him. "I don't know if you will ever be able to share any of it with me, but please know this, I cannot undo the things you have seen. I can only be here for you to lean on and ask for support." Susi was holding both of his hands in front of the open trunk of her car. He grabbed her shoulders and wrapped his arms around her again.

"It was so horrible." He sounded almost cold. "How can human beings do such horrific things?"

They just stood there talking for a few minutes and decided to have lunch on the way home. Sammi hadn't come with her mom. They had planned to surprise her at school, so Susi had not told her that he was coming home that day. Susi had made the arrangement with her sixth-hour teacher. They stopped at a small diner. Neither had to pay for the meals. A small group of Marine Vietnam vets sitting at the next table took care of, as one of them said, their own. Lance's eyes became glassy. He did not expect any of this.

By one in the afternoon, they were at the school. The principal met them and apologized for the small entourage. Sammi sat in the second row, and the door to her classroom was behind her. The principal walked in first and pretended to speak with the teacher. The students began chatting amongst themselves. Sammi exchanged notes with the girl sitting next to her when she stopped, looked up, and turned around. There was her father in the back of the room by the door. She leapt out of her seat and ran to her dad. Lance knelt down to catch her. Several teachers and other staff silently made their way into the room when Lance entered, and they all had their phones set to record the amazing homecoming.

Sammi clung to her dad and cried; so did he and her mother. Less than an hour later, Sammi had been excused for the rest of the day and was on her way home with her parents. When Lance and Susi went to bed that night, it was the first time he returned from a deployment and didn't want to make love. He just wanted to fall asleep in her arms. He laid his head on her chest, and she stroked his head gently until he drifted off. Much to her surprise, he woke her sometime around four in the morning. He wanted her.

He was off for the next three days, so in the morning she just let him sleep as long as he wanted. Sammi was happy it was Friday and she'd have the weekend to talk sports with her dad. At breakfast she told her mother that she was sure that this was going to be one of the longest days…ever, not just because it was the last day, but she would rather have stayed home and talked with Dad.

Susi knew that he'd seen horrible things. He usually slept still and peaceful, but the night before he'd been tossing and turning, mumbling things she didn't understand. When he woke up and came to the kitchen for his morning coffee, he told her that he felt exhausted, even though he had slept almost ten hours.

"Despite everything," he said, grabbing Susi and wrapping his arms around her, "being able to hold you again is worth all that shit."

Susi looked up at him. "Any chance you can take some leave so we can escape for a bit?"

"Let me see what I can do. I think I have three weeks or so that I can take." He kissed her forehead.

"Honey, I need to tell you something, got a minute?" Susie asked. She poured herself another cup of coffee and sat at the kitchen table. Lance joined her.

"What's on your mind, my love?" He slid his hand under her shorts and she playfully swatted it away.

"Focus," she instructed him with a smile. He assured her that he was focused, just not on the conversation. She urged him to give her a few minutes and he complied. "I need you to understand that I realize the Navy wants you guys to disconnect, have no feelings and emotions," she said, clearing her throat. "But that is not the case with most guys. I'd say the majority will end up with some kind of issues. Obviously, I am not married to the entire Navy. I am happy with the sailor I have." This was getting difficult. She paused and took a sip of coffee.

"What are you getting at, honey?" It was obvious he was getting impatient.

"What I'm trying to get at is that I've known you for a lot of years. I know what you were like and what you are like now. We have always been able to talk openly and not keep secrets from each other. I would appreciate it if you talk to me about the things you saw and had to do, the things that caused you to toss and turn last night." She took a deep breath and waited.

"Thank you, Susi, you truly are my rock. Maybe we can take a little time tonight after Peanut goes to bed."

Susi chuckled. "Good luck with that. She is halfway through her last day at school, and I bet she is already on pins and needles to get home to talk sports with her dad."

"Sports? Really? Like what?" Lance inquired.

"Mostly football. She has developed a strong liking for the Seahawks and is already itching for pre-season to start. She has taken up roller blading and she is on the cross-country running and the swim team. I think that's all of it." Susi scratched her head and thought.

"Wow, she's a little busy body. That's awesome. Total tomboy? No girlie stuff?" Lance wanted to know.

"Oh yes, she went to the Christmas dance with a boy that she really likes, and she looked like an angel. Remember, I sent you that picture of her?"

He remembered. Just after three that afternoon, Sammi came running in the front door, dropped her backpack on the table by the door, and looked for her dad. He suggested that they get out of Mom's hair and go have some ice cream and talk. They were back in time for dinner, and Susi could tell they had a great afternoon. The conversation about the Seahawks was in full swing during dinner, and Susi couldn't help but smile at her two honeys.

"Oh, hey, Mom, can I still visit Tracy in Seattle?" Sammi stopped her conversation with Lance in mid-sentence.

"Of course, did you two make plans yet?" Sammi told her that they were going back to Disneyland as well as Six Flags. Since Sammi had been six, she would go to Seattle for a week or two at the beginning of summer break to hang out and get spoiled by Tracy.

When Sammi had gone to bed, Lance and Susi made themselves comfortable on the deck with a glass of wine and soft music, watching the waves roll slowly across the sand. Slowly, Lance began telling Susi the horrors he'd witnessed: the night Baker shot himself, the young Marine who'd thrown himself on a grenade, and all the other nightmares. He told her about how he'd sneak on the roof to listen to music and think about her.

"I hope you never have to witness anything like that ever again," she whispered. She could tell he was crying. "I'm here for you, baby."

"I know, my love," he whispered. "I felt you when I'd lay on that roof. Feeling you so near, even though you were so far away, was what maintained my hope." She knew that just having conversations may not be enough, but she would have to see how he managed.

FOURTEEN

Enough Is Enough

"Behind every strong sailor, there is an even stronger family who stands by them, supports them, and loves them with all their hearts."

A WEEK AGO, LANCE talked to the detailer to request going back to the desert. It had been the first time in all the years that Susi and he had been together that they argued. It ended with Sammi accusing him of wanting to get himself killed, and all three of them went to different parts of the house unhappy.

"Can I come in?" Susi knocked on Sammi's door.

"Yeah." Susi opened the door a little and peeked in. Sammi was sitting on her bed crying. Susi sat on the bed next to her and wrapped her arm around her daughter. Sammi slid down and laid her head on her mom's lap. "Why does he want to go back there? Does he not understand or care how much we worry about him? We've seen and heard enough of what's going on, and it sure doesn't seem like anyone is coming back from there without some kind of mental or physical damage."

"Yes, he does understand, baby girl," Susi said softly. At that very moment she didn't know how much more she had to give, how much deeper she could dig to help her husband and daughter.

"Sit up, honey," Susi told Sammi. When she did Susi slid off the bed and got on her knees in front of her daughter. "Listen, baby, life can be total shit sometimes. The life I had before your dad was worse than shit. It was the fungus that feeds on shit." Susi cringed at the memories trying to creep into her mind.

"Mom!" Sammi was shocked. "I've never heard you talk like that."

"You haven't seen me after five margaritas," Susi joked, got up, and took Sammi's hand. "Come on, we need to let your dad know that we love him and support whatever he needs to do."

Sammi looked at her mom. "You know something, Mom? You are literally the strongest woman I have ever met. I don't know where you get all this from. I hope I can be as strong as you when I need to be."

"You already have been, baby." Susi squeezed her daughter's hand.

Moments later Susi was knocking on her own bedroom door but didn't wait for an answer. Lance was sitting on the floor with his back against the bed. He wouldn't look up. "I'm sorry."

Susi could see he had been crying, something he didn't use to hide. Susi and Sam sat on the ground with him, one on each side. Sammi took his left hand. "I'm sorry, Daddy. I respect and love you so very much. I should not have said what I did. I know I can't undo what I said, but please know this: I will support whatever decision you make no matter how hard it is for me. Please forgive me." She put her head against his shoulder.

Susi didn't give him a chance to say anything.

"Honey, I know you need to do this, whatever the reason may be," Susi said, placing her head on his other shoulder. He kissed both of his girls' heads. "I am scared enough for both of us. We need you; I need you; you are my whole world." Susi took his hand and squeezed it. He pulled his arms up and wrapped both Sammi and Susi in his arms.

"I shouldn't have turned this into an argument," he said. "I hear what other guys have to deal with at home, what they worry about when we're deployed. Often it screws their concentration and focus on the mission and they end up getting hurt or cause someone else to get hurt." He took a deep breath. "Neither of you have ever given me a reason to worry about anything. When I'm gone, I can completely focus on my job, and that is the thing I am so thankful for. Honestly, girls, I don't know if my detailer will even let me go back. If not, it's okay, and if I can go back, I promise you both I will be done when I hit twenty years."

"Are you serious?" Susi looked up at him.

"Yes," he said, clearing his throat. "It's time I focus on you guys. You have been here for me, no matter what, for all these years. You have dealt with things without any support. You've had small health issues and I wasn't here, and I've missed nearly every milestone in Sammi's life. Nothing good has come out of this war, and way too many good guys have been lost. I'll find out tomorrow, and if it's a no-go, we can start talking about the next chapter of our lives."

Sammi wiggled out from under his arm and wrapped both of hers around his neck. "So, you might be here for my graduation?" Sammi was grinning from ear to ear. Lance nodded. Susi had a feeling in her stomach she couldn't shake. Something was off, something she couldn't put her finger on, but she knew it wasn't good. She glanced at Lance. Susi was worried, the love and joy she used to be able to see in his eyes had been replaced with darkness, pain, and sadness. What would she need to do to get that back? She knew right now was not the time to say anything, but she needed to convey to him again that she was always here to listen to him no matter what. Anything else could wait. His well-being would always take precedence.

"Sammi said it right when she said we can't undo what's been said, but I want you both to know that I will never allow something like this to happen again." He looked at both the girls, and Susi could see how much he was hurting.

"It's okay, Daddy," Sammi said soothingly. "I know you have a lot to deal with." Sammi hugged him. "You know, I hear it at school the way you do at work. Kids are always complaining about their dads or moms being gone. Some of them think they can get away with more if their dad's not there. There seems to be little consideration for the parent who's at home and has to take care of everything nor any thought to the one deployed."

"I'm very proud of you, Sammi," Susi told her daughter. "You have been a joy in my life since the day you've been born. I really don't know how Dad and I got this lucky to have such an amazing daughter."

"Hey, girls, what do you think, wanna go to dinner?" Lance suggested.

The girls agreed and got ready. It never took either of them very long to get ready for anything. They lived in jeans and t-shirts with ponytails, very low maintenance, something Lance had been thankful for since Sammi was a young teen.

Four hours later they were back home. They had gone to Beach Bums Bar and Grill for dinner and then walked along the beach for nearly two hours. Sammi explained things about seaweed and other oceanic facts that made both her parents scratch their heads. Susi loved her daughter's passion and commitment to learning.

"I wonder who she got that from?" Lance teased his wife. "Certainly not me. Are you ready to head to bed?"

"Can I have just ten more minutes of your time?" she responded.

He sat back down on the couch. "What's up, honey? I can see something is really eating at you."

"Baby, please just be honest with me." He hugged her. One thing she had always treasured was their honesty with each other and their ability to talk about anything. She knew the events of earlier that night might make it difficult right now, but she hoped that wasn't it.

"Honey, we have been together for nearly fifteen years and I remember the night we met as if it was yesterday," she continued. "The first time I looked into your eyes, there was such spunk and such a love for life. Now all I can see is pain and sadness. It scares me."

"Baby..." Lance tried to interrupt.

"Let me finish, please, this is difficult," Susi insisted and took his hand. "For nearly fifteen years I haven't cared what life threw at me. I handled it. Never in a million years would I have thought to let you know if there was a hiccup that needed dealing with when you were deployed. I knew the things you had to deal with were so much worse, but those things have taken their toll on you. I first noticed this after the plane crash on Guam. Please, honey, if there are things you are worried about, things you don't know how to deal with on your own, please talk to me."

"Thank you, my love, that means a lot." Lance leaned over to kiss her. "Let's go to bed." He winked at her and got up and headed to the bedroom. Susi remained on the couch, staring into emptiness. She'd read enough about veterans and active duty military taking their own lives despite urges to get help from families and loved ones. There had to be a way she could do something for him. For now, she would have to let it go. There wasn't really anything she could do at the moment anyway.

He was already in bed when she got to the bedroom. "What took so long?" he asked.

"I'm sorry, my love, I just got lost in my own thoughts for a moment," she explained, leaning over to kiss him. "I'll be just a minute." She grabbed the t-shirt he'd been wearing and headed for the bathroom to brush her teeth and get ready for bed. She slipped out of her clothes and into his shirt. Moments later she was in bed and sat on his upper thighs.

"You know how much I love you, right?" she asked and leaned over to give him a little kiss on the nose.

"I have a pretty good idea," he replied, then grabbed the back of her neck and pulled her in to kiss her. She could feel him get hard, and that was exactly what she had wanted. She pulled away from his grip and softly slid under the covers. He put both his hand behind his head and sank into the pillow while Susi did her magic. Several minutes later Lance stopped her. She peaked out from under the covers. "Is everything all right?" she asked.

"Oh, absolutely, my love. I was just hoping we could make love." He smiled at her. She crawled out from under the covers and lay next to him. He wrapped her in his arms and started caressing her from her neck to her breast. Susi felt as if the bed was disappearing beneath her. He hadn't kissed and touched her like that in a long time.

A little while later, they lay asleep in each other's arms.

****

Lance came home the next day and Susi could tell something was wrong. He didn't talk much and seemed irritable. She let him have his time to change and then she would find out what was going on. He came into the kitchen just minutes later and got a beer out of the fridge.

"What's going on, babe? Did you find out anything?" She had a suspicion what the answer would be.

"She feels it's not a good idea for me to go back. She said she thinks I have too much going on and she wants to make sure I'm safe," he said angrily while sitting down.

Susi stopped working on dinner and turned to stand behind him. She wrapped her arms around him and kissed the top of his head. "Honey, I know that was not what you wanted to hear. I'm so sorry, is there anything I can do to help?"

He shook his head. "I'm just gonna watch TV for a bit. How much longer till dinner?"

Susi told him it would be another twenty minutes or so and he should just relax. He got up and walked toward the living room. She was sure that she heard him mumble that at least now she would get her way and he'd get some lame assignment. She pretended not to hear but made up her mind that he would need to get help. He was getting more and more angry and depressed.

Sammi came home and before she had a chance to ask anything, Susi pulled her aside and let her know what was going on. "Is he okay?" Sammi whispered. Susi gave her a so-so gesture and they left it at that.

At dinner Susi suggested that he make a tee time for the next morning. It was Saturday, he didn't have duty, and the forecast was promising. "I'll go play a round with you if you want, Dad," Sammi chimed in. That seemed to take his thoughts off the issues, and Susi nodded at her while Lance wasn't looking.

Bright and early the next morning, father and daughter headed out. Lance had told Susi that they would stop for breakfast and if she wanted, she could meet them at the club for a late lunch. "Sounds great. Just send me a text when you are on hole sixteen and I'll head that way."

Paradise Point Golf Course was thirty to forty minutes away depending on traffic and by the time she got there, the two of them were already sitting at a table discussing their game.

"This kid is a killer," Lance announced. He seemed in much better spirits than he had been in for some time.

"Dad's just getting old and rusty," Sammi joked.

"Oh my," Susi chortled. "That sounds like a challenge to me. I have to meet a cake client in the morning. Why don't you two play again?"

"Sounds like a plan to me," Lance agreed, winking at his daughter. "You just got lucky today, little miss."

"Oh really? We'll see about that," Sammi countered and gave her dad a pat on the back.

By the time the two golfers came home the next day, Susi had already made it home from her appointment and had dinner in the Crockpot. She enjoyed the warmth of the late summer sun out on their deck with a good book and a glass of wine. Lance and Sammi took turns yelling for her as soon as they came in the door, and it only took a moment until they noticed her outside.

"Got any of that left?" Lance asked and pointed at the wine bottle. Susi laughed and confirmed that there was plenty. Lance went inside and came back with two glasses.

"Who's the other glass for?" Susi wanted to know.

"It's for Sammi, we have to celebrate."

"Dad, really?" Sammi chuckled and hugged him. She smirked at Susi. "I got two birdies and an eagle today."

"Oh wow, that is worth a celebration," Susi concurred.

"This kid can play some golf, I tell you," Lance declared. He seemed over the moon. He acted the way he used to when Sammi was little and she learned to ride her bike or not fall when she was on roller blades.

"Maybe you two need to play more often," Susi suggested. "It seems to do you both a lot of good."

****

They took that suggestion to heart and played golf every chance they had. Lance was back to work at Naval Medical Center Lejeune when someone overheard him talk about what a fantastic golfer his daughter was. Before he knew what had transpired, he and Sammi were invited to play golf with two of Lance's co-workers the following Sunday. They were really pushing it in October but got lucky.

Lance called Susi after the game and asked her to come to the golf course. Sammi had just beaten her dad and the other two guys. Those days seemed to set the tone for the remaining year and beyond. For the next two years, Lance's depression seemed to have vanished. He and Sammi had become very close, and when the weather wasn't good enough for them to play on a course, they were in the garage hitting balls into a net or playing golf on Sammi's play station.

When it came time to pick a new duty station in 2008, Lance announced that he would retire. He was not interested in being an independent duty corpsman on a submarine. It was time to help his daughter develop her golf talents and be there for his wife when she needed him. For twenty years she had been the backbone of this family, and it was time for him to take over and let her spread her wings in her career. On May 31, 2009, he officially retired. His ceremony was beautiful. Both Susi and Sammi couldn't help but cry. Sammi had just turned eighteen in March. She'd been offered several full scholarships and waited on her mom and dad to decide where they wanted to settle down.

Neither of them had to give that much thought. They wanted to go back to Washington State. Sammi applied at the University of Washington and was quickly accepted. Since she would be going to campus in Seattle, Lance and Susi decided to buy a house somewhere within reasonable travel time. Both of them knew Sammi wanted to live on campus, and they dreaded it but gave in. They knew they had to let her start living her life, and it was time for the two of them to explore the world together.

Within a year they had purchased a house with three acres in Silverdale, just across the Puget Sound from Seattle. Once again it was an older house, built in the late seventies, and this one needed work. Everything from all the flooring being re-done to painting, new bathrooms, windows and a huge garden where Susi could plant everything she wanted. They had bought Sammi a Jeep Wrangler as a graduation gift and it fit her tomboy personality perfectly. Sammi came home on Fridays and headed back to campus on Sunday night. Life felt good, but little did Susi know at that very moment in time that Lance's depression had started flaring again.

He had seen a doctor at the VA in Seattle while Susi was at work. It took nearly four months to get the appointment, and they did nothing more than prescribe him a mild antidepressant. There was no mention that he should attend counseling or be tested for potential PTSD. He'd also started drinking more, in secret. He had no intention of hurting Susi or Sammi, but he felt so numb and dead inside some days, and it seemed as if it was happening more and more often. Susi had noticed that he'd been having some trouble sleeping and had asked him about it. He often had neck and shoulder pain at the end of the day. She got him Tylenol PM to help him with the pain and sleep. If she had known about the alcohol and antidepressants, she may have been able to avoid the storm that was brewing.

FIFTEEN

The Suicide Attempt

*"The minute you think of giving up, think of the reasons
why you held on for so long."*

J UST AFTER BUYING THE house in Silverdale, Susi started working
at Sluys Poulsbo Bakery. It was supposed to be part time, but she always ended up working a bit longer. Lance had still not figured out what
he wanted to do. He'd talked about getting his master's but never really
followed up. She would need to take some time off and take him to Germany. They had talked about going before he had to go to Fallujah, but
nothing ever came of it. Susi did get things worked out with her parents,
and they talked once a week on the phone. She had told her mom that she
was worried about him, and she'd had a long conversation with Tracy.

"There seems to not be anything left but the shell of the man I fell in
love with all those years ago," Susi told Tracy. "I knew that after the
plane crash on Guam he wasn't quite the same, but he was far from
where he is now." She paused and took a deep breath. Now that they
were near Seattle, it was easy for Tracy and Susi to meet for lunch or
just coffee. They tried to meet at least every other week at Starbucks on
First Avenue and Pike Street.

"Have you tried talking to him about what you see?" Tracy asked.

"I have a couple of times, but he excuses his behavior with pain and
being tired." Susi was near tears. "I don't know what to do, I don't
want to lose him."

Tracy reached over and held onto Susi's arm.

"You know how affectionate he used to be, how carefree and playful? None of that is left. I can't even remember the last time we made love," Susi added.

"Maybe when you get home, you can try starting a conversation and see where it leads, at least it's worth a try," Tracy suggested.

When Susi got home that night, he was sitting on the couch watching TV.

"Hey, baby, what are you up to?" she playfully asked and kissed him. He reached up, took her hand, and laid it against his face. "How's Tracy?" he asked.

"She's great," Susi replied, resting her head on his. "She was wondering if we want to meet her for dinner at Ivar's on Friday. Well, her and Max."

"Sure, that would be great. Did you have anything in mind for dinner tonight? It's getting to be that time." He smiled at her and bent his head back to be able to kiss her. They agreed on pizza, and Susi ordered one. After they ate Susi sat on the couch, and Lance asked if he could rest his head on her lap, which she gladly let him do.

"I wish I could still show you how much I love you," Lance said. "Nothing about my feelings for you has changed. It has just become so difficult to express that love." Lance squeezed Susi's leg. "I wonder almost daily if I haven't become more of a burden to you than anything else."

"Honey, please don't say things like that. You are and will never be a burden. You are the love of my life and you are going through a hard time. We'll get through this, I promise." Susi leaned down and kissed his forehead.

"Are you sure?" Lance insisted. "I honestly think if it weren't for me, you'd have a much better life. You wouldn't be stuck at home with the broken version of me."

"Honey, please look at me," Susi pushed. Lance turned so he could look up at her. "You mean the world to me; you are my very breath and heartbeat. I would rather have this life with you than any other life imaginable."

A teardrop fell and landed on Lance's cheek. "I hate to be the cause of your tears. I hate that I have become the reason for your pain instead of helping you. You deserve better than this. You need to be with someone who can love you the way you need to be loved."

"Don't say such things!" Susi shouted, then frowned. "I don't mean to cry. You know how sappy I can be, and you are by no means my pain."

"Are you sure, my love?" He reached up and gently touched her face. "I just don't want to hurt you anymore," he said.

Susi leaned down and kissed him. "Honey there is only one thing that hurts me and that is the thought of losing you."

They finished the movie they were watching and headed to bed. The next few days seemed to be better. He seemed less down. Friday morning came and Susi was getting ready to head to work.

"You remember about dinner tonight, right?" she asked him.

"Yes, ma'am," he answered and gently smacked her butt.

"Why don't you give me a ride to work? I'll text you when I'm done, and we can head straight to the ferry from there. I think we should aim for the one at a quarter after four," Susi said and returned the butt smack. Lance agreed and they headed out. After he dropped her off, she stood outside for a moment. She had the strong feeling that something was not right. Even after a couple hours at work, she could not shake the feeling. She needed to call Lance. After dialing his number, she waited for him to pick up, but there was no answer. Susi tried to continue working, but her concentration was at home. She just knew something was very wrong.

"Jake, do you have a minute?" she asked her boss in his office.

"What's up?"

"I'm sorry, but I need to get home. Something is wrong. I cannot explain right now, I just know." Susi seemed rushed.

"Do you need a ride?" Jake asked.

"Sure, if you have time." Susi was grateful he had offered. She didn't want to take a cab.

He had someone take over for Susi, and they went out the backdoor to his car. She was glad he didn't ask any questions and kept the conversation to small talk. Twenty minutes later they pulled up in front of her home. She thanked Jake for the ride and assured him that he didn't need to wait. Lance's car was in the driveway.

Susi went inside and called out his name but got no response. She checked the kitchen, he was neither there nor in the living room. Deep fear and panic set in. She ran up the stairs, threw open the pale oak door, and found him lying on the floor in the bedroom in front of their bed, an empty bottle of Captain Morgan next to him along with the empty container of Tylenol PM, his antidepressant, and a container of oxycodone, both empty. Susi had not seen the drugs before. She started to panic but knew she had to stay calm. She checked to see if he was breathing while she called nine-one-one.

"*Nine-one-one, what is your emergency?*" the dispatcher asked.

"My husband took an almost full container of Tylenol PM, antidepressants, and oxycodone. I'm not sure how many of those he took, and he emptied a bottle of rum. He is barely breathing, and his pulse is very weak."

"*I have paramedics on the way to you. What is your name and your husband's?*"

"His name is Lance, Lance Wells, and I'm Susi, same last name." She had a hard time speaking. Her mouth felt dry, her voice shaking as much as her hands. "Please hurry, I don't want to lose him."

Moments later she heard the siren and she ran downstairs to open the door. Two paramedics came in and followed Susi upstairs. They quickly assessed the situation, put him on oxygen, and moved him to the stretcher. Several police officers also arrived in the house, asking Susi what she knew about the attempt.

"I had no idea that he was on oxycodone or antidepressants. He must have gone to the VA to get them while I was at work," she cried. The paramedics brought the stretcher with Lance downstairs. "Can I ride with you, please?" she asked.

"Of course," one of them stated. Susi turned to the cop. "Look, he is not crazy. He has been through hell, a major plane crash, and two wars that would fuck with anyone's head, so please do not treat him like a criminal. That is not what he needs. He needs compassion and understanding."

"Ma'am, there are laws and we have procedure we need to follow," another paramedic told her.

Susi walked out and asked them to shut the door behind them. "Right now, my husband's life is in danger and I'm getting in the ambulance with him. If you have any other questions for me, then you'll have to meet me at the hospital," Susi coldly stated and got into the ambulance. One of the cops asked the paramedic which hospital they were taking him to and was told that Lance would be transported to Harrison Medical Center in Bremerton.

Susi sat in a seat next to Lance and held his hand. He was unresponsive, and she knew that she had never been so scared in all of her life.

"Honey, please don't leave me. I love you with all of my heart. You are my everything." Tears started rolling down her cheeks. "We can work through this together. I will do whatever you need me to do, just please don't go."

She felt an ever so slight squeeze on her hand and informed the paramedic about it. Within twenty minutes they arrived at the ER. He was taken to one of the rooms, and nurses quickly attended to him along with a doctor. Seconds later Lance went into cardiac arrest. Susi was ushered out of the room while a crash cart was brought in. Susi sank to her knees outside of the room, sobbing. She laid her hands on the floor, and for the first time in her life she prayed.

"God, if you're up there, please don't take him from me, please, I'm begging you. He is my everything." She remained on the floor. Moments later a nurse helped her to her feet.

"Let's go back in," the nurse said and smiled at Susi. "We got him back."

"Mrs. Wells, may I have a word with you for a moment?" the ER doctor asked. Susi looked through the window in the door and then turned towards the doctor, all the while trying to watch Lance through the little window. She was trying to dry her tears, but it was difficult.

"Any idea if he is struggling with anything?" the doctor inquired.

"He said a few days ago that he felt he was a burden and that he didn't want to hurt me anymore," she told him. "I tried to explain that he doesn't hurt me and that he is not a burden, but, as this clearly shows, he didn't believe me. I didn't even know he was on antidepressants or the oxycodone."

"We're going to call the VA and see what we can find out," the doctor said. "We are generally required to have a security guard in the room with a suicide attempt. I'm gonna see if I can bend the rules a little and just have someone right outside the door. The last thing he needs right now is to have someone make him feel worse." He paused for a moment. "Mrs. Wells, I'm going to be honest with you. Of course, it's a little too early to tell. We will have to run some tests, but there is a chance your husband will have liver damage as well as potential kidney damage from this. We will also need to run an EKG, and he will have to undergo a psychological evaluation as soon as we can get the counselor here and Lance is fully awake."

Susi nodded. "I understand. I just know that the policies in this state are not friendly when it comes to dealing with someone suicidal, and I know I do not need him to end up feeling embarrassed or ashamed due to actions from the hospital staff."

He told her that he agreed with her. Sadly, there was nothing they could do other than to play it by ear with each patient, and that was even risky. He advised her that she could go back into the room and he would get back with her as soon as he had an answer from the VA. Susi went back in and pulled a chair next to the bed. Before she sat down, she leaned over and kissed Lance's lips, eyes, and forehead. She gently caressed his head.

"Baby, I don't know if you can hear me or not, but I need you to know how very much I love you and how very important you are to me." She again kissed his head and reached down to take his hand.

"I know there was a time in my life when I was so hurt inside but couldn't explain to anyone what I was feeling, so I didn't ask for help." She wiped her nose with a tissue she'd pulled out of her pocket. "I wonder if that is how you feel, you just can't explain it." Holding on to his hand her gaze drifted around the room. It was grey and cold, informative posters, boxes of gloves, and equipment. Through the small window in the door she could see the security guard standing to stretch his legs. *Someone his age shouldn't have to work anymore,* she thought to herself. The beeping of the monitor Lance was attached to brought her attention back to him as she felt a slight squeeze from his hand.

A nurse came in to check his vital signs and told Susi that Dr. Burrows would be with her in a moment. He'd just gotten off the phone with the VA.

"Mrs. Wells," Dr. Burrows addressed Susi, "I talked to the VA and they were a bit vague. I deal with that a lot. I did find out that your husband has been on antidepressants for several months. He was just put on the oxycodone about two weeks ago after a diagnosis of severe cervical stenosis."

"What? Cervical stenosis?" Susi asked. She'd never heard of that before. She wished she could stop crying.

"It is a condition in the neck," the doctor explained. "It happens frequently in people who have spent many years in the military. What happens is that the neck's protective spinal canal narrows due to degenerative changes or trauma. Carrying heavy loads can add to the situation. They are trying to get him scheduled for a neck fusion."

Susi was stunned. How could he have not told her about any of this? All of this must have been the reason why he said he didn't want to be a burden.

"I should really call my daughter and let her know what's going on," Susi stated while looking at her watch. It was just before one in the afternoon. Sammi would still be in class. She would have to call the administrative office. A nurse stayed in the room with Lance while she stepped out to make the call.

The security guard stopped her and said, "Ma'am, I am sorry you have to deal with this." He looked sincere and concerned. "I lost my veteran son with PTSD to suicide. I hope your husband pulls through and gets help."

"Thank you," Susi replied. "Honestly, sir, I think I need a hug."

"That you can have." The older man hugged her, and she knew that it was as comforting to him as it was to her. She thanked him again and then walked a few steps down the hall. Moments later she had the administrative office at the University of Washington on the phone and explained that she needed to reach Sammi Wells, that there had been an accident with her father, and he was at the hospital. Not five minutes later, Susi's phone rang.

"Mom? Is Daddy okay?" Sammi asked anxiously.

"Sweetheart, I need you to try and stay calm." Susi was reluctant to say what really happened but had to tell her. "Sammi, Daddy tried to commit suicide. I was able to get home in time to find him. He's not awake yet."

"What? Why? I'll be on the next ferry. Do you want me to call Tracy? Which hospital are you at?" Sammi shot out one question after the other.

"Yes, please call Tracy, and we are at Harrison Medical in Bremerton," Susi confirmed. "Just let them know at the front desk who you are here for and they'll send you back." Finished with the call, Susi went back in the room.

Lance was still sleeping. The nurse smiled at Susi and told her she'd be back in a little while to check on him. Susi went back to his side and took his hand. As soon as she had done that, she saw tears running down the side of his face.

"Honey, can you hear me?" Susi asked. The nurse stopped near the door. Lance nodded. The nurse told Susi she was getting the doctor and walked out. Lance opened his eyes a little and looked at Susi. "I'm so sorry." He held on tightly to her hand. "I just didn't want to be a burden to you anymore."

"I don't ever want to be without you, no matter what happens, not ever," Susi whispered to him. The door opened and Dr. Burrows along with the nurse came in.

"How are you feeling?" the doctor asked Lance. He raised his hand and shook it side to side as to say so-so.

"Lance, I talked to the VA and found out that you are supposed to be having neck fusion surgery soon, is that correct?" Dr. Burrows continued. Lance nodded. "I understand it has not been scheduled yet."

Lance nodded again. "I understand they are trying to get you in with a neurosurgeon in town since they are rather backed up," the doctor stated. "Are you okay with me taking the tube out? It should make talking a lot easier." Lance nodded and the doctor followed the procedure. He looked down at Lance. "Bet you've done this a time or two?"

Lance tried to smile.

"Do you understand that you will need to speak to a psychologist, and we will need to run kidney and liver tests to make sure there is no damage?"

"Yes, Doctor," Lance replied, swallowing hard. Susi could tell how embarrassed he was.

"Honey," Susi said gently, kissing Lance's cheek, "please know that no one is judging you." She told him that everyone was concerned about his well-being, that Sammi and Tracy were on their way, and that she would not leave his side no matter what.

Moments later a technician came to take Lance for a CT scan of his liver and kidneys. He told Susi that they would bring Lance back to the room, but it would take about thirty to forty minutes before they'd get done. They would also need to draw some more blood for the next batch of lab work.

Susi told the nurse that she would go to the cafeteria and get something to drink and then come right back to the room. Thoughts were racing through her head. What did she do wrong that he didn't tell her about the visits to the VA, the surgery he needed, and the depression? Had she become so disconnected that she didn't even notice the desperate need her husband was in? How could she have let this happen? She hoped that she would get a chance to speak with the psychologist alone. If not she would make an appointment with someone as soon as possible.

She walked back to the room bringing coffee for the security guard. Just as she got there, she heard Sammi call out to her.

"Mom?"

Susi turned around. Both Tracy and Sammi were there. Susi felt a flood of relief and began crying again. Sammi ran to her mother and hugged her. "Is Dad okay? Please tell me he's still here." Susi nodded, and they just stood there and hugged. Tracy gave them a minute and then joined them. The three of them walked into the room. Lance hadn't been brought back yet, but Dr. Burrows joined them seconds later.

"Doctor, this is my daughter, Sammi, and my best friend, Tracy," Susi stated as she pointed at each of them.

"I can't say it's a pleasure to meet you," said Sammi. "Is my dad going to be okay?"

"I just got his last bloodwork results back," the doctor said. "Everything looks good but his liver counts." He cleared his throat. "He must have been drinking heavily for some time. I'm waiting for his CT scan results. We'll talk some more about that later. He should be back at any moment. I'll be back in a little while." He left the room and seemed to be in deep thought.

Susi looked at Sammi and Tracy and began to cry again. "How did I not see this? He's been drinking hard liquor for months behind my back. On top of that he'd gone to the VA. He has cervical stenosis and needs neck fusion surgery. They put him on antidepressants months ago and recently started him on oxycodone for his neck and shoulder pain. How did I not see this?"

"Mom!" Sammi knelt in front of her mother. "This is not your fault. Please don't ever think this was you're doing in any way."

"She's right," Tracy said in an almost whisper. "You know the last two years you were with Gene, I always worried that you might harm yourself, but never in a million years could I have seen this coming. I've known Lance as long as you have. He has always been such a happy-go-lucky guy."

The door opened and the technician that had taken Lance for his tests was bringing him back. Lance looked at his daughter and Tracy and felt a rush of shame. Sammi waited for the technician to attach the monitors, and then she gave her father the best hug she could.

"Do you know how much we love you? How much you mean to all three of us?" she asked, looking into his eyes, and began to cry.

"I'm sorry, baby girl." He fought the tears. "I'm so sorry. I feel so lost and empty and I didn't want to be a burden to your mom anymore. She does so much, and I just slow her down with my needs."

Before either of the women had a chance to say anything, there was a knock on the door, and it opened. A man entered and introduced himself as Charlie Neese. He was the psychologist who had come to evaluate Lance and talk to him about his intentions with the attempted suicide. He explained to the women that he needed to talk to Lance in private, but Lance told him that he wanted Susi to stay. She needed to hear what he had to say because he felt he had hidden too much for too long.

****

Sammi had been studying psychology and would have loved to stay in the room for learning purposes, but this was her father. She had to give them space. "I have never known two people who loved each other more than them two," she said to Tracy, but it seemed aimed at no one in particular.

"I hear you, sweets," Tracy replied. "From the moment they met, they have been inseparable. I questioned your mom in the beginning and thought she was moving too fast. I literally had no idea how much and how deeply they fell for each other the moment they first touched. It's been over twenty years."

They sat in the cafeteria waiting. Sammi told Tracy it could take a minute.

"How do you know so much already?" Tracy asked. "You are only in your second year."

Sammi laughed. "I'm taking some advanced classes, so next year I may be able to go to the graduate year and start my doctoral degree sooner."

Tracy shook her head. "Anyone ever mention to you that you are a straight-up overachiever?"

"Of course, but I'm not, I just get bored easily," Sammi snickered.

They looked at each other and started laughing.

****

Lance was answering the questions from the psychologist.

"How long have you been thinking of taking your life?" he asked.

"A couple of weeks. I retired from the military a while ago and I just can't seem to find any purpose in my life," Lance replied. "There was a lot of work on the house and when that was all done and this pain started, I lost my foundation."

"You are on antidepressants, so the VA is aware of your depression. Did they suggest counseling?" Charlie asked.

Lance shook his head. "No, I even asked about it, and they told me it would take months before they could get me in with someone and I should just take the medication. I've been on that for almost seven months and they just started sending me a stronger dosage." Susi tried hard not to cry again; she couldn't believe what she was hearing. He gave twenty years of his life to the Navy and this was the thanks he got? Unbelievable.

"Have you started receiving benefits yet?"

Lance had been. "I'm seventy-five percent disabled right now," he said. "After the neck fusion, I'll suppose they'll bump me up to one hundred." Lance took a deep breath, "I used to run with a friend along the berm when we were in the desert and I tripped and tore my meniscus, they did three surgeries to repair it and then a partial knee replacement. That put me at twenty-five percent. Just before I got out of the Navy I got diagnosed with sleep apnea and that put me at seventy-five percent.

"How do you feel about your wife? Your marriage?" Charlie looked at Susi. "This is the question I wished I could have asked in private. Are you prepared that you may not like the answer?" Susi nodded.

"I can leave the room if you would rather answer this in private," Susi told Lance.

He shook his head. "No, I need you to hear this because you deserve to hear the truth."

He turned to Charlie. "My wife has been there for me from day one. Never once did she say I needed to pay attention to her wants and needs. Never once did she fight with me about wanting to stay in the Navy another three years. She's never complained about where we had to move, and she made a home for us at every duty station. She is my rock, the glue that holds our family together. For twenty years she has put my wants and needs ahead of hers. She is everything I could have ever asked for and I am eternally grateful for that. If her first husband hadn't cheated on her, I may not have been lucky enough for her to fall in love with me."

Susi smiled at her husband, and Charlie seemed to ponder the answer for a moment.

"Then why attempt to kill yourself knowing she would find you? Hold on a moment." He turned to Susi. "How did you find him so soon?"

"He had dropped me off at work and was supposed to get me later. It was right after he dropped me off that I got this sinking feeling in my stomach. I tried to ignore it, but it just got stronger. After two hours I couldn't get a hold of him and I panicked. My boss gave me a ride home. I just knew something was very wrong," she told Charlie.

"You really do have very deep feelings for Lance, and you are very connected to each other. I have no doubt that you two have a rare connection that allowed you to sense his distress," Charlie said. "So now, Lance, why would you want to end your life when you have someone who loves you so deeply?"

"I've been feeling more and more like a burden; I just sit at home and do nothing. She goes to work and takes care of the household. I'm just there. I know she would never tell me if she wanted me to let her go, but I've seen it time and time again with fellow veterans. They get out and within a year, their wife is gone because he no longer has anything to offer. That's how I feel, like I have nothing left to offer her," Lance admitted.

"How do you feel about that, Susi?" Charlie asked.

"I'm sad that he feels that way. He has so much to offer. Just knowing he's there at the end of the day, I can lay my head on his chest at night. We take walks hand in hand. I would love to help him find an educational aspect he's interested in. He got his bachelor's in business while he was on active duty. He could get his master's and do something with that, but he needs to heal first. He's seen so many horrific things. I'm no psychologist, but I would be sure he has PTSD. I will do whatever I can to help him get better."

"Lance, I'm going to recommend you start counseling as soon as possible," Charlie said sternly. "I'm going to give you a list of clinics, and I need you, not Susi, to follow up and schedule appointments. You need someone who can treat you for PTSD even if the VA has failed to diagnose that issue. You will have to call me within seventy-two hours after you are released and let me know who you have made an appointment with. If I do not hear from you, I will have to send authorities to get you, and we will have to treat you in an inpatient facility."

"Why?" Lance asked.

"You tried to end your life, and, in this state, we make sure you get the help you need one way or another. Under normal circumstances that security guard would have been in this room, but your wife assured us that this was just a desperate cry for help and that you really did not want to die." Charlie was skeptical.

"She knows me, I honestly think she knows me better than I do, but yes, her assessment is absolutely true," Lance stated. "I can tell you she will not rest until I have made that appointment, and she will make sure I go."

"I'm going to ask this again now. Why would you want to die in a manner that would make your wife find you?" Charlie stared at Lance waiting for the answer. Lance's face turned red, and Susi could see the tears well up in his eyes. All he could do was shake his head. "That may be something you need to address in counseling," Charlie added.

"Charlie, I've read some stuff about EMDR therapy for PTSD and things like that," Susi stated. "Do you think that would be beneficial for Lance?"

He smiled, aware of eye movement desensitization and reprocessing therapy for these cases. "Yes, EMDR would be perfect if the therapist diagnoses Lance with PTSD." He turned to Lance. "You should definitely mention that you need to be assessed for possible PTSD."

Susi gave Charlie her cell number as well as Lance's and promised that he would be in touch within a couple of days. Charlie shook their hands and told them that it would have been a pleasure to meet them under different circumstances and that Sammi should get in touch with him when she is ready for her internship.

Lance and Susi both thanked him as he started walking out the door. Sammi and Tracy were standing outside. "I told your mom and dad to have you get in touch with me when you are ready for your internship," Charlie told Sammi.

"Oh, wow, Mr. Neese," Sammi said. "I really appreciate that. I'd really like to work somewhere where I can help veterans."

"I'll get you set up when the time comes. In the meantime, you might want to check into doing some volunteer work at the King County Mental Health clinic. They can always use volunteers, and it will give you credits and a foot in the door."

Sammi was thrilled. Tracy had already gone back into the room, and the nurse had come in right after her.

****

"I have your discharge papers," the nurse said to Lance. "Do you feel ready to go home?"

Lance nodded but felt a bit uneasy. He felt ashamed that he hadn't been honest with his wife. Honesty had been such an important aspect of their marriage. He really didn't understand his own thinking. She had never judged him, had always supported his decisions. She had been the best wife a man could hope for. Had the events of Guam and the desert messed with his brain that much?

"Will you please help me make the counseling appointment?" he asked Susi, feeling like he was going to cry. He needed to get back to trust her the way she had always trusted him.

****

Before they left the hospital, Susi had called Jake and told him that Lance had been in accident and she needed a few days to take care of him. Luckily, Jake didn't ask about details and told Susi to take all the time she needed. She felt exhausted, as if she hadn't slept at all. When they went to bed that night, Lance laid his head on her shoulder and had his arm wrapped around her, holding on so tight, it felt as if he was afraid to let go.

By the time Lance came downstairs in the morning, she'd been sitting outside enjoying the cool morning air with her cup of coffee. There was just something magical about the time just before sunrise, before the whole world was awake. In the last few years, she had used that time to find strength to keep going. Tracy had been her voice of reason; more than once she had said she missed the days when it was just the two of them. Tracy and Max were having issues because Tracy had been single for so long and she had no idea how to share herself with anyone. Susi talked her into getting help.

Susie asked herself, What do I need? I need him to love me the way he used to, I need him to make love to me, I need to feel his body against mine. I miss my husband. Only moments later Lance joined her on the deck with a cup of coffee in his hand.

"Can I tell you something?" he asked. She nodded. Some part of her wished she would have had more time to herself. Lance set down his coffee and kneeled down in front of his wife.

"I am so sorry to have put you through this. I am so scared of losing you. I would understand if you wanted to leave. I've not made life easy and you have been so patient, for year after year." He stopped.

Susi looked at him and cried, "I have told you time and time again if you need to talk, I'm here. Behind my back you went to the VA to get medication. Where is the trust?"

"Can you forgive me?" He had tears in his eyes. Nothing he had experienced now seemed as scary as the thought that he had completely pushed her away.

"Of course, I forgive you," she said, taking his face in her hands. "I want my husband back. Is he still in there?" Lance smiled and nodded yes. He told Susi that in a little while he would call and schedule an intake appointment. They spent the day talking, working in the yard, reading, cooking together, watching TV for a little while, taking a walk, and then going to bed. Susi didn't want to push anything right now. She wanted to give him the chance to go to his appointment and explain what had happened and what led him to it.

Twenty-four hours later he had scheduled an appointment at Peninsula Psychological Center. They had matched him with a counselor who was very familiar with PTSD, trauma, and suicidal tendencies. He had also talked to an admission counselor at Strayer University to start his master's. Susi was proud of him; the night before his first appointment he seemed anxious.

"Everything okay, honey?" she asked.

"Yeah, just a little nervous about the appointment tomorrow." He tried to force a smile.

"Would it help you if I go with you? I mean, I can't go into your appointment, but I can drive with you and be there when you come out." She put her hand on his arm. The idea was welcomed, and by his sigh, Susi could tell that he felt a little relieved.

They were already in bed and Susi was about to doze off when he said, "I honestly cannot remember what had even brought me to this point. I knew that there were issues I needed to work on and possibly resolve. I want to be the husband you had fallen in love with all those years ago. The gentle, loving man you have so faithfully supported through all those deployments and traumas. You have never complained and have stood firmly by my side no matter what life dished out. I really think you deserve better than this broken-down mess."

Susi wasn't sure if he'd wanted her to hear that or if he had just made the statement out loud, thinking she was asleep.

****

He was in good spirits in the morning. Susi had gotten up a little earlier to make him his favorite breakfast of biscuits and gravy. When he came down to the kitchen, she was in the process of refilling her coffee cup. He took the cup out of her hand and set it on the counter, then he wrapped both his arms around her and hugged her like he hadn't done in... he couldn't remember how long. Susi laughed at his playfulness. They had breakfast and an hour later were on their way to the appointment. Once in the waiting room, Lance got quiet. Susi helped him with the paperwork, and shortly thereafter the therapist came to get him.

"Lance?" Tall, black hair and blue eyes, a scruffy beard and gentle expression, he held out his hand, and Lance shook it. "I'm Jeff, wanna follow me?" Lance nodded, and the two men disappeared behind the door. An hour later Lance was back in the waiting room and actually smiling.

"See you next week," Jeff said before shutting the door.

"You seem to have perked up quite a bit," Susi observed.

"Yes," Lance affirmed. "He is awesome, not that I have anything to compare him to, but he is a retired veteran also. It's really easy to talk to him, and he suggested for me to do the EMDR therapy, which you had talked about at the ER. He said that it is a very effective therapy style for people with severe PTSD. He gave me some information about it." He held up a couple of brochures to show Susi.

Susi's hope had found a way back and something, she didn't know what, made her feel confident that he would find his way back to her. When they got home, they did some work in the garden and then went to Home Depot. Lance wanted to add some more raised beds in the garden, so he wanted to go check on lumber. That evening they went to an early dinner. They took the 4:15 ferry and went to their favorite place, Ivar's. Max and Tracy met them there. When they got home, Lance opened a bottle of wine and turned on some soft music. He poured a glass for each of them and then took his wife in his arms and began slow dancing with her. Susi was beyond happy; she couldn't remember the last time he had danced with her. They sipped their wine, danced some more, and then Lance picked her up and carried her to the bedroom. For the first time in months, maybe even longer than a year, he slowly undressed her and made love to her the way he had done in their first year of marriage. She held onto him and when she had a chance, she looked deeply into his eyes. She saw a glimmer of the spark that used to be her husband, she knew he was still there. It would take a little time, but he would come around. She was patient, she would wait.

"What do you think about taking two or three weeks for ourselves and go visit my family in Germany?" Susi announced as they lay in the dark.

"Really?" Lance questioned. "That would be great."

Susi sat up and turned on the lamp on her end table. "Let's see how things go with counseling and what needs to be done with your neck and go from there. They've seen so many pictures of you that they already feel like they know you. We could Skype with them this weekend if you want."

Lance agreed with his wife and told her he looked forward to meeting them.

SIXTEEN

Retirement Life

"I'm not telling you it is going to be easy; I'm telling you it will be worth it."

Lance had been in therapy for nearly five months. Jeff had started EMDR therapy with him, and Susi read everything she could get her hands on in regard to the subject. EMDR had been used for combat veterans for some time, and since 9/11 it had also been used on first responders and people who had endured trauma. From what Susi learned, there were eight phases to this therapy, which helps people change how they see and respond to traumatic memories, deal with present triggers, and learn to address triggers and overcome them.

"So how does that work exactly?" Tracy inquired. She had come over for one of her occasional visits to help her unwind from the craziness of the city.

Susi took a deep breath. "Well, it is really interesting. The processing part of the whole thing being more of a way of digesting horrible things that have happened in a different way, specifically in the brain. Meaning that what has been learned will be stored with healthy, appropriate emotions and beliefs and will no longer result in negative body sensations. The negative emotions and behaviors are caused by unresolved negative experiences, and those can lead to anger, violence, suicide attempts, and substance abuse. The ultimate goal of EMDR therapy is to leave the person with perspectives, emotions, and understandings that will lead him or her to more healthy behaviors and interactions. So far, I am really thrilled with the results."

Susi refilled her coffee and let her mind wander off for a moment. "He doesn't startle as easy and has become more trustworthy towards others again," she said. "Something that Jeff and I had both found odd was that his trust and emotions toward me never really changed. Jeff explained to me that it is highly common for someone with severe PTSD to become violent towards their loved ones, completely unwillingly to cooperate."

She continued explaining to Tracy that all too often people affected by severe trauma, like combat veterans, are trained to not feel, to not give in to their emotions. Then later, when they are done with their service and are falling apart emotionally and mentally, they cannot ask for help because in their minds that makes them weak. That is what they learn, what is drilled into them in boot camp.

****

Over the next few weeks she became more and more curious about exactly what was going on and she wished she'd had more time to dedicate to learning all she could, but Lance developed other health issues. More and more often, his arms and hands were falling asleep. Susi had made multiple phone calls to the VA, and they finally ended up going there to find out what was going on with the surgery he was supposed to have. It had been months and there was still nothing happening. They were even told that they had to re-evaluate the condition. He would wake up in the morning and have needles and pins in his arms. They scheduled an appointment with his primary care doctor at the VA in Seattle, and he referred Lance to a neurosurgeon in town after yet another MRI confirmed the suspicion of cervical stenosis. The times Susi left the VA being able to do nothing more than shake her head in disbelief multiplied with each visit.

They were so backed up with similar cases at the VA hospital that they first considered sending him to San Diego for the surgery, but it didn't look any better there. Susi was beyond thrilled that he would not be treated at the VA for a spine issue.

Just before he had retired from the Navy, he had been diagnosed with sleep apnea and had to wear a CPAP mask to sleep. The first one he had was horrible, and Susi felt as if she were sleeping next to Darth Vader. She had to wear ear plugs just to be able to tune out the noise. He had recently gotten a new one and it was much quieter.

"I really want to wait until after New Year's to have the surgery," Lance told Susi at breakfast. "Sammi is coming home, and I'd like to get your folks over here to visit since we still have to wait a bit to go over there."

It was the end of summer. The days were getting shorter, the air had more of a chill, and ever so slowly the leaves began to change color. It was the beginning of Susi's favorite time of year. She loved spring as well but not as much as fall. The end of a year always seemed sort of a renewal. Lance had built a beautiful three-tier deck. On the first they had a table with umbrella and six chairs, on the second a firepit and six more chairs, and the third was a narrow walkway to the hot tub they had installed. A few feet away from the deck was a small pergola which in spring was covered in a beautiful blue wisteria. The whole garden had been turned into a small paradise.

She would get up early, make her coffee, wrap a flannel blanket around her, and go outside to watch the fog rise over the trees. They had six hundred acres behind them that had been made a wildlife preserve several years ago. No one would build behind them. She sat there looking at the morning fog and thought back on all the times she felt scared, lost and alone, no one to talk to when she'd learned about her husband's pain. She'd always gained strength from her weekly chats with Tracy, and she had told countless young Navy wives that there were two things they needed to be the heart and souls of their husbands' well-being. First, they must be faithful, despite what peer pressure demanded, be strong and stay your course, be the one who makes a difference, and second, they need to find a true friend. Maybe there is someone from their childhood who they have stayed in touch with over the years, someone they'd met while the family was stationed somewhere else, someone they'd gotten really close to. It is so important to have someone to talk to, someone who understands what you are going through and is willing to listen. Not try and fix your problems or hand you solutions but listen, really listen. She'd gotten a call from Katy some months ago and learned that Katy had started an off-base support group for wives who dealt with the issues of PTSD, grief, traumatic brain injury, and other challenges. They had grown from five original members to over 150 and three locations.

By Christmas the surgery had been scheduled for January 8. Much to Lance and Susi's surprise, Sammi brought a boyfriend home at Christmas for them to meet. She had met Mike at a club in Seattle.

"You don't go to clubs," Lance stated directly.

"I don't, Dad." Susi hugged her dad and kissed him on the cheek. "One of the guys from the golf team got awarded a scholarship, and the team decided to take him out. I wasn't really going to go, but they asked me to be the designated driver."

"So, Mike, what do you do?" Lance looked the young man over, trying to be as much of a dad as he could.

"Daddy, really?" Sammi scolded him, and they both laughed. Mike failed to see the humor. "He's just trying to give you a hard time," Sammi told Mike and took his hand.

"Sir, I'm a master-at-arms here at NAS Bangor." Mike proudly extended his hand, and Lance took a hold of it and shook it. He smiled at Susi. She knew that Lance was pleased. Mike must have had a firm handshake.

"Did you really expect anything else?" Susi asked her dad.

"I guess not," Lance confessed and turned to Mike. "What's your rank?"

"E3, sir."

Lance told Susi later he felt Mike was so nervous that Lance could hear his heart pound. "At ease, son, I'm not going to bite."

"Sorry, sir. Sammi told me you were FMF and, I mean, well... wow." They all laughed.

"Looks like you have a fan club, honey," Susi quipped. The doorbell rang, and Susi sat down her dishtowel to go answer the door.

"Who could that be?" she mumbled to herself. Moments later she let out a screech, and someone at the door shouted, "Surprise!"

Susi couldn't believe her eyes. There could not have been a better Christmas present. Lance and the kids came to see what the commotion was about, and as soon as Sammi saw who was at the door, she shouted and ran to greet the visitors. *"Oma, Opa, was für eine Überraschung (what a surprise)!"* She hugged her grandparents again and again.

Susi looked at Sammi. "When did you learn German?"

"I've been taking a class at school, and I use Babble!" Susi just shook her head.

"Let them come in," Lance said and made his way to the door to greet his in-laws.

"It is so nice to have you here, how did you get here? Did you rent a car?" Lance inquired.

Peter, Susi's father, shook Lance's hand and hugged him at the same time. "I don't trust myself to drive in that crazy traffic," Peter stated. No sooner had he finished his sentence, than Tracy and Max peeked in from both sides of the door. "I guess you know how we got here now?" Peter remarked.

Susi cried, "I can't believe this. What an amazing Christmas gift. Oh my God, how am I going to feed everyone?"

"Why don't we get some pizza tonight, and we have time tomorrow to plan Christmas Eve and Christmas dinner," Lance suggested.

Susi grinned; she knew he was in pain, but she also knew that she had her husband back, at least most of him. Once Susi had her parents situated in the guest room, Mike and Sammi in Sam's old room, she sent Lance and Max to Total Wine to get celebration supplies.

"Don't you think your dad might want to rest for a bit?" Lance asked her.

"He told me that he slept fairly well on the flight, and he really wants to have a beer with the boys before going to bed." She smiled at him and patted his butt.

Susi ordered pizza and made herself comfortable on the couch with her mother, daughter, and best friend.

"I honestly never thought I would see this," Tracy stated and pulled out her phone to take pictures. Helene began asking Sammi about her boyfriend, and Susi informed her that they had, in fact, just met.

"You're kidding," Tracy spouted. "How long have you known him?"

"About two months," Sammi said, scratching her head. "Since he lives on this side of the sound and has a crazy schedule, we are somewhat limited, but he calls me every Sunday night."

Susi and Tracy looked at each other and started laughing.

"What's so funny?" Sammi wanted to know.

"Did your mom ever tell you that your dad used to call her every Sunday night? He never missed a single Sunday no matter what," Tracy told Sammi. "We were living in Arizona, and your dad was at Great Lakes at the time."

"I had no idea, really, Mom?" Sammi looked at her mother. Susi nodded and smiled.

"Back then I felt like the week couldn't go by fast enough," Susie explained to her daughter. "That phone call on Sunday was the best thing and helped me through so much." Sammi watched as her mother drifted off to past memories.

"There is so much of your life we missed," Helene chimed in.

Susi hugged her mom. "Don't think about that, Mama. You've been able to see your granddaughter since she was still somewhat little, thanks to Skype, and we talk a lot. You didn't miss the best time of my life, did you?"

Helene shook her head. Susi hugged her mother's neck and kissed her cheek.

Moments later the guys were back with boxes of beer and wine that would last them till New Year's, maybe even longer than that. Lance had caught the pizza delivery at the door. Susi remembered one of the bins in the garage had paper plates in it, and she went to find them.

She was back moments later, the paper plates in hand.

"How long are you going to be here?" Lance asked Helene and Peter.

"January twenty second, if that is okay with you?" Helene stated.

Susi and Lance looked at each other; they had hoped to keep the surgery secret at least over Christmas.

"Is everything all right?" Peter wanted to know. "I told you we should have checked with them first!" he told Helene.

"No, no, Dad, you can stay as long as you want, we love that you are here," Susi reassured them. "Lance has to have an operation on January eighth, and we won't be able to do anything for a few weeks after that."

The whole group stopped talking and looked at Lance.

"I have to get a neck fusion done," Lance stated and shrugged his shoulders. Peter and Helene didn't understand what he meant, and Susi translated what they needed to know to understand the procedure. Peter had worked in medicine most of his life and knew what she was talking about.

The mood seemed to have been affected by the news, but Lance picked it right back up by telling some jokes. Peter was happy he understood and didn't need Susi to translate everything.

Peter and Helene didn't last past nine, at which time they excused themselves and headed to bed. Around ten Tracy and Max left. They had a lengthy drive back to Tacoma and promised to be back for breakfast in the morning.

Susi, Lance, and the kids stayed up a while longer. Susi and her daughter managed to finish almost another whole bottle of wine.

"Well, I better get to bed if I'm gonna make breakfast for this crowd in the morning," Susi commented.

"I'll gladly help you, Mom," Sammi said.

"Mike, are you going to stay or head back to the barracks?" Lance asked.

"Of course, he's gonna stay," Sammi announced, not giving Mike a chance to say anything.

"I'm sorry, babe," Mike told Sam. "I really didn't bring anything to change into or even a toothbrush."

Without much thought Sammi told him to just go get what he needed.

Lance and Susi told him he could stay if he wanted to and if they were going to run to the barracks to get his stuff to please be quiet when they got back. Neither Lance nor Susi heard anything after their heads hit the pillows.

****

The next couple of days seemed to fly by and there was so much laughter in their house. On Christmas Eve, a little while after dinner, Susi excused herself to go to the restroom. When she was coming back down the stairs, she stopped in the shadows just to observe her family. For a moment she thought back on the first Christmas in America, how sad she had been that all communication had been lost with her parents, that she sat by a fake tree with nothing on it but lights, and Gene was out getting drunk. What she would have done that night to be back home. But right then and there, she remembered if just one moment in her prior life had changed, she would not be where she was at this very moment. For the first time in her life, she actually felt gratitude for the way her life had gone before Lance. For the first time, she realized that had even one minute changed, she might be in a different place right now.

It hadn't been that long since she'd almost lost Lance. She remembered running into him and the wine all over his uniform. The spark in his eyes, those beautiful blue eyes, so full of life. The Navy had taken so much from him. They took the spark out of his eyes, the joy for life out of his heart, a little bit with each deployment, a little bit with each person he had to patch up and send back into combat only to zip up his body bag a few days later. Pachelbel's *Canon in D* began to play on Susi's Christmas music play list. She remembered that Lance had told her he would listen to that when he snuck on top of the building in Fallujah. She let the tears roll down her cheeks; they weren't tears of sadness or pain, but tears of happiness and joy.

"Honey, are you all right?" Lance was at the bottom of the stairs looking up at her. She smiled at him and came down the remaining steps, wrapped her arms around his neck, and placed her head on his shoulder.

"I love you so very much," she said. "I have loved you from the moment I first looked into your eyes, and there is nothing better that could have happened in my life than that wine on your uniform." She kissed him.

Both of them noticed how quiet the room had gotten, and they both turned at the same time to look at their guests.

"Everything okay, you two?" Tracy wanted to know. They both nodded and rejoined their guests. They spent the day playing board games, taking a long walk at Seabeck beach park, and the evening was spent talking about various aspects of their lives, which, if anyone really thought about it, might have seemed mundane. There was no drama, no fear, just comfortable lives.

A little after seven o'clock, Tracy's phone rang, and she excused herself and walked into the kitchen. "Tony!" Lance and Susi both went to the kitchen. "Put him on speaker," Lance demanded. Tracy hit the button and they all yelled, "Merry Christmas," together.

"Lance, hey man, how are you?" Tony seemed happy at the other end.

"I'm great," Lance said, looking at Susi. No need to tell him about the upcoming surgery.

"Well, I have some news for you guys," Tony announced. "Kinda been waiting for Christmas to let you know." He paused.

"What's up, brother?" Tracy spouted. "You're not getting married, are you?"

"Yes, ma'am." They could hear him smiling at the other end.

"What? Who?" Tracy yelled.

"You'll meet her New Year's Eve, we'll be in Seattle," Tony stated. "You all wanna meet for lunch that day and we can make plans for the evening?"

"We are, obviously, all at Lance and Susi's. Her parents are here from Germany," Tracy let him know, "and Sammi is here with her boyfriend."

"We can figure it out and get back to you tomorrow, does that work?" Lance asked. "Are you still on Guam?"

"Yeah, we are heading out on the twenty-eighth and stopping in LA to spend the day with my fiancée's sister. I can call you from the airport." Tony was so thrilled to be able to talk to all of them, and they all could hear it in his voice.

"You're not even going to tell us her name?" Tracy asked.

"Nope," Tony replied.

"You know you suck, right?" Tracy told him.

"Tracy," Susi said, "let the guy be, you'll meet her in a couple days."

"Fine!" Tracy pouted.

Lance and Susi let them talk for a few more minutes and then they opened Christmas gifts and had dessert. They finished the evening with childhood stories of Christmases they remembered, and Susi enjoyed listening to her mother talk about her holiday memories. There was so little she remembered; she had been too young. Her dad talked about hiding in the basement one Christmas because the air raid siren had gone off. Two month later, Dresden got bombed. They had gone into the basement as they had done many times before and by the time they came back out, there wasn't much left of the house they had lived in.

The day after Christmas, they took the ferry from Port Townsend to Coupeville and went walking near the Deception Pass bridge. Though Helene was afraid of the height of the bridge, she managed to walk across it with help from Peter and Lance, and she loved looking up at the bridge from the beach below. Both Helene and Peter loved the quaint tranquility of Coupeville, and they decided to come back after New Year's and before the surgery.

Susi had put dinner in the Crockpot before they left that morning, and she just had to put the final touches on it when they got home. They spent the evening playing games, and at some point, Sammi decided she wanted s'mores. Her grandparents had no idea what s'mores were, so Lance went outside to start a fire and Sammi could make s'-mores for her grandparents. While Helene didn't care for them at all, Peter loved them, especially with a glass of red wine.

On the thirtieth of December, Helene's birthday, Lance and Susi de-cided to treat her mother and the whole group, and they all went for dinner atop the Space Needle in the beautiful Sky City restaurant. Helene was beyond impressed. What she couldn't do though was go out onto the observation deck. She enjoyed the view from the inside, and Susi sat with her while the rest of them froze their butts off admiring the lights of Seattle in the dark. By the time the group got home that evening, Helene could not do more than have a glass of wine before heading to bed. She told Susi and Lance that she had not been that spoiled in a long time and thanked both of them again.

The arrangement had been made to meet Tony and his mystery women at Ivar's for lunch on the thirty-first. The small group took the eleven o'clock ferry over to Seattle and walked along the waterfront for a little while. They were supposed to meet at twelve thirty, so they had some time.

"Are they always so accepting with anyone new in their family?" Mike asked Sammi as they were walking behind Susi and Tracy. Susi had to smile about the comment but did not say anything.

"Yeah," Sammi said out loud. "I can honestly not remember them ever being standoffish or distant. I think moving every three years probably had a lot to do with it."

Lance talked Helene into riding the big Ferris wheel and she held on to him as if her life depended on it. Peter and Susi were in the cabin with them, and Susi was thrilled that her mom had agreed to get on the ride. She just avoided looking down and was excited to see the view from atop the wheel. She told Susi that she felt she'd missed a lot of things because of her fear and maybe sometimes things did look a lot better from the top.

After the Ferris wheel ride, they made their way to Ivar's. Tracy, Max, Tony, and his fiancée were standing by the doors. She seemed a bit timid and stood partly behind Tony. The usual hugs were exchanged and then Tony took her hand. "Everyone this is my fiancée, Lucy Meyers. Lucy, this is Susi, Lance, Susi's parents, Helene and Peter, Sammi, and I have not met this young man." He gestured to each person as he named them off. Sammi introduced Mike and everyone hugged Lucy, welcoming her to the family.

"Well, let's go inside," Susi suggested. "It's a bit chilly out here, and I think we are all ready to eat." Lance pulled one of the gold-trimmed doors open, and one by one they went inside. Tracy had made the reservation. The table was ready for them and they were quickly seated.

"Lucy, tell us a little about you," Tracy requested. Lucy looked at Tony for reassurance and he nodded.

"I'm a nurse at the naval hospital on Guam. That's where Tony and I met a little over a year ago." She cleared her throat. "I was married before but only for two months. My husband was killed in Afghanistan two months after we got married." The group was dead silent, none of them knew what to say.

"It's okay, guys," Lucy added. "This happened a few years ago, and I went through grief counseling so I could start over. I love Tony. He's amazing and I can't wait to be his wife." There seemed to be a sigh of relief that went through the group.

"Have you guys set a date and made all the plans yet?" Tracy asked.

"We were thinking May," Tony replied. "I've already put in for leave for mid-May, and we thought if you were able and willing to help organize, we'd like to get married here, in Washington."

"That's fantastic," Tracy announced.

"I wanted to ask you two," Lucy looked at Susi and Tracy, "would you be willing to be bridesmaids for me? I know we just met, but I honestly feel like I already knew you from everything Tony told me about you."

"Absolutely," the two women said almost in unison. "I'm guessing your sister will be your maid of honor?" Tracy added.

"Yes," Lucy confirmed, "that's why we stopped over in LA. I wanted to ask her in person."

"Wow, one by one everyone is getting married," Sammi pronounced, "even the ones we thought would never take the step."

Drinks and appetizers had been served, and Lance toasted the new member of their extended family. Moments later the entrees arrived.

"Mom," Sammi addressed Susi, "you have been eating the Pier 54 cioppino for as long as I can remember coming to Ivar's."

"What can I say?" Susi smirked and popped a mussel in her mouth. "I love it."

Two hours later the group made their way out of the restaurant. Lance and his bunch had to hurry if they wanted to make the next ferry.

"Are you guys coming to the house in a little while?" Susi wanted to know.

"Yes," Tracy replied. "We've got a reservation at the Oxford Inn. I think it would get really crammed if we all tried to stay at your house."

"No, it won't," Susi offered. "My parents are in their room, Sammi and Mike in theirs. We have the two reclining couches and the comfortable air mattress. Everyone is covered. Besides, do you really want to drive after midnight?"

"I guess not," Tracy agreed. "Are you sure it's not too much work?"

Susi told her it was no bother at all and that settled it. On the way home, they stopped at the store to get chips and snacks for the evening. She had put chili in the Crock-pot for anyone who would be hungry later. She figured that would most likely be everyone, especially the guys.

The evening went fantastic and, as it had become customary, just after midnight they sat in the living room and watched Dinner for One. By two, everyone was asleep and comfortable. As she so often did, Susi woke up around four. She pulled a blanket off the bed and opened the door that lead to the deck just off their bedroom. The sky was crystal clear and the deep black was covered with millions of stars. She heard their resident owl hoot, and she smiled as she closed her eyes and took a deep breath, filling her with joy and deep gratitude for all the good in her life.

"Honey, how are you doing?" Lance whispered from inside.

"I'm fine," she responded.

Moments later he wrapped his arms around her from behind and kissed her neck.

"Aren't you freezing?" Lance whispered. Susi just shook her head and smiled. "Just having a moment with the old owl."

"I'm gonna have to have a word with the critter." Lance gently swayed. "Not sure what he's thinking having a nightly affair with my wife right under my nose." They both chuckled, and Susi suggested they get back into bed. No one seemed to be in a rush to get up in the morning, and Susi managed to bake fresh rolls and biscuits without waking anyone. When she began cooking bacon and sausage, bodies started to stir under the covers. Moments later Tony, Lucy, and Max were in the kitchen and getting started with a cup of coffee.

"Is it okay to shower downstairs?" Lucy asked. Susi told her to go ahead and let her know that she had put towels in the bathroom. Before she'd made it back to the kitchen, Lance and Tracy had also gotten up.

Mike and Sammi were the last ones to drag themselves to the breakfast table, but once everyone was there, the conversations picked right back up where they had left off the night before. By early afternoon Tracy, Max, Tony, and Lucy had to say their good-byes. Their flight was scheduled to depart at six thirty that evening. They would be heading to Hawaii and from there to Guam. Tracy pulled Susi aside and told her to let her know if she needed any help when Lance had his surgery or the days following. Susi appreciated the offer and told her she may need her to take her mom to the store on her day off but that might be all.

****

Early on January 8, Lance had to check in at the hospital. They were there by seven thirty. Susi helped him get changed, and they waited for the surgeon and anesthesiologist. They didn't have to wait long. The surgeon was first. He greeted them and gave them both the quick version of the procedure. Moments after he left, the anesthesiologist came in and went over his part of the surgery with Lance. While he was still there, a nurse came to take Lance to the operating room.

"I love you so much and I will be right here when you're done," Susi said, hugging Lance.

"I love you too, honey." He squeezed her hand. "Everything will be fine."

With that he was taken away, and Susi was instructed to wait in the family waiting area. She had been given a piece of paper, which had Lance's patient number, and she could follow him from the OR to recovery. She had also been told that the surgeon would be out to talk to her once the surgery was completed. She went to the cafeteria, got a cup of coffee, and then went to the waiting area where she pulled out her Kindle and tried her best to focus on the book she was reading. The room was cold with white walls, green couches, some grey chairs, and a table with assorted magazines. Nothing that would encourage a person to relax. After an hour or so, the texts began dinging on her phone, family and friends inquiring about the progress. She sent out a group message and let everyone know that it would be at least another hour and that she would let them know when the doctor had come to talk to her.

Tracy messaged her and let her know that she'd taken the day off and was at their house with Peter and Helene having tea, and they would be heading to the store for dinner supplies shortly. She told Susi that her mom wanted to know if there was anything in particular she'd like for dinner. Susi said she would have to think about it, but she'd be okay with a surprise.

Just before noon the surgeon came to talk to Susi. He let her know that the surgery went well, and Lance was on his way to recovery. He explained to her that Lance had an incision on the back of his neck that was about five inches long and had a drainage tube which would stay in until the next day. Susi waited about another half an hour, and then she went to the nurse's station to ask if she could wait in the room. She wanted to be there when they brought him in. The nurse told her that was fine, and Susi found her way and made herself as comfortable as possible. She got her Kindle back out, set it on the small table, and got out her phone to let everyone know what the doctor had said.

Moments later a nurse rolled the bed with Lance into the room. He mumbled something she couldn't understand.

"Hi, hon..." Susi stopped. She was shocked. Lance looked very pale and had dried blood trails in four places around the crown of his head.

"What the...what is that?" she demanded to know from the nurse.

"Did they not tell you that they were using a halo?" The nurse seemed embarrassed.

"What's a halo? And no, they did not." Susi grew more and more irritated but kept her voice low.

"I will have the doctor come talk to you right away." She hooked the monitors up and disappeared. Moments later the doctor came into the room. "You had a question?"

"I guess you could say that," Susi told him, obviously irritated. "What is with all the blood on his head?"

"I'm sorry you weren't told about this before. I can see how that would be scary," he assured her. "In order to do the procedure, we had to turn your husband on his stomach and secure his head with, what we call, a halo. It is a piece of equipment that holds the head in place via four screws. They did not anchor in the skull but went through the layers of skin." He waited for a reaction from Susi, but she was still focused on what he was saying.

"He won't even have a scar from those, but I do apologize that you were not told about that and that he wasn't cleaned up before he was brought to the room." With the last remark, he looked at the nurse who had brought him in from recovery. He showed Susi the incision and drainage tube and told her he would be back in before he went home for the night. Both he and the nurse left the room, and Susi found a cloth, got it wet, and gently cleaned Lance's head. By the time she got to the third puncture, the nurse came back with a couple of washcloths and a towel.

"Would you like me to do that?" she asked.

"No, it's okay, I don't mind at all," Susi replied and forced a smile at the nurse.

"Honey?" Lance whispered. "Are you here?"

"I'm right here, babe," she said softly and kissed his head. "I'm just wiping your head off a little to cool you off." He drifted away again.

The nurse told her that he would still be out of it for a little while, but it shouldn't take too long. She was right. When he snapped out of being drowsy, he was as goofy as he could be with all the stuff attached to him. The nurse put some pain medication into his IV, and minutes later he began to sweat profusely. Susi and the nurse tried to cool him with cold washcloths and ice cubes, but nothing seemed to help. The nurse told them that it would just have to run its course, and she went to talk to the doctor about changing the medication.

Early evening the nurse brought a menu for Lance to choose something light for dinner, and then she gave him another dose of pain medication, this one strong enough to help him sleep. She told Susi that he would be out for some time. Susi took the opportunity to take the prescriptions to the pharmacy to have them ready by morning, and she went home for a little while to have dinner and get some essentials for the night. She found her parents sitting with Max and Tracy and a bottle of wine.

"I'm gonna stay at the hospital for the night and bring him home tomorrow, is that okay?" she asked her mom.

"Of course, honey," her Mom replied and got up to hug her. "How is he doing?"

"I guess, given the kind of surgery he just had, he's doing all right, looking a bit rough though," Susi said. She ate and chatted with everyone for a few minutes before heading back to the hospital. Lance was still out. She put on her sweats and tried to make herself comfortable on the fold-out chair. When he was restless and called for her, she got up and laid her head gently on his. She didn't want to go near his shoulder, as the drainage tube was draped over his right one. Though not much, she did get some sleep, and while in moderate pain he had stopped sweating by morning and was in reasonably good spirits. By noon they were at home, and Susi had him in bed resting while she ran to the pharmacy to pick up the prescriptions. She was glad her dad was there to keep an eye on him. The next two days were a little rough, but they'd been through worse.

By the time Helene and Peter had to go home, he was back on his feet. He still had to wear a special collar to keep his head steady, but overall he felt better. Her parents made definite plans for Lance and Susi to come over in the summer, so they could all go to Italy for a few days or maybe the south of France. On the way home from the airport,

Susi and Lance stopped at Ivar's for dinner and reflected on how just a couple weeks ago they'd been there with eight other people.

"If someone would have told you twenty something years ago, when you were in the midst of that crappy marriage with what's his name, that you would be in Washington with your awesome husband, daughter, and a nice extended family, what would you have said?" Lance asked sheepishly.

"I would have told them that they need to get help or something because they were off their rocker," Susi responded with a smile.

"I don't know about you, but after everything is said and done, I could not have asked for a better life than what I've gotten with you." He took her hand and kissed it.

"You know, I agree one hundred percent," Susi said, "and I am ready for the next battle."

"Oh? What's that?" Lance asked her.

Susi reminded him that this whole thing with his neck should increase his disability percentage, as he had told her, and that dealing with the VA could turn into a nightmare.

Things with them had not exactly been easy.

They were in for a long fight.

SEVENTEEN

The VA and the Fight for Rights

"The pessimist complains about the wind, the optimist expects it to change, the realist adjusts the sail."

A FTER ALL OF THEIR guests had returned to their respective parts of the world, Lance and Susi took a month to do nothing other than enjoy their home, the mountains around them, and the new Siberian husky puppy they had just gotten. Lance had started physical therapy and his overall health had improved tremendously. He knew the neck fusion wouldn't be a permanent solution, that at some point he may have pain again and may need more treatment, but for now he felt good.

"I suppose we need to get some help getting the paperwork in for your additional claim, what do you think?" Susi asked over breakfast.

"We should be able to find answers on the VA website, and there may be a way to upload all the papers," Lance answered. "We can check after breakfast."

They cleaned up together and were at one of their computers in no time. Everything they needed to know to add to his existing disability claim was there. The website had explanations for everything. His first claim, the sleep apnea, gave him an automatic fifty percent disability rating. He'd also had an issue with his left knee. When he was deployed to the desert, he had gone running frequently, and one particular day he'd tripped in a pothole, felt a pop, and knew he had torn his meniscus.

The knee issues had added another twenty-five percent to his disability rating. Those had been simple to file, as they were close to the end of his time in the Navy and he was still active duty, but now he was retired.

Lance called the VA in Seattle. They made an appointment for him to get the paperwork in and get the claim with the neck issue started. This should push him over one hundred percent. Both Susi and Lance were really hopeful that the VA would get everything taken care of. They had no reason to think otherwise.

"Hi, sweetheart, Dad and I are going to be at the VA in Seattle tomorrow morning," Susi told Sammi over the phone. "Would you have time around noon or so for lunch?"

"Sure thing, Mom" Sammi said. "Is it okay if Mike joins us?" "Of course, I'm sure your Dad will be happy to see him," Susi told her daughter.

The VA center in Seattle was over an hour drive. The appointment was at nine thirty in the morning, but with morning rush-hour traffic, they would have to leave the house earlier to get there on time. Lance figured two hours just to be on the safe side. That would give them time to grab coffee and get over the Narrows Bridge.

The appointment did not take more than an hour. Susi was really good about keeping records, and everything pertaining to this appointment was neatly in a file, which they could copy and submit.

"I have to say I have not seen any medical file organized this neatly in a very long time," the VA representative said, and Susi smiled.

"Thank you," Lance stated, "That's all my wife's doing. She worked in a doctor's office for many years, and it was her job to organize everything and to put all the information into computers when all that first started."

"Well, then that makes sense," the older woman said. "Don't expect this to go super-fast. We are really overloaded at the moment, but you should have your increased pay and backpay within ninety days."

"Ninety days, that seems a bit long but okay," Lance commented.

There really was not much else they could do at the time. They left the VA and made their way to Japonessa where they would meet Sammi and Mike for lunch. The four of them had a good time and sat at lunch for nearly two hours.

"I really don't want to drive all the way around again," Lance stated. "Let's just take the ferry across." They had two options for their way home. One was the one-hour ferry ride from Seattle to Bremerton, which was overall the least stressful. The other meant getting back on I-5, down to Highway 16 and then Highway 3 to Silverdale. That meant lots of traffic. They decided on the ferry ride.

More than three months went by and there was no word on his claim. Lance checked his e-benefits, but there was nothing there. He called the VA and was told that nothing had been received. A week later he was back at the VA center, trying to find out what had happened to all the paperwork he had dropped off over three months ago. They profusely apologized and stated that with the heavy workload they had, the paperwork must have gotten misplaced. Lance could send it in or upload it through his e-benefits. He did both and again was given a three-month timeline. A few weeks later he got an email stating that certain forms were missing, and he needed to upload everything again, which he did. Two weeks later he checked the status and there was nothing there. He uploaded everything again and waited. At least this time it said something like in progress that went on for over two months.

He then called the VA and asked what was going on. He told them that he had been waiting in excess of ten months. Again, they apologized and asked that he please be patient. It was confirmed and reconfirmed that all paperwork had been received, but everything was in complete standstill. Four more months passed. They checked the e-benefits website, talked to the VA center, and the best they got was to be patient.

"If we didn't have our savings to rely on and my small income, and what you are getting from the VA, we would be in deep shit now," Susi said one night as they sat outside by a campfire sharing a glass of wine.

"You can say that again," Lance added. "If we had to rely on that income to make ends meet, we would have lost the house and everything else by now. I do not understand how they are getting away with this."

After they had been put off for another three months and then were asked to submit all the paperwork again, they had both had enough. They submitted another copy online and took one to the VA center. After that they called Sen. Patty Murray's office. One veteran who had overheard their dilemma at the VA had waited for them outside and then told them they should call the senator's office. He had done the same and had his increase in disability and backpay within less than a month.

They took his advice, and the next day Lance called.

"You have been waiting how long?" a shocked young man in the senator's office asked.

"Almost seventeen months or so, I believe. All I keep getting is the runaround. We have literally submitted everything electronically more than five times and taken it all in to the VA center more times than I care to remember," Lance told the person.

"Lance, can you do me a favor?" the young man asked. "I know you've submitted everything time and time again, but send me all of your information via email along with a letter explaining what's been going on the last seventeen months."

Lance agreed and as soon as they hung up, he got busy sending everything. It took a little time and he was relieved when everything had been sent. Thirty days later Susi sat down to calculate their monthly budget and check on flight prices, as they planned to go to Germany that the following summer. She logged into their bank account and she gasped.

"Lance!" she yelled.

He was in the kitchen in seconds.

"What's going on?" he asked.

"Look at this!" She pointed at the bank account page loaded on her computer. Lo and behold, all seventeen months of backpay had been deposited.

"Tonight, we are going out for Lobster," Lance simply stated. "Call the kids and see if they want to go." He squeezed Susi. "Thank you so much, my love. I couldn't have done all this without you."

Susi hugged him as hard as she could. "Let's book our flight and surprise my mom on her birthday instead," she suggested. Lance loved the idea and asked Susi to call her aunt to see if she could pick them up, not tell her parents and help with the surprise. On December 24 Susi called her mom, who said she would have sworn that they were going to be there that day. On December 27 they got on a flight to Iceland where they would have a three-day layover. It was something Icelandair offered.

"I have never been so cold in all my life," Susi said when they walked out of the airport just after six in the morning trying to find a cab. They ended up taking a bus that would drop hotel guests off at various locations. When they got to their room at the Icelandair Hotel Natura, Susi hoped she'd get a little sleep before the sun came up.

The room was warm and welcoming; beige and brown wallpaper and off-white wainscoting made the room seem almost elegant. A small table and chair sat across from the bed which had inviting down blankets and pillow. The huge picture window provided a view to the front of the hotel which was outside of the city. They had been told that in Iceland New Years was celebrated for several days so they should be expecting fireworks.

She woke up at nine thirty and it was still pitch dark. Around eleven the sun made a formal appearance only to be gone again just after three in the afternoon. The enjoyed a day at the blue lagoon, which was beyond amazing.

"Now we have to get out of this fantastically warm water and walk about twenty something feet in freezing temperature," Susi commented. "How do you suppose I do that without freezing?"

Lance smiled and kissed her nose. "Honey, would you like me to go get your robe and slippers?"

"Would you, please?" she asked sweetly while keeping herself submerged up to her chin.

The next day they went on a tour looking at all the sights, the Godafos waterfall, which was nearly covered in ice, the continental divide line through which they walked about a mile, and the Strokkur geyser. It was all incredible. That evening they were booked on a northern lights tour, but sadly it was cancelled due to bad weather.

The morning of the thirtieth, Susi's mom's birthday, they were on their flight to Frankfurt at seven thirty but had not departed yet. Susi called her mother from her seat to wish her happy birthday.

They finally arrived at the front door of her parents' house at one in the afternoon. They had picked up flowers on the way, and Susi told Lance to stand by the door. Peter answered and knew what was going on since he was in on it. He told them that Helene was taking a nap but he would get her to the door.

"Happy birthday, Schwiegermama," Lance announced. Susi was hiding behind her Smart Car waiting for all sorts of happy noise, recording the whole thing with her phone. There was nothing. She came out behind the car, walked toward the door, and saw her mother just sitting on a step inside the door in total shock. The surprise had worked.

They had a fantastic time. Lance enjoyed the small town of Herborn and getting to meet all of Susi's aunts, uncles, cousins and one remaining grandmother. They really enjoyed New Year's Eve the next day. January first they met Peter's sister, as well as her children and their spouses. On January tenth they flew home. Sammi and Mike picked them up, and they both looked like cats who ate the canary.

"What's going on with you two?" Lance wanted to know.

Susi looked at Sam and knew something was up. She seemed to be a bit fidgety.

"Oh my god, you guys got engaged?" she squealed with delight and grabbed Sammi's hand.

"What?" Lance didn't seem as excited.

"Oh, stop, you silly man." Susi nudged him, and he started laughing.

The next few months everyone was busy. Susi and Sammi went dress shopping, planned decorations, a theme, and all the other details. Lance was busy helping a couple of other veterans getting their claims through. He'd learned a valuable lesson, and it seemed the VA had implemented a new system. Anyone filing for a new claim was supposed to have it processed within thirty days. Of course, that didn't quite happen, but as far as Lance knew, no one else had to wait seventeen months. He finished his master's degree and was playing with the idea of pursuing a doctoral degree.

The day of the wedding arrived. Sammi and Mike had decided to have their ceremony right there in Lance and Susi's yard. Sammi had put a lot of work into building an arch out of pine branches, and she and Lance had built sort of an altar for candles and flowers to be used during the ceremony. Everything had turned out as they had hoped. They had all the attendants at their house and in local hotels. Susi had hired her favorite hairdresser to come to the house to do the hair for the bride and her attendants.

The caterer had set up, and to keep things quiet during the ceremony, they did as much of their prep as possible beforehand. The instrumental version of Ozzy Osbourne's *Dreamer* began to play as Sammi and Lance made their way down the aisle. As they stopped so Lance could give his daughter's hand to the man who was about to become her husband, one of the catering assistants dropped a tray on the concrete by the back door. It startled everyone but Lance and Sammi. Susi smiled. She knew she had her husband back, the man she had fallen in love with all those years ago.

Sammi and Lance on her wedding day, November 2018. Lance will always be the most important person in my life; he has touched my life in ways no one else ever has. He supports everything I do and all of my dreams no matter how crazy they are. I love how small my hand is in his, I love how my head feels on his chest. There is nothing unrealistic about us!

Author's Note

A Word About the Navy, the VA, Veterans Homelessness, Veteran Suicide, and Marriage Commitments

"To care for him who shall have borne the battle and for his widow, and his orphan." —Abraham Lincoln

I N THE 2019 MOVIE *Sgt. Will Gardner*, actor Max Martini portrayed an Iraqi war veteran who did all he could to make an honest living only to be cheated. He had lost his wife and son in an attempt to find his way back to a normal life. His ways were not always honest or ethical, but that is not the point. The movie is deeply touching and portrays a reality most of America has learned to turn a cold shoulder to. While Sgt. Gardner has an amazing adventure, in the end he ends up on some steps in Washington D.C. with a cardboard sign stating, "Veteran, please help."

The last frame of the movie, before the credits, makes the following statement:

> *Although it is impossible to gauge accurately, findings estimate approximately 50,000 veterans are still homeless on any given night in the United States of America. A recent DoD report states that 383,947 Veterans have been diagnosed with war related Traumatic Brain Injuries (TBI) since*

the year 2000. The VA Inspector General's report revealed that 307,000 veterans died while awaiting healthcare claims [as of the time I wrote this book]. *The VA National Suicide Data Report claims that the average number of veterans who die by suicide each day remains unchanged at twenty.*

Whether the suicide rate remains unchanged at twenty or twenty-two is up for debate, does it really matter? That number should be zero. Attempting to speak with someone at the National Suicide Prevention Hotline, the veteran has to wait as there can be up to sixty-one people ahead of them. At the VA lifeline chat, they have to complete a self-check quiz and input a special code before they can communicate with someone who can help. The quiz itself takes about ten minutes and then they receive this message: "A VA chat responder will review it [the quiz] and leave a personal response for you on their secure website, usually within 10-15 minutes. If the volume is especially high it may take up to 30 minutes. The Responder will offer options for follow-up that could be helpful."

After that it is up to the veterans whether they want to enter into a chat with a counselor.

It would be my guess, having lost family and friends to suicide, that someone who is on the verge of taking his or her own life, someone who is making one last attempt to find just one person who cares, will not wait in line for sixty-plus other people or take a quiz on whether he or she wants to die or not.

I started the quiz. There are twelve or more questions. They have to all be answered to move onto the next one. They are multiple choice questions (e.g., "not at all," "some of the time," "a lot of the time," "most or all of the time") and already the first question has ten sub-questions. According to the VA, the Veterans Crisis Line has answered over 1,625,000 calls since 2007. The questions I have are how many who called were put on hold, how many who called had to wait, and for how many was having to wait one minute too long? This is not acceptable.

The year 2018 finished with the highest number of suicides in the past six years: 138 Army soldiers, 68 Sailors, 58 Airmen, and 57

Marines. By the way, the Navy is the only service that publishes its data, including possible suicide rates, online as of 2018. I came across multiple sites that stated that more than fifty percent of those who chose to commit suicide had some kind of contact with the military health system within the ninety days preceding their death. Contact may have included various behavioral health appointments, pharmacy visits, primary care visits, and other types of contact. The VA and the Department of Defense (DoD) claim that they have made significant changes in suicide prevention, mental health education, and treatment. Then why is the suicide rate still as high as it is, especially with active duty members? There are many who believe that their claims (VA and DoD) are nothing more than lip service.

Mrs. Gudrun Cordle wrote an article for the U.S. Naval Institute Blog, published on April 26, 2019. The article, titled "The Navy's Stress Problem—A Spouse's Perspective," calls on the Navy to wake up. Favoritism and politics have gone over the top in today's Navy. Mrs. Cordle has experienced the reality of the power of the politics in the Navy herself. She thought she was having a heart attack when she called her husband who told her he was on his way to a meeting and for her to call 911. He caught himself before she hung up and told her he was on his way. They made it through that, according to her, just as they did six deployments, cancer, arthritis, and all the challenges a twenty-five-year Navy marriage brings with it. Her husband retired this year (2019), and she is glad to have him back without the pressure of the Navy. In her article she shares the story of an acquaintance of her husband's who had taken his own life after having left his family in D.C to complete a tour on the waterfront. A couple of the ships in his command had done poorly during an inspection.

The Navy, as well as the other branches of the military, claim to be family friendly. We are no longer in the days of spouses not being general issued equipment.

Mrs. Cordle shares another example: A ship was on deployment when the executive officer (XO) received notice of an emergency back home. The incident pushed him into depression, which even the ship's corpsman could not tackle. The commanding officer had to make a decision; he was familiar with the politics. The XO could still get his own command but if the CO reported the depression issue of the XO, his career would be over. The CO chose a different route. He sent the XO on emergency leave with the condition that he seek professional help as soon as he got there. The CO apparently had no faith that the Navy would treat this person without prejudice and stigma.

There are countless Navy policies, as well as the other military branches', which conflict the description on how mental health is treated, and it is really no different than any other illness. A master-at-arms or someone in nuclear operations can lose their clearance if they are put on antidepressants or seek counseling or help for mental health issues. It is not hard to imagine how many of those serving are hiding their issues and suffer from depression that can potentially turn dangerous.

While there were about 120,000 homeless veterans in the United States in 2018, there were less than 8,000 shelter beds for the same number of veterans. A search on the subject brings as many conflicting results as any political debate currently on TV for the 2020 election. One website actually claimed that in order to end veteran homelessness, we need to have a clear understanding of who is at risk and why they end up on the street. Here is a thought: In order for a veteran to get his benefits he/she has to have an address. No matter what the percentage of homeless veterans is, they cannot get the benefits they earned without a bank account, and they can't get a bank account without an address.

Veteran women are twice as likely to become homeless as non-veteran women. In 2016 over fifty percent of all the sheltered homeless veterans were age fifty-one and older. The number of homeless veterans age sixty-two and older increased by more than fifty-four percent between 2009 and 2016. More than fifty-five percent of veterans who are currently in sheltered homelessness have a disability and have, at some point, received health care from the VA, and more than twenty-eight percent have been diagnosed with depression. Thirteen percent have post-traumatic stress disorder (PTSD), nineteen percent deal with alcohol abuse, and twenty percent have received a diagnosis of drug abuse. Often these drugs were initially prescribed by a VA doctor.

Someone recently asked if the VA takes care of homeless veterans. Well, maybe somewhat. They do claim that over 40,000 homeless veterans receive compensation of some kind, like pension, each month. Really? If someone lives on the streets, has no address and no bank account, how can he or she receive any benefits? The VA cannot deposit any money if one doesn't have an account at some bank nor can they send a check if one doesn't have an address, so how are they paying benefits? Sixty-eight percent of all homeless veterans reside in some way in principle cities, fifty-one percent have disabilities, and fifty percent have serious mental illness while seventy percent suffer from substance abuse. Fifty-seven percent are white males compared to the general homeless population of thirty-eight percent, which are non-veterans, and fifty percent are age fifty-one and older compared to nineteen percent non-veterans.

According to Wounded Warrior Project (WWP), there are as many as one in three veterans living with PTSD. WWP had to go through major changes in the last couple of years after a scandal in the media, which caused some damage to the work they do for veterans. As of June 2019, WWP reports that in excess of eight million Americans live with PTSD, and the latest survey shows that almost seventy-eight percent of the veterans served by WWP report living with PTSD. WWP helps those who have served through their connect-serve-empower mission. They will go above and beyond to help those who have served, in many ways more than the government who send them into war in the first place. They do not just help those who served but also the family support system. They understand that those who support the warriors need care as well.

There is also Team Red, White, and Blue (Team RWB), an organization whose motto is "To enrich the lives of America's veterans by connecting them to their community through physical and social activity." Team RWB has county chapters in every state across the country, and they welcome anyone who wants to become an active part with the organization to help veterans. They are always putting together athletic events for all skill levels and help veterans in any way they can.

****

It was not that long ago that during the holiday season, I came across a homeless veteran on a street corner in Silverdale, Washington. I called a local community service to get him to a shelter and while he had to wait, I sat with him and listened to his story. He had served three tours in Iraq, he served in the battle for Fallujah, he'd lost two dear friends with the same improvised explosive device (IED) that took his left leg. While we waited, I got him coffee and a burger. It made him cry. He told me not one single person had even looked at him that day, or the few days prior.

He showed me a picture of his little boy; his son was two years old the last time he had seen him when he came back from Iraq. His son and ex-wife live somewhere in Oregon with her new husband. He said he wondered if she would even tell his son about his dad. He is not allowed to see him due to his mental health issues. After a little over an hour, his ride to the shelter arrived. I wanted to listen to more about his life, his story, but I was glad that he would have an actual bed to sleep in that night. The young man who picked him up told me that they would keep him until they found a permanent shelter for him.

I recently stopped at a rest stop along I-5 between Vancouver, Washington, and Seattle, when Sammi and I met a homeless veteran who fits the over age fifty-one group. We gave him five dollars and a hug. He smiled and wanted to share his story. We told him that I am a veteran's wife and Sammi just married an active duty Navy guy last November. I told Sammi as we continued on the road that I wished I could have sat there and just listened to him. He told me that he doesn't look for handouts, he just wants people to see him. The ones who do are either veterans themselves, a family member of a veteran, or an active duty military member.

One thing has come to light that makes many of us doubt someone with a sign that says "Veteran, please help." We have all seen the news segments and social media videos showing incidents of "stolen valor."

The Corpsman's Wife

In 2013 President Obama signed a law making it a federal crime to claim to be a recipient of military decorations, medals, or to ask and receive money, property, or other benefits received through military service. As a veteran's wife I'd like to think I can spot an imposter, or at least I hope so. I can only hope and pray that karma will take care of those who claim they suffered while they served when they never even wore a uniform.

As a whole we have and continue to fail those who protect our rights. The media coverage of Operation Iraqi Freedom has made us all numb to global suffering. Countless books and movies have shared the stories of warriors who perished and will be remembered by no one other than their families and those like them.

****

The negative aspects of some military wives described in this book are very real. I have encountered many who change the color of the light bulb by their front door to let the single guys know that hubby is deployed, and groups of wives who go on manhunts as soon as their husband is on deployment.

Lance is also very real; he is the love of my life. I am proud to be his wife, I am proud for all he has done with his life, and I am glad that I can be here to help him heal from everything life and his Navy service has brought down on him. Though we met the same way Susi and Lance did in the story, and our Sammi was conceived that night, our lives, sadly, went differently. Though we remained close and dear friends for twenty years, we were not married until 2013. Sammi is our sweet little girl. Well, she's not little anymore. She's a married woman; but you guessed it, she is not a fictional character, and she has been a proud Navy wife since November 2018. She did not know her father until she was twenty-one, and while Lance knew she existed, he had no idea she was his daughter.

Oh, now I suppose you want to know the details. Well, I'll give you a few. When Lance got to San Diego in January 1990, I had decided to

252

tell him about the baby. We were on our weekly call and I told him that I had something special to tell him. He said the same. I told him to go first and he told me that he was getting married. When he asked me what I wanted to tell him, I told him it wasn't that important and congratulated him. I was crushed. I'd really thought he felt the same about me that I felt about him. We talked about it later and he figured I wasn't going to leave my job. I was also still married to someone else and had two older children. If he would have asked me to, I would have packed them up and gone to San Diego, but at this point that is irrelevant. I am glad that Sammi was raised with old-fashioned values and she knows how to appreciate and support her sailor.

Someone whom I admire recently made a lot of sense of the history of the last sixty years for me. Here is what he told me: Seventy years ago, World War II ended, and the veterans came home to parades and being celebrated. PTSD, then called battle fatigue, existed but not to the level of today. Life was good and the country's moral fiber was strong. The 1960s and 1970s brought the sexual revolution and the desire of the younger generation to express their individuality. These were the adult children of those WWII veterans, and Woodstock was their festival. Move forward another generation to the 1980s and 1990s, the introduction to technology, computers, and the fear of AIDS. By the end of 2000 close to 450,000 people had died from the disease, and for a moment we seemed to find our morals again.

People were scared to share brushes or use public restrooms. Though I was not able to find any evidence, I did live through that time and can say that couples became closer again through the sheer fear of catching the disease. People who might otherwise have cheated just talked to their spouses, and some even rekindled their marriage or got divorced.

Then it hit us: mobile phones, My Space, and by 2006 there was Facebook, and the fact that we seemed to replace our personal computers and cellphones every year, or at least every two years. The "throwaway" generation had been born and spanned for the first time in history, over more than one generation. The LGBT movement had gained tremendous ground, and the general mindset had become this: If it doesn't work for ME, if it doesn't serve ME, if it's not in MY best interest, then I'm not interested. Yet the millennials seem to have dropped the long-standing divorce rate. Either way, with the dawn of technology we also faced the dawn of diminishing patience and understanding. That combined with the throw-away mentality created havoc.

Think of it this way, you just bought that new iPhone and it's awesome. Six months later there is the next one. Now your old one isn't so awesome anymore. You are newlywed, everything is perfect. Fast forward six years and he doesn't pay attention to you anymore, he's gained a little weight. Someone else pays attention to her at work and someone else doesn't mind that little extra weight, and affairs are started without either of the partners saying, "Can we please do what we need to do to find the love we once had?" There is not a single state left where the no-fault divorce is not practiced. This started in 1970 in California and spread across the country. It is rare for two partners to admit to each other that things just aren't working, and they need to divorce but can remain friends.

Twenty to forty percent of marriages end because someone cheated, how is there no fault? Fifty to sixty percent of men and forty-five to fifty percent of women cheat on their spouses. Forty-two percent of those who cheated did it more than once. I'm going to share the top ten reasons why people divorce, all of which are avoidable and can be worked through:

1. Infidelity.

2. Money.

3. Lack of Communication. Keep in mind, life happens, you have to make time to talk to each other.

4. Constant arguments. If one or both of you are unhappy, it will result in constant arguments. Talk to each other!

5. Weight gain. Now if that is not ridiculous, I don't know what is. If the outside of your partner is that important, then maybe you should not be married in the first place. A lot of people may even consider you shallow.

6. Unrealistic expectations. Who can really say if anyone's expecta-

tions are unrealistic? They may not match yours, but does that make them wrong or unrealistic? Well, maybe if you marry a super model and you can't accept that he/she will most likely not look that way when they are fifty-plus, that is an unrealistic expectation.

7. Lack of intimacy. This one might actually hold ground. If you've been given the cold shoulder for months, maybe even years, I'm not talking just sex here, this is about emotional and physical intimacy, ignoring your partner's need for sex for no apparent reason for any length of time can be a solid reason for divorce.

8. Lack of equality. If one partner feels they do more than the other in a marriage, that can spell trouble. A man may feel that his wife who is home all day with their kids doesn't really do anything. On the other hand, she may feel that him sitting at a desk all day while she has to chase after the children all day, cook and clean, and run errands, makes him lazy. They are both right and they are both wrong and they must communicate with each other.

9. Not being prepared for marriage. A large number of divorced couples actually claimed that they were just not ready. Of those, most divorced between the fourth and eighth anniversary.

10. Abuse. This is the one reason which should, above all others, lead to divorce. Love has nothing to do with being physically abused on any level. This is also the hardest to walk away from, and I speak from experience.

****

If you are married, engaged, or dating someone in the Navy, or any other branch of the military, you need to know life in the military is not the same as in the civilian world. Your significant other, whether it be your husband or your wife, will at some point be deployed, and the one thing they will need more than anything is to know that the one they love is there for them, that things at home are fine because he/she is taking care of things. They need to be sure that you will not stray, that you will be faithful and as committed as your great grandparents were to each other. If you ask anyone who has been married for forty or more years how they made it, they will tell you two things:

1. They worked through the problems no matter what with mutual respect, compromise, and understanding.

2. They communicated with each other. Problems happen in every relationship and ignoring them doesn't make them go away. You need to talk to each other and work out problems. If all else fails, find a good marriage counselor.

When you are out on the streets of Seattle, Portland, Los Angeles, San Francisco, Phoenix, Denver, Chicago, Washington, D.C., or any other major city in the country, be mindful of your surroundings. If people look like they need help, they most likely do. Don't just look the other way. A smile and a brief conversation can often make all the difference.

About the Author

S ABINE CHENNAULT CAME TO the United States in 1981, and she has been creating stories since her teen years in Germany. Mother to three children and grandmother to four grandchildren, she lives with her husband, Lance (Retired Navy Corpsman), and their two Huskies in Washington State. Sabine has degrees in Culinary Arts, English Literature, and Family Counseling. She is the author of two books: *The Corpsman's Wife* and *Sam and the Pixie: Finding Faith.*

hellgatepress.com